DAD BOD

— NAILED —

Jasinda Wilder

NAILED

ONE

"I'M NOT SURE WHAT YOU WANT ME TO TELL YOU, Laurel," Audra says, scooping a ridiculous amount of guacamole onto a corn chip. "I can't say I know him very well, but what I do know, I like. He seems like a great guy."

I sigh, and take a sip of my skinny margarita. "Not helpful."

She shrugs, popping the chip and guac into her mouth, speaking after she's chewed a few times. "Sorry. I told you I wouldn't be much help."

Audra is on the shorter side at five-five or five-six, but she's insanely fit, strong, and toned, as well as curvy in all the right places; with platinum blonde hair in a swept-back pixie cut and sky-blue eyes, Audra is the potty mouth of our group, the one always making inappropriate but hysterical jokes, and innuendos that can be downright salacious.

Nova, the other new girl of this foursome besides

me, just laughs as she listens to our exchange. And as she listens, she uses the tiny black straw to poke at the lime floating on the top of her margarita. Nova is a red-haired Amazon woman, standing six feet tall with fiery red hair that is draped in a thick braid over her right shoulder. She has electric blue eyes and she's built like a goddess in every way—absurdly well-endowed in both her tits and ass, as well as being ripped in a way that speaks to her intense dedication at the gym.

"Why are you looking for reasons to dislike him, Laurel?" Nova asks me.

"Because he vanished on me, and if he did that once, he'll do it again, and I'm not interested in playing those kinds of games," I reply. "I don't want to like him. I want to dislike him so it'll be easier to forget about him."

Imogen grins at me. "I might have something for you. I'm not sure how much reason this is to dislike him, but it may be a little bit of a red flag."

Five-seven, with rich auburn hair and eyes the green of grass lit by the summer sun, Imogen is built somewhere between Audra and Nova—curvy and gorgeous and fit, but not as powerfully built or ripped as Nova, nor as shredded as Audra.

I lean forward. "Do tell!"

The other three lean forward as well, and Imogen

laughs. "You guys are like TMZ at the slightest whiff of gossip!"

I wrinkle my nose. "I'm not after gossip for the sake of gossip, I'm after legitimate reasons to blow off Ryder McCann."

Imogen snorts. "Because that's *so* much better than just wanting to gossip."

I nodded, intentionally ignoring her sarcasm. "You're right, it is, though I'm not just digging around in his past out of morbid curiosity. I have my reasons."

Imogen rolls her eyes, sips her margarita, and then pops her lips. "Well, this is just what I heard from the other guys the first time I hung out with them all." She lifts a shoulder. "So I don't know how true or accurate it is, or how far it goes. But…apparently, Ryder has a thing for, as he put it, the crazy chicks."

I blink. "He has a thing for crazy chicks?"

Imogen nods. "According to him, they're fun to date because crazy chicks are also—and I'm quoting him here—'crazy in the sack.'"

I sit back with a huff. "Men are pigs."

Audra is cackling, now. "Honestly, though, if that's true, then it's probably a good thing I met Franco first, because according to some of the guys I slept with before Franco…I'm a crazy chick."

Imogen, sitting beside Audra, smacks her on the arm. "You are not."

Audra just stares at Imogen. "Bitch have you *met* me? I've probably slept with more guys than all three of you combined."

"That just means you're a slut," Imogen says, laughing. "Not crazy."

I widen my eyes at the insult, but then Audra starts laughing.

"Former slut," Audra says, holding up a finger. "*Reformed* slut. I have found love, left behind my slutty ways, and am now a kept woman."

Nova snickers. "I don't think that means what you think it means, Audra."

Audra frowns. "Kept by a man, duh—a one-man woman."

I reach across the table and pat her on the head, patronizingly. "You may wanna Google 'kept woman' before you use it again."

Audra looks around at everyone, and since all of us are laughing, she huffs. "Fine, then. Enlighten me."

"Kept woman is the archaic term for what we call a sugar baby," Nova answers. "It's basically a woman who dates and sleeps with a wealthy older man in return for a lavish lifestyle. Not exactly prostitution, since it's not direct payment for sex, but that's the implication."

Audra reddens. "Oh. Yeah, that's not what I thought it meant."

We all laugh, and then Imogen wraps an arm around Audra, kissing her loudly on the cheek. "Oh, Audra. There's absolutely no one like you." She snickers again. "I love that you're…ahem…a kept woman."

"I didn't mean it that way," she snaps. "I meant committed to one man."

Imogen is still laughing, leaning against Audra, who is stiff with embarrassed anger. "I know, I know—I'm using your term. I'm not making fun of you, honey."

"Feels like it," Audra huffs, and slams the rest of her margarita and then looks around for the waitress to order us another pitcher.

Imogen sighs. "That's just because things with you and Franco are still new, and you're a little defensive about your relationship. I get it."

"I'm not defensive," Audra protests. "I'm just…" she sighs, throws up her hands. "Fine! I'm defensive about it. But it's weird! I've spent the last twenty fucking years avoiding relationships like the bubonic plague, and now suddenly I'm in one, and it's serious, and I'm living with him and we're saying I love you and it's fucking *weird*, okay?"

"That's a lot of fucking," I mutter, repressing laughter.

Audra arches an eyebrow at me, smirking. "You have *no* idea how much fucking Franco and I do." She wiggles her eyebrows, and all of us laugh at the silly gesture. "We're like teenagers, I swear. He woke me up at two in the morning with a hard-on the size of goddamn Texas shoved between my ass cheeks."

Imogen just stares dreamily at the ceiling, sighing dramatically. "I just love that, don't you?"

Audra rolls her eyes. "Not when I have to be up at five to get ready for work and he kept me up until midnight trying to fuck through half the positions in the Kama Sutra."

I nearly spit out my drink, and it ends up spraying out of my nose instead. "Ouch! That burns...shit!" I dab at my nose and hold the napkin over my mouth as I cough around the aspirated alcohol. "God, you two are *terrible!*"

Nova and I, both single, exchange glances of equal parts amusement and annoyance.

Nova shakes her head. "You really are a nasty woman, Audra."

"I have one of those Nasty Woman T-shirts, actually," Audra says, "so I take that as a compliment."

Nova just laughs. "Good, because I meant it that way." She scoops salsa, chomping the chip noisily. "I'm just cranky because I'm currently *not* being woken up with a giant cock between my ass cheeks, so I'm low-key jealous and being bitchy about it."

Audra focuses intently on stirring the guac with

a chip. "I can think of a cock that might want to get buried between your ass cheeks. And—I'm just guessing here—but I imagine it's probably pretty giant. I mean, the rest of him sure as fuck is."

Nova colors. "I have no idea what you're talking about."

Audra frowns. "Oh come on! I know I saw you and James macking on each other at the barbecue."

Nova shakes her head again. "Who says 'macking' anymore?" She waves a chip. "And that's a nonstarter. Not talking about it."

"Well then you can't complain about not having a dick in your ass, because I saw how James looked at you," Audra says. "And if nothing else, he *definitely* wants to put his dick in you."

Nova scratches at the table, her pale skin almost as red as her hair. "I don't want a dick *in* my ass, thank you very much. Just sort of…wedged between the cheeks." She won't look at any of us. "And I'm serious, I'm not talking about…that. Or him. Or anyone else as it pertains to me, or my love life. Which is nonexistent, and that's all you nosy bitches need to know."

Audra holds up her hands. "Fine, fine. I'll let it go. But only because we're new friends and I'm not ready to piss you off with my tendency to be a pit bull about getting the juicy details."

Imogen cackles. "Enjoy it while it lasts, Nova.

Once she decides she wants to know something, you're better off just telling her, because she *will* get it out of you."

Nova narrows her eyes. "Not out of me, she won't."

Turning to Audra, Nova says, "You've met your match when it comes to stubbornness."

Audra narrows her eyes as well, and this escalates until they're both basically just squinting. "Nobody, and I mean *nobody*, can out-stubborn me." She stabs a finger at Nova. "Try me, bitch."

Nova, somehow, manages to keep a straight face. "You're on…bitch."

I just watch all this. "You're both being so…aggressive…about this. Can't we all just get along?"

Imogen snorts, eyeing me. "Ever the peacemaker, huh, Laurel?"

I shrug and nod. "Typically, yes."

"So, does Ryder having a thing for crazy chicks count as a reason to not like him?" Imogen asks, turning the conversation back to me.

I sigh. "Maybe? I mean, I'd like to say that him having a thing for crazy chicks just because they're good in bed is a solid reason, but he's a single guy, so that's sort of par for the course. It's just a bit…sleazy, maybe."

Audra frowns at me. "It's not sleazy, he's just

being honest about what he wants—some red-hot boning."

I almost spit out my drink again. "Stop doing that!"

Nova hands me another napkin. "And also, just because he said that crazy chicks are crazy in bed doesn't mean it's *good* sex." She glances at all of us. "I think we can all agree that *crazy* sex and *good* sex aren't necessarily the same."

Audra eyes her. "So—spill."

Nova lifts an eyebrow. "Spill what?"

"Examples, bitch! Crazy sex versus good sex."

Nova looks around at all of us, and then sighs. "This is codified girl talk, right? This doesn't leave this booth?" We all chorus our agreement, and Nova grins. "So, in college, there was this guy I was crushing on, like really hard. He was in my anatomy and physiology class, and we'd actually had several classes together, since we were both in the medical program. He was…not my usual type. I'm a tall girl, right? And I've been into powerlifting since high school—I was the first girl to compete with the powerlifting team in my school's history, actually. So, I'm not just tall, I'm strong. Which intimidates most guys, right? Especially guys who work out, oddly—they're worried I'll show 'em up or something stupid, I guess. Even more curious is that the guys who aren't intimidated by my size, strength, and build are, historically, the skinny guys who don't work out.

"Anyway, this guy fit that bill—long hair, beard, wore socks with Birkenstocks, played hacky sack in the quad—that kinda guy. But he was cute, and funny, and we tended to sit near each other a lot."

Audra pretends to snore. "We don't need the backstory, hon. Get to the juicy shit."

Nova sighs. "Fine. To make the story shorter—for those with attention span deficits—he ended up being an absolute *maniac* in bed. Not super well-endowed, but *damn* did he make up for it with sheer… just…*wildness*. He was insatiable, and like, insanely creative. He wanted to try things I'd never heard of, all these weird positions and shit."

"Like what?" Imogen asks.

"Like, once, he wanted to try the…um…butter churner." She blushes scarlet again, focusing on crumbling a chip into pieces.

Audra splutters. "He did not. Really?"

Nova nods. "He certainly did."

"And?" Audra is, of course, all ears.

"And…it's uncomfortable and amazing at the same time. It's not the kind of position you can just hang out in for very long, but it's intense in the moment." She grins lopsidedly.

Imogen and I both have similarly lost expressions,

and Imogen is the first to admit ignorance. "Um, sorry, but what's the butter churner?"

Nova cackles, and is now ripping up a napkin into shreds. "It's, um…you—meaning, the woman—you're on your back, with your butt up in the air. Like, you're sort of resting on your neck. Sort of like doing the bicycle? And he's standing over you, or kneeling on a couch or something, and going at it downward."

Imogen glances at the ceiling as she tries to picture what Nova is describing. "Wow. That sounds… not great."

Nova shrugs and makes a face. "If you have a pillow under your neck and he's got the right angle, it's actually really great. Stimulates your G-spot like nothing else." She grinned. "He also wanted to try what he called the couch twerk. Which was another weird one that I ended up liking a lot more than I thought I would. He sits upright at the edge of the bed, and you have to kneel on him, facing the same way as him with your feet under your butt. And then you bend forward and put your hands on the floor and…yeah. Talk about getting *deep*. It's hot because you have all the control over pace and rhythm and everything. All he can do is sit there and feel good while you decide how fast or slow you want it."

Audra blinks. "Wow. That's a new one for me."

Her grin is lascivious. "I know what Franco and I are trying tonight."

I laugh, glancing at Nova. "So, that was crazy sex, needless to say."

"Right. It was always like that—crazy positions, super energetic and athletic and fun." She shrugs. "But not...*good*. Like, it was adventurous and fun, and I always got there in the end, but it was fun more for the novelty of things and how crazy he was about everything. But it wasn't *good* in terms of sheer sexual satisfaction."

Imogen nods. "I can understand that. So what was *good* for you, then?"

Nova sighs. "My ex."

"Ex what?" I ask.

Nova shrugs. "Does it matter?" She pours salt onto the table and traces designs in it. "It was rarely adventurous—cowgirl was about as exotic as it got, for the most part, but it was just...*good*. He could just make me feel *amazing*."

I nod in agreement. "I totally sympathize. My ex-husband always wanted to 'spice things up' with weird stuff. Standing up and bending me over random objects and...just weird, random positions that felt a little kinky but honestly didn't make me feel any better in terms of gratification. It was really more about him and me putting a Band-Aid on our dying marriage. Using weird positions to mask the fact that things had stopped working between us. But then my ex-boyfriend, Derek, who I dated a few years after Paul and I divorced—we had great chemistry. We didn't need weird stuff, because it was just good."

Audra snorts. "If it was so good, why aren't you with those guys?"

Imogen whacks her on the shoulder. "Because good sex doesn't mean a good relationship—you should know that better than any of us."

Audra tips her head to one side. "True, true. But then you have to talk about *great* sex. I think if you have a great relationship, you're going to have great sex."

"I don't know about that," Nova said. "What constitutes great sex *or* a great relationship? How do you quantify that?"

Audra just grins wickedly. "Great sex is simple—crazy sex that's intensely gratifying, with feelings." She shrugs. "A great relationship? I'm not sure I could quantify that one."

Imogen holds up a finger. "I can. It's when you're crazy in love, and you're totally committed to each other for life. It's when the sex can be totally vanilla but still satisfying and intense, so trying new positions is just icing on the cake, because you don't need the crazy stuff to feel good. It's having the best of all the worlds. When you don't even need to *have* sex to be totally gratified and happy—you're just... happy to be near each other."

Audra holds up a hand, and Imogen high-fives her. "Preach, sister!" Audra says, laughing.

Nova and I just exchange irritated glances.

"Well, I guess I wouldn't know what that's like, would I?" I snap.

Audra gives me a long stare. "You could, though."

I narrow my eyes at her. "Don't." I point a finger at her. "Do *not*."

She holds up her hands palms out. "I'm just saying—between the four of us, the worst thing we could find to say about Ryder is that he has a thing for crazy chicks—and thus, crazy sex. Which would work in your favor, because crazy sex is always worth it, even if it doesn't lead to good sex or a great relationship."

I sigh, scrubbing my hands down my face. "You had to go there?"

Audra just grins at me. "You know it. If there's a there to go to, I'll go there, and probably ten steps beyond it."

Imogen laughs. "That is God's own truth!" She side-hugs Audra. "Nobody can make a totally innocent situation dirty as fast as you."

"It's my specialty, what can I say?" Audra says, with a cutesy shrug and expression.

"Ten Hail Marys?" Nova suggests, laughing. "Or...maybe ten Hail Marys per guy you slept with?

Audra cackles. "I'd be saying Hail Marys for the rest of my life!" She smirks at Nova. "Going by the stories you were telling, though, I don't think you're too far behind me."

Nova just smirks. "Wouldn't you like to know? Nobody knows my number."

Imogen frowns. "Her number?"

Audra fishes a credit card out of her purse. "The number of guys she's slept with."

Imogen laughs. "Oh. Well...I can tell you my number with one hand, and I'm not sure if I should be embarrassed or proud of that."

I hold up my hand for a high five. "Same! Single digit partners sisters."

Imogen high-fives me. "Unlike Señora Slutty Buns here," she indicates Audra, "who would need to use both hands, both feet, both tits, and most of the hairs on her head to count, like, half of her sexual partners."

Audra glares. "Are you slut-shaming me, Imogen Catherine Irving?"

"Yup!"

Audra breaks into cackles, leaning into Imogen.

"Fair enough." She turns serious, her eyes on me. "I think you should just get it over with and sleep with Ryder."

I huff. "He stopped answering my calls and texts. Just…poof. Gone. Nothing. Nada."

"So?" Audra gestures at herself and then Imogen. "We know where he works."

"So, I'm not going to chase him. If he stopped wanting to talk to me, I'm not going to force it."

"He's just chicken because he likes you." Audra flags down the waitress. "One more pitcher, and the bill on this card." She hands the waitress her credit card before any of us can protest.

"Hey!" Imogen snaps. "We're splitting it!"

"Not anymore!" Audra slaps the table. "I've made an executive decision for the group—we meet here once a week, and we take turns paying the entire bill. It's a standing date, no breaking it for anything except the most important events."

The other three of us exchange glances, and then Imogen nods and shrugs. "I'm in."

"Me too," Nova says. "I needed this in a bad way."

"I'll probably have to take out a loan to pay for it with the way we drink, but I'm in too," I say.

The waitress comes by with another pitcher of skinny margaritas and the bill for Audra to sign, and then, for some reason, all attention is on me.

"What?" I ask. "Why is everyone looking at me?"

Imogen smirks, tapping me on the tip of the nose. "We're waiting for you to tell us what you're going to do about Ryder."

"Nothing. I'm going to forget about him."

"So why did we come here, then?" Audra says, frowning. "I thought this was about talking you into fucking him."

I choke on margarita yet again. "No! I said it was about talking me *out* of fu—out of thinking about him."

Audra just snorts. "Bullshit."

I roll my eyes. "It's not opposite day, Audra."

Nova raises a finger. "I'm with Audra on this one. You wouldn't have brought all four of us out to talk about Ryder unless you secretly, deep down, wanted us to talk you into seeing him again."

"You went on, what, four dates? You go out with your girlfriends to get over a serious boyfriend, not a guy you went on four dates with." She shoots me a questioning glance. "Did you do anything with him?"

I shrug, shaking my head. "Not really."

Audra's eyes fix on mine. "Not really? What does that mean?"

I blush. "It means we made out a little, and that's it."

Nova laughs. "You messed around, you mean."

Audra moves her fist toward her mouth and pokes her tongue against the inside of her opposite cheek. "Yeah…*messed* around."

"We kissed, mouth to mouth, and that's *it*," I say, feeling my cheeks burn.

Audra's eyebrow arches. "After four dates all you did was kiss?"

I shrug. "I move pretty slowly, and I told him that up front. I've got a son, so I have to be careful about who I let into my life."

Audra snickers. "Maybe that's why he ghosted? You didn't put out soon enough."

Imogen slaps her on the arm again. "She told him up front that she wanted to take things slowly."

"Yeah, but only kissing after four dates? That's glacially slow." Audra gives me a grin that says she's just giving me crap.

"It's totally normal," I say. "Fucking on the first date is what's unusual."

Audra nods as if in agreement. "That's why I didn't date. I just fucked."

"I fuck, hard," Imogen quotes, making her voice deep and gruff, and we all cackle. "You're out of your league with this one, Laurel."

I laugh. "Oh, I know."

Imogen pours the last of the margarita into our glasses. "You should at least find Ryder and talk to him, see why he suddenly stopped answering your messages. There's got to be some kind of logical explanation."

"What if his explanation is that he just doesn't like me?" I ask.

"We get together again, and the margarita pours are a little heavy in your favor," Nova answers. "And we ask for double the tequila."

I just laugh. "If you get me hammered on tequila, you'd better be ready to babysit me, because tequila-drunk Laurel is…a handful."

"I think that's just the nature of tequila," Nova says. "It has that effect on everyone."

I sigh. "I don't want to want his explanation. I don't want there to *be* an explanation."

"Why not?" Audra asks.

"Because I like him too much, and I just know he's only going to ghost me again, and I'll be even more invested by that point."

Audra smirks. "When you called me, what you said was that you had fallen for him."

I glare. "That was me being emotional—and tipsy. It was an exaggeration. You can't fall for someone after four dates."

Audra and Imogen just laugh, exchanging significant looks.

"What?" I demand.

They just laugh all the harder.

"Keep telling yourself that," Audra says. "It's not true, but it may let you sleep at night."

I sigh, because the evidence does seem to be in their favor.

And it *was* a little bit more than a kiss that happened between us that night.

He knew it, I knew it, and chances are, that's why he vanished on me.

UGH.

I just *know* this isn't going to turn out well. But I'm a sucker for punishment, it seems, because I'm all too aware that I'm going to go talk to him.

"You'd better make it triple the tequila," I say with a long sigh. "I have a feeling I'm gonna need it."

TWO

I CHECK MY MAKEUP IN THE REARVIEW MIRROR OF MY CAR, purse my lips, make sure I don't have any lipstick on my teeth, and then angle the mirror downward. I plump my breasts, tugging the top down a little and pushing the girls up, and then huff in irritation at myself for putting so much effort into this. I rearranged my schedule today, skipping lunch and condensing things so I'd be able to leave before seven in the evening—and made sure Nate's babysitter could stay later than her usual six p.m.

And I'm dressed to kill: tight knee-length black skirt that shows off all the work I do in the gym to keep my butt tight and some fairly plain but comfortable black heels that add to the effect the skirt has on my butt. I paired the skirt with a peach-colored top that leaves my arms bare and shows off just enough of my expensive cleavage—meaning these great tits are displayed to maximum advantage, with the aid of the low-cut top and a push-up bra. My hair is brushed to a glossy sheen and hanging in loose spirals around my shoulders. My makeup emphasizes the pale green of my eyes and my naturally tan skin—which is a gift of genetics from my Sicilian mother…along with a heck of a temper and a voracious appetite for carb-loaded foods.

Assured that I look as good as possible, I straighten the mirror, take a few calming breaths, and then shut off the car. I step out, close my car door, and tug my skirt down a bit…then huff and tug it back up, letting the hem sneak up just above my knees. This isn't about seduction—the opposite, if anything—but it won't hurt to use what advantages I have, right?

It's seven on a Friday evening, and I have it on good authority that Ryder McCann is in this building—Billy Bar. A dive bar with a reputation for being crammed to capacity most evenings, serving stiff drinks at decent prices, and bouncers that only step in and break up fights if they threaten to damage the décor. Billy Bar is a former Pizza Hut building with new blacked-out windows and a cool new paint job. I've never been inside before, but a few of my coworkers have and they swear it's nicer inside than you'd expect. The parking lot gives me anxiety, though—or rather increases my feelings of being out of place. My car is a five-year-old BMW 4 series convertible that I bought pre-owned as a reward to myself for getting promoted to regional manager—it's white with a tan interior, and there's a booster seat in the back, and the inside is clean. The rest of the vehicles in the lot are, almost exclusively, either Harley-Davidson choppers or big masculine chest-thumping, macho-mobile pickups, most of which have lift kits and oversized tires, racks for ladders, enormous silver toolboxes in the beds, grille guards that could withstand a charging rhino, LED light bars, and interiors cluttered with soda bottles and fast-food wrappers and cigarette cartons.

Yeah, my little Beemer is out of place.

But Ryder is here, and it's a public place. Not exactly neutral, as this is his favorite bar, according to Imogen and Audra. In fact, this is where all four of the Dad Bod Contracting guys come to drink. Today, though, it's just Ryder, and maybe James—neither Franco nor Jesse was certain of James's whereabouts.

I march into the bar, mentally repeating my orders to myself:

Keep an open mind; listen to what he has to say; don't get sucked in by those mesmerizing hazel eyes…

And most importantly—don't end up in bed with him.

I repeat this in my head over and over again as I enter Billy Bar and stand just inside the entrance, scanning the interior. It's hypermasculine—an entire motorcycle hangs on one wall, with light fixtures made from car parts and industrial steel tubing, exposed beams and ductwork, giant beer signs and mirrors and neon tube lettering. Hard rock is blasting just loud enough to be an assault on the ears, but not so deafening that you have to shout to be heard. Most of the clientele is male, bunched in clusters with pints of beer and tumblers of whiskey clutched in fists with scarred and tattooed knuckles. There are plenty of women, but most of them seem to be paired up with other men, clinging to bare, burly arms and nodding at their every word with vapid giggles.

Ugh—I'm being judgmental.

I'm sure they're nice intelligent women.

He's hard to find—Ryder is huddled into a corner booth, alone, sipping from a beer and, strangely, doing nothing else. Just sitting there with his beer, alone.

I let out another deep breath and then cross the bar, twisting and shimmying between clusters of men—most of whom give me a once-over…and a twice-over…and a thrice-over, and more than a few lingering stares as I walk past. I feel so many eyes on me that I'm half tempted just to bolt right back out that door.

"Hey, babe. You must be new here," a rough voice says.

I look up at the enormous, tattooed, bearded

man blocking my way. "Hi. Yes, I am, and I'm actually meeting someone, so…"

He just stares down at me—or, rather, at my breasts. "He can wait. Have a drink with me." It's not really phrased as a request.

I glance past at Ryder, who is in the act of taking a long pull of his beer and then pausing to skim the bar with his eyes.

He sees me. His eyes widen, and then abruptly narrow.

I'm hemmed in on all sides by clusters of men, some of whom have noticed me, some of whom haven't. Short of shoving or kicking—and making a scene I'd rather avoid—there's no way past the man in front of me, who does not seem at all inclined to move.

"Like I said, I'm meeting someone, and I'm afraid I've already kept him waiting, so if you'll excuse me…"

His laugh is a dark, ugly snarl of amusement. "This ain't the place you go meetin' boyfriends, sweetheart. Whatever he's paying you, I'll pay double."

It takes a moment to fully comprehend what the man is implying, and then when I finally do, anger rifles through me. "Excuse me?" I hear my voice go high and shrill, as it does when I'm pissed. "What exactly are you implying?"

He reaches for me, a big paw wrapping around my waist and yanking me toward him. "You heard me. I'll pay you double whatever he's paying. Been a few days since I've gotten my dick wet, and your mouth looks awful pretty."

I shove him backward as hard as I can. "Get off me!"

A thick hand covered in reddish hair and freckles shoots out, latches onto my assailant's wrist and clamps down until his knuckles go white. My assailant grunts, and I watch as Ryder steps forward, twisting his hand until my assailant hisses. Ryder's unruly thatch of bright red hair is tangled in front of one hazel eye, and a small mischievous smile curves his lips.

"Don't apologize to the lady," Ryder says in a voice as hard as nails and crackling with threat. "Seriously, I'm begging you, don't do it."

The other guy is as puzzled as I am; his voice, when he finds it, is tight with pain. "Wh-what?"

Ryder's other hand is empty, hanging loosely at his side—he's giving off the impression that he's barely exerting any effort. "I really, *really* don't want you to apologize to my friend." His grin turns positively scary. "Because if you don't apologize right the fuck now, I get to pummel you into a bloody pile of dog meat."

"I'm—I'm sorry, lady. I'm sorry. I'm sorry."

"Beg her to forgive you."

"For—forgive me—please forgive me."

Ryder's knuckles are pale, his hand trembling with the power of his grip, which has the man's arm and wrist and elbow all twisted in the wrong direction until it's obvious that with one quick jerk, Ryder could snap multiple joints at once. "Tell her what a piece of shit you are."

"I'm—I'm a piece of shit."

"A puny, pathetic, filthy piece of shit who couldn't get pussy he didn't pay for if his life depended on it."

"A puny—"

I touch Ryder's arm. "Enough," I interrupt.

Ryder's eyes flick to me, to the man writhing in pain, and then back to me. "I heard what he said."

I hate that a part of me finds this thrilling. "So did I. You've made your point—you've avenged my honor."

His grin is quick but amused, and then he turns to the man, releasing him with a shove. "Take a swing—I fucking dare you."

The man just stumbles away, shaking out his arm, looking pissed but unwilling to push it. With an ugly glare back at me and Ryder, he lurches out the door.

Ryder just smirks at me. "Fancy seeing you here." He indicates the booth he was sitting in. "I'm over there."

I follow him over and slide in opposite him—Ryder must be some kind of preferred patron or something, because a waitress appears almost immediately—she's young and pretty, with brown hair and blue eyes and a cute smile for Ryder that I'm surprised to find isn't at all flirtatious.

"Another beer for you, Ryder?" Her tone is familiar, personal.

Ryder nods. "Yeah, I'll have another."

Her eyes go to me, friendly and welcoming. "And for your friend?"

He glances at me. "Laurel?"

"I'll have a gin and soda with a slice of lime."

When she's gone, Ryder turns his hazel eyes on me, brushing a lock of hair out of his eyes with a thumb. "So. What brings a classy broad like you to a dump like this?"

I snort. "Classy broad? Not sure if that's an insult, a compliment, or both." I look around. "And I wouldn't call this a dump. It's nicer in here than I expected."

Ryder laughs. "I think most people expect it to be either a strip bar or a dirty hole in the wall."

I snicker. "Well, that is pretty much what I would have expected, just looking at it from the outside."

The waitress returns with our drinks; Ryder

thanks her and then turns to me. "So. What are you doing here?"

I just grin and shrug. "This can't simply be my favorite bar to come to alone on a Friday night?"

Ryder snorts. "Not likely." He gestures around. "I helped Billy with the renovations of this place—all four of us did, actually—and I've been coming here every weekend since then."

"Oh. So you're saying you'd know if I'd ever been here before."

"I'm saying the clientele of this place is almost exclusively contractors—the only women that ever come here are with a date or looking for...well, not a date, and let's just leave it at that." He scratches at his beard. "So...why are you here?"

I sigh. "I had it on good authority that you'd be here."

He nods, sips his beer. "I see." His smirk is cocky and annoying and knowing. "Stalking me, huh?"

I roll my eyes at him. "Stalking would be crazy, and I'm fairly certain I'm not crazy." I fix him with a stare. "Maybe that's why you stopped answering my texts."

His eyes narrow. "Who have you been talking to?"

I counter his question with one of my own. "Why did you stop responding?"

He laughs. "A Mexican stand-off, it looks like."

"I think a Mexican stand-off has to be more than two people," I say.

He nods. "Ah, true." His eyes search mine, and then make a brief but noticeable trip downward before sliding away to scan the crowded bar. "So how about this—we both answer each other's questions at the same time."

I snort. "That's stupid."

"Okay, well then, you go first. Who have you been talking to and what did they say, and why were you asking them about me?"

I arch an eyebrow. "Nice try. You go first."

He huffs in annoyance. "You promise you'll actually answer if I do?"

I nod and hold out my hand, and we shake. "Promise," I say.

"All right, but before I answer I gotta know how much of the unvarnished truth you think you can actually handle without getting mad?"

I wrinkle my nose. "How am I supposed to be able to gauge that without knowing what the truth is?"

Ryder's brow furrows, which shouldn't be attractive, but is. "Oh. Good point."

"But let's assume I can handle the truth, the whole truth, and nothing but the truth."

"So help you God?"

"Nah, this isn't court."

He laughs. "Fine, the whole truth, then." He takes a long, fortifying drink of his beer, and then levels his eyes at me. "I had a couple of reasons. One, you'd made it clear from before the first date that *if* wc had sex, it'd be well after you'd gotten to know me, and that things would be moving slowly. So, no sex on the first date or even the fourth or fifth. Which was fine—seriously, no big deal. But four dates in, I knew I couldn't keep my end of the bargain."

I frown. "What do you mean?"

"I just couldn't do it. I'm too fucking attracted to you. When we kissed after that fourth date, it took literally everything I had to not pressure you into sex."

I blink at him. "So you just stopped answering my texts and calls?"

"It wasn't just that."

"But wait, pressure me? What does that even mean?"

"It means—"

"Were you worried I couldn't resist the pressure? That I wouldn't be able to say no if I wasn't ready? Seriously, I don't see how that leads you to just vanishing on me."

Ryder sighs. "I told you, it was more than that."

"Then do elucidate, please."

Ryder frowns. "Elusi-what?"

I roll my eyes. "Don't act dumber than you are."

"For real, I don't know that word."

Elucidate," I say, pronouncing it clearly: el-*OO*-sih-dayt. "Explain. Make clear."

He nods. "Got it. Elucidate." He hesitates. "That kiss sort of freaked me out a little."

My heart thumps. "Me too." I meet his eyes. "Why did it freak you out?"

"It just…it felt…weird." He sighs, waving a hand. "I don't know how to put it. More intense than I'm used to? I don't really know."

"Like there was a connection between us just from the kiss."

He nods. "Yeah, pretty much. And just to be honest, Laurel, I'm not sure I'm ready for anything with a connection that strong."

I snort. "You're forty-something years old, Ryder. If you're not ready now, when will you be?"

"Forty-three. And…never?" He grins, though, and I'm not sure if that's a joke.

I tilt my head. "You're not covering the truth by pretending it's a joke, are you?"

He sighs. "See? You're not supposed to be able to see through my bullshit that easily."

"But I can," I say, smirking. "So don't bother bullshitting me."

He grunts in amused annoyance. "Today is kind of an anniversary for me, which is why I'm here alone—I'm drowning my misery."

"Anniversary of what?"

"My divorce."

I nod. "Ah. That I totally understand."

"Yeah, I guess you would."

I smile sympathetically. "So, was it a messy one?"

He lets out a sarcastic bark. "Are they ever not messy?"

"Good point," I say.

He eyes me. "You don't really want to hear this story, do you? Isn't it bad form to talk about exes?"

"On first dates or early in the relationship, yes, but this isn't a date, and we don't have a relationship because you ghosted me."

He heaves a sigh and then takes a long drink of his beer. "I didn't ghost you."

"Not sure what else you'd call abruptly cutting off all communication without warning or explanation."

"I just did explain."

I frown. "Yeah…because I stalked you here and demanded one."

He snorts a laugh. "So you admit you stalked me?"

"Well, if you must know, I asked Audra and Imogen to ask Franco and Jesse where I could find you, and they told me. So, it wasn't that hard."

"I mean, I *am* here pretty much every night."

I lift an eyebrow. "Every night?"

He shrugs. "Billy serves good burgers, and cooking ain't really my thing." He lifts the pint glass in his hand. "Most nights, I have one or two, sometimes three. I'm not a heavy drinker, if that's what you're wondering."

I lift both hands palms out. "I wasn't judging." I laugh, then. "Nicely done, by the way."

He makes a face that's somewhere between a puzzled frown and an amused grin. "What?"

"Avoiding answering my question."

He blows out a breath. "Fine. Yes—it was messy. From start to finish, the whole fucking relationship was messy. The way we met, hooking up, dating, getting engaged, getting married, getting divorced, the whole thing was an unmitigated fucking disaster."

I blink, eyes wide. "Wow. Okay."

He gestures at me with his pint glass. "You asked."

I nod. "I did." I roll a hand. "Continue."

"Why do you want to know?"

"Curiosity?"

He laughs. "Morbid curiosity, then." He pauses for a moment, thinking. "All through high school and trade school, I had a weird nickname: Bob Vila."

I laugh. "Like, the guy from the tool commercials and *This Old House*?"

He snorts, nodding. "That's the guy. You know why they called me that?"

"Because you were into construction?"

"Electrical work is not the same as construction, FYI. And no. Jesse was the first to call me Bob Vila, back in...tenth grade? Eleventh? Somewhere in there. It was because I was always dating these girls who were, according to James, Jesse, and Franco, fixer-uppers." He uses air quotes around the phrase. "Meaning, the really messed-up girls from shitty backgrounds who I thought needed me to save them."

I grimace. "Oh. That's...fun."

He laughs. "It's a complicated psychological thing. I guess I just wanted to feel needed—at least that's what the therapist I saw after my divorce told me." He shrugs. "It was a series of train wrecks, to be honest. One girl after another was messed up somehow and would get needy and clingy and weepy and I'd end up breaking up with them because I'd realize they needed more fixing than I could provide, and I'd promise myself the next girl I dated wouldn't be needy."

"Yet they always were," I suggest.

He nods. "Exactly. And then I met Amy. I was freshly single, coming out of another relationship with a girl who was…well, let's just say popping Norco like Tic Tacs was the least of her issues."

"Yikes."

"Yeah. So I met Amy at a bar, and we hit it off. Flirting, lots of back and forth, I thought she was hot, she seemed to like me, seemed fairly normal, no obvious signs of crazy. And trust me, I was getting good by that point at seeing signs of crazy." He concentrated on his glass. "So, we, uh…hooked up. I was determined that's all it would be—remember, I was less than two weeks out of a relationship that had really taken its toll on me. Only, I messed up—I stayed the night. Not intentionally, but still. We'd been drinking, and it got late, and I meant to get up and go home, but ended up passing out instead."

"Let me guess, she had a boyfriend."

He smirks. "Not quite. We'd gone back to her place after the bar—again, seems normal, right? Only, I wake up, and she's not there, and there's a chick standing over me, staring down at me looking pissed, and it's *not* Amy."

I frown. "Huh? Like, you slept with the wrong girl?"

He laughs. "No, god no—I wasn't *that* drunk. The girl was totally different, brunette to Amy's blond, tall to Amy's short—a totally different person. And she was seriously pissed off, because she'd stayed the night at her boyfriend's house, came home to get her books for class, and found a random dude naked in her bed."

I break out into laughter. "What? How does that happen?"

He shakes his head. "It turned out the girl whose bed I was in—Shelly, her name was—realized I had hooked up with Amy...her former roommate. Shelly had kicked Amy out because she kept stealing money, not paying rent, and doing other crazy shit."

I blink. "Wow. Quite an impression. So...how did you end up in Shelly's bed?"

"Amy was still between apartments, and needed somewhere to bring me so we could...you know. And apparently she'd kept a copy of Shelly's key, and somehow knew Shelly would be at her boyfriend's that night, and figured Shelly wouldn't mind us using her bed."

I make a disgusted face. "Um...gross!"

"I know! I was mortified. But apparently Shelly was fairly familiar with Amy's bullshit and wasn't too surprised. She told me to let myself out and feel free to not come back. I'm assuming she threw away her sheets once I left." He laughs.

I shake my head. "Wow. So...you ended up *marrying* this Amy girl? The one who stole from her roommate, kept secret copies of keys, lied about being homeless, and brought you to her ex-room-mate's apartment for sex?"

He laughs, nodding. "Yep, I did."

"Wow. Do tell how *that* happens."

"She was…convincing. I'm not justifying it, mind you. I knew it was a bad idea, I knew it was only going to get me into trouble, but I was…addicted, I guess. Because she *really* needed me. All the guys were like, 'danger, danger, abort, abort—this chick is fucking nuts,' but I just couldn't resist." He sighs. "She was a deadly combination of hot, good in bed, and needy." He frowns at me. "Sorry, I'm just…telling the truth."

"No need to apologize—I did ask." I laugh, shaking my head. "She must have been *really* hot and *really* good in bed for you to overlook that amount of crazy from the first hookup."

He nods. "Yeah, I guess she was. I don't know if I can even explain it or rationalize it now, honestly. I just… I couldn't help myself." A pause. "That's kind of par for the course, how things with her started. Only…it got worse. She was bipolar but refused to get diagnosed properly, refused any kind of medication, and insisted her self-medication worked fine… that being copious amounts of alcohol, pot, and whatever pills she could get her hands on, but mostly a lot of boozing."

I wince. "That never works out well."

He shakes his head. "No, not at all. We got married after dating for eight months—which again, all the guys pleaded with me not to do, and I ignored them. So, there I was, married at twenty-three to a bipolar, alcoholic, pill addict with a lot of emotional baggage. I never really knew much about her past because she'd never talk about it, but I knew it involved sexual abuse of some kind, probably physical abuse, chronic homelessness, and who knows what else. But she put on a good show, you know? When she was up, she was *way* up. Super bubbly, full of life and energy and joy and just…an infectious wildness. She made you feel like anything was possible. You never knew where the day would take you when she was on an upswing. She was totally unpredictable—which was part of the fun. She'd decide to go roller skating in the rain, or drive around topless at eighty miles per hour, or break into a YMCA in the middle of the night to go skinny-dipping. And she'd always get away with it, somehow. Looking back, it was miraculous we never got arrested, because she did some crazy illegal shit, and I was always right there with her. But when she was up, she was invincible, and she convinced you she was, and the facts seemed to agree with her—she never got hurt, never got arrested or caught, and the crazy shit we did was always a hell of a rush."

"I can see how that'd suck you in," I say.

"Right, well, the downswings were the polar op-posite…thus the term bipolar, I guess. When she was down, the world was ending. Life was meaningless. She became, in her own mind, the most horrible, useless, disgusting, fat, ugly, sad sack of shit walking the face of the earth. When she was up, drinking and drugs were just icing on the cake, enough to loosen her up and add to the fun. But when she was down, she got vicious with it. She'd kill fifths like you and I would polish off a bottle of beer, and then she'd pop a handful of pills or smoke a bunch of pot. And she'd…" He sighs. "These benders would last for days. I couldn't stop 'em, couldn't slow her down, and couldn't rein her in. She'd vanish for days on end, and after a year or two of living through the cycles I started to learn that she always ended up in the same places. There was this park which must have been near where she grew up or something, because she'd always crawl into one of those yellow plastic tubes that connect one part of a play structure to another. I found her there by accident once—I happened to be driving past the park looking for her, and just hap-pened to look at the exact right moment to see this shape in the tube, wearing what she'd been wearing when she'd run off three days before. After that, I'd find her there eight out of ten times."

I wince. "Yikes."

"Yeah." He's quiet for a while, and I don't rush it. "Those benders…man, they started taking their toll, and I'm talking financially, too. Eventually, her luck started to run out."

"Uh, oh," I say, hearing the heaviness in his voice.

He nods. "Yep. She got in a car wreck—totaled the used Hyundai I'd bought her, and miraculously didn't hurt herself or anyone else. That was the beginning of the really ugly period—I told her that she had to get help. She agreed, tried to cut down on her drinking, promised she'd see someone. And she did, a couple times. And then she started feeling better—the upswing of her cycle, and was convinced she was all better, and quit seeing the doctor, quit taking the meds she was prescribed to manage her mood swings."

"That never ends well," I say.

He shakes his head. "Nope, but it's part of the cycle. You hit an upswing and mistake it for being fixed and decide you can manage without the meds, and then the next time you shift to a downswing, it's a huge crash, and it's nastier than ever. She got trapped in this cycle. I refused to buy her a new car until I was sure she was clean and stable, and it took about two and a half years, but finally she convinced me she was okay." He's not drinking his beer, just swirling it, staring into it. "So, like an idiot, I believed her and bought her a car. A used Wrangler. I guess in the back of my mind I sort of knew she wasn't fixed, because the Jeep I bought her was older, and not in great condition, but I'd had to pay the fines for the wreck, and my insurance premium went up, and business was getting a little sketchy for reasons outside my control, so things were tight, but she wanted a job and she really seemed to be more stable than I'd ever seen her."

"It didn't last, huh?"

He barks a laugh, a bitter sound. "It lasted six months. And, to be honest, those six months were the best of our relationship. She was working, she was fairly level, didn't drink all that much or smoke or pop pills, she was happy, she was affectionate, business started to pick up again." He sighs. "And then she got a DUI. She was over twice the limit, in the middle of the day. I took care of it—paid the fines, bailed her out of jail, got her car out of impound, went to court to get her fines reduced, which cost a mint in lawyer fees. And then, bam, less than two months later—two months of her going to AA once a week, and I know she went because I took her and waited outside and picked her up—she got another DUI. This time, she took my truck in the middle of the night—she was hammered *and* stoned and decided she needed food to sober up, and she went to Denny's."

"Ryder, god…how much more could you have taken, at that point?"

He sighs, a pained expression on his face. "I loved her, Laurel. We'd been together ten years by that point. How could I just abandon her? She'd get herself killed without me."

I winced. "God, that had to be hard."

"There aren't really words for it, honestly. Yeah, I thought about leaving her all the time. But I kept coming back to the question of what would happen to her without me?"

"So what was the breaking point?"

"She led the police on a high-speed chase through a quiet suburban neighborhood, hammered off her ass. And then, while on a high-speed chase, she popped a handful of pills, threw them down with a slug straight from a bottle of vodka she'd bought with loose change, and OD'd. Behind the wheel. I think at this point she was trying to kill herself, she just didn't have the...I don't know, courage? That's the wrong word, but I don't know what the right word is, just that she wasn't going to cut her wrists or shoot herself, so OD-ing behind the wheel was her way of trying to end things, I think. Only, her luck held out one last time—going ninety through an intersection she rear-ended a car. The other driver was seriously injured, but Amy didn't have a scratch. The lucky part was that the other driver didn't die, which was a miracle, considering how bad the wreck was."

"Jesus, Ryder."

He laughs bitterly. "Sorry you asked, now, aren't you?" He sighs. "There was no avoiding jail time for her, this time. The costs piled up, my debt increased, and I was getting desperate. I knew it was only a matter of time before she killed herself or someone else. So, when she got out of jail, I gave her an ultimatum. She had to get clean and stay clean, or I'd leave her."

"Good for you."

The bitter laugh, this time, was painful to hear. "Yeah, if I'd only had the balls to keep it. I gave her the ultimatum in the car on the way home from jail. Mistake, that was—a *big* mistake. She opened the car door and unbuckled—and we were on the freeway doing seventy-five. Stone-cold sober, she told me she'd kill herself if I ever left her."

I exhale sharply. "Oh, wow."

He nods. "Yep. So…I mean, I wasn't surprised, but she was dangling a foot out the door of a moving truck, threatening to throw herself out if I didn't promise to stay with her, so I promised."

"God, Ryder."

He takes a sip, finally, but a tiny one. More for something to do to cover his emotions than anything. "Part of her sentence for the crash was court-ordered mandatory rehab, the kind you can't just check yourself out of when you feel like you're all better. The rehab…that was the last straw for me, financially. I ended up having to sell my business to keep from going bankrupt, had to sell the house, my truck, everything except my tools and this old, beat up, rusted-out piece of shit antique I'd salvaged as a project. I'd been fixing it up on the weekends, and I had it running, sort of. It wasn't worth anything, so I couldn't sell it, and it ended up being my only mode of transportation. The tools, the truck, and my personal effects were all I had left. I had this month-to-month lease at a dumpy apartment while I figured shit out, and that's when everything blew up."

"What do you mean, blew up? How much more blown up could things get?"

"Right? Broke, unemployed, all but homeless, my wife in rehab? Couldn't get any worse, huh?" Another bitter laugh. "I got divorce papers in the mail."

I rear back in shock. "What?"

He nods. "That was my reaction. I thought it was a cruel joke or something. Until I got the letter the next day—she'd sent the letter at the same time as the papers, but the papers arrived first for some reason. Her letter basically said rehab had shown her how much of a mess she'd made of her life and mine, and how she finally had to face the reality that she'd never be able to get clean if we were together because I'd keep bailing her out, keep fixing things for her. She apologized for everything, promised she was going to get better, and that if I had to move on, she'd understand, but she hoped I'd wait for her."

I shake my head, struggling for words. "Wow. I mean just…wow. Was it real?"

He nods. "I called her. She told me it was the only way she'd survive, that she had to face her demons on her own, and she had to know she didn't have me to keep fixing things for her." He rubs his face. "And I realized she was right. I'd gone bankrupt—or all but—trying to save her. So…I signed the papers. The day the divorce was final, I got a call from Jesse saying that James's wife had died, and that he needed us. Well, considering I was basically at a dead-end anyway, I packed my shit, put my furniture in storage, and moved in with James, Jesse, and Franco. I went to work for James and, eventually, put my life back together again."

He tosses back his beer, and then glances at me.

"So," he says. "Your turn."

THREE

I STIR MY DRINK WITH THE LITTLE BLACK STRAW—I'D BEEN so wrapped up in Ryder's story that I'd forgotten to drink it, and now the ice is melted and the lime is floating soggily on the surface.

"My story is sort of similar," I say. "Just less…"

"Batshit crazy?" Ryder suggests.

I nod. "Yeah, pretty much. I dated some disasters in high school and college—mistakes and assholes, bad boys and bastards. Think of the girl who seems to have a nose for the worst possible guy she could pick…that was me. So then I met Paul. He was nice. Not a bad boy, not an asshole, not a drunk or a drug addict."

"Sounds great on paper," Ryder says with a grin. "What was wrong with him?"

I poke at the lime in my drink. "It kind of sounds lame, now that I've heard your story." I laugh. "I should've gone first."

Ryder chuckles. "Let me guess: mood swings?"

I nod. "Yep. The official diagnosis, obtained during our belated and ill-fated attempt at marriage therapy, was bipolar disorder with narcissistic tendencies."

Ryder winces. "Ouch."

"Yeah. So basically, everything was about him. When he was depressed, it was my fault and my responsibility to make him feel better, and when he was feeling good, he was invincible and perfect and expected me to go along with all his crazy ideas or I was a bad wife."

"What was his brand of crazy?" Ryder asks.

I laugh—bitterly, yes, but with amusement gleaned from hindsight. "Oh man, you name it. He woke up in the middle of the night about six months after we got married and decided he needed a tattoo, so we drove through the night into Chicago and got matching tattoos."

He looks me over. "So where's yours?"

I snicker. "I managed to talk him into letting me get a tiny little infinity symbol on my left hipbone. By tiny, I mean it could've fit on my index finger."

"Can I see it?" Ryder asks with a smirk.

"No, because I got it removed the day the divorce was finalized." I angle my left hip upward, shove down the waistband of my skirt and point at the faint outline where it had been. "That's all that's left."

"That's not all that crazy," Ryder says. "So far, I win."

I cackle. "Oh, you're gonna win, no question about that." I wave a hand. "He bought a motorcycle, once. We were all but broke, because he was between jobs and I was working three jobs to make ends meet. He was on one of what I called his wild hair swings, where he would get a wild hair up his ass about something. That time it was thinking he'd...I don't know, become a motorcycle racer or something. So he takes the money we'd saved—*I'd* saved—so we could afford a down payment on a modest house that didn't have a leaky roof and wasn't surrounded by crack dens, and bought a crotch rocket."

Ryder tries unsuccessfully to suppress a laugh. "Wow. What a dick."

"Yeah, and he'd bought it used from some guy he'd met at a bar, so there was no returning it." I sigh. "He crashed it two weeks later and broke his leg."

"That sucks."

"Yeah, and he totaled the bike, and we didn't have insurance, so we were out the money I'd saved, the motorcycle was trashed, and we owed a bunch of money for his hospital bill." I shake my head. "That's about average for Paul on his wild hair part of the cycle. He'd get a crazy idea and spend money we didn't have on something we didn't need. He'd drag me out of bed in the middle night, get himself hurt, and put us more into debt."

"And his downswing?"

I take a long sip of my watery drink. "Basically he became the most morose, depressed, verbally and emotionally abusive asshole to ever walk the earth." I pause. "And, if we're telling the truth, the whole truth, and nothing but the truth…he was also insanely sexually demanding during his downswing. When he was manic, he rarely even thought about me or sex—he was too excited about whatever his latest cockamamy idea was. But when he was depressed, he became convinced the only thing that could make him happy again was me…only, it never worked. It just made him more depressed and angry—usually because I'd done something wrong. I came too soon, or too late, or I failed to read his mind about what position he wanted…" I blush, trailing off. "I shouldn't be telling you this."

"Amy was the same way," Ryder says. "On a depressive cycle, she was the neediest person alive. I couldn't keep up—honestly that's hard to admit, as a man, but it's just the truth. She…needed me more frequently and more intensely than I was capable of sustaining. I mean, sex four times a day every day for a month straight *sounds* like fun, especially when you're in the middle of a dry spell, but the reality is…"

"Exhausting? Mentally, emotionally, and physically draining?" I suggest.

He nods, looking grateful that I understand. "Exactly. I'm totally capable of keeping up with that for a week, two weeks, but after three weeks I start to need some breaks, and maybe some snacks."

"So, you're not an inexhaustible sex machine?" I joke.

"I'd rather you know the truth now than find out later," he says, going with it. "I'd hate to disappoint you."

"All joking aside, I get it." I find myself unable to look him in the eye as I say this. "Paul was the same way. And…I always thought I revved pretty high in the libido department. To be honest—I always struggled with feeling like my previous boyfriends didn't want me as much as I wanted them so, at first, Paul needing me like that was refreshing. But when it turned into weeks and months of him wanting sex two, three, four times a day, I just…I got burned out. But if I turned him down, it would…" I trailed off.

"Make the depression and anger even more vicious?" Ryder suggests. "Turn it on you. Make it your fault."

"Exactly."

Our eyes meet, understanding and empathy

shuttling between us.

I smile. "I honestly never thought I'd meet any-one who would actually be able to understand the whole thing."

Ryder laughs. "*You* didn't?"

I wince. "Good point." Another silence, this one less amicable and more awkward, more tense. "So. Now what?"

Ryder looks away. "Honestly, I don't know if us sharing the whole bipolar ex thing makes me feel any better."

I frown. "It doesn't?"

He shakes his head. "The problem I'm having isn't that I don't like you or that I'm not attracted to you—the problem is, I didn't need another reason to feel even more connected to you."

I sigh slowly, pinching the bridge of my nose. "Ahhhh. So you're like Audra."

He blinks. "What? How do you mean?"

"Allergic to anything resembling a serious relationship."

He scratches his fingers through his thick red beard. "Oh. I don't know about allergic, but it's defi-nitely something I've avoided since Amy."

"Which is why you only sleep with the crazy chicks?"

He chuckles. "I don't *only* sleep with crazy

chicks. It's just what I seem to gravitate to, for whatever reason."

I arch an eyebrow at him. "You can't really be that lacking in self-awareness, can you?"

He's silent a moment. "Meaning what?"

"Meaning you absolutely *do* sleep with crazy chicks by intentional design. They're safe. A crazy chick burned you, broke your heart, shattered your ability to trust, and left you broke. Therefore, by sleeping with the crazies, you're certain to be safe from falling in love again, because there's no way in blue hell you'd fall in love with another one."

He rocks back in the booth, staring at me through narrowed eyes, his jaw grinding. "You don't play fair."

I shrug. "I'm way past the point in my life where I'm gonna play games or mince words, Ryder."

"I see that."

"I'm not crazy, and you know it. I'm a risk—that's why I scare you."

He leans forward, eyes blazing. "I'm *not* scared of you, Laurel."

I smirk. "Oh yes, you are. Have the balls to admit it, Ryder."

Ryder's hazel eyes crackle and spit sparks. "It's not *fear*. Risk-aversion isn't fear. Risk-aversion is prudence, and that's it."

I have to laugh at that. "Oh, that's rich! Risk-aversion is prudence? You're delusional."

He frowns, truly upset, now. "Oh, and you're not?"

"Risk-averse? Yes. Delusional? No." I tap the table. "I fully admit my choice in men since Paul and I divorced has been less than stellar. Honestly, my choice in men my whole life has been abysmal. I know that about myself. That's why I'm afraid to let myself really, truly like you—that's why I went out of my way to find reasons *not* to like you. The answer to your initial question, by the way, is that I asked Audra, Imogen, and Nova for things about you that would make me like you less. I'm worried you're harboring some inner asshole-ness that I'm not seeing. I didn't see Paul clearly until it was too late. Like Amy, there are resources available to him to help manage his bipolarism, but he chooses not to use them—he refused to see anyone, refused to take medication no matter how I begged him. We both know using the term 'crazy' is unkind and unfair, and that what our respective exes suffered were illnesses they couldn't control. But if Paul had been willing to try to manage his illness in a healthy and constructive way, it probably would have worked between us. He had moments where he could be wonderful—especially where Nate was concerned."

I sigh. "And you seem rational and sane and interesting, and god knows I'm attracted to you, but I'm scared, and that's why I'm being so cautious. I'm just terrified I'll fall for you and you'll turn out to be just as much a mistake as Paul and all the other guys I've dated since then. I'm embarrassed to admit it but, sadly, every one of them ended up being an asshole in one way or another."

Ryder tugs on his beard. "Well, I think I can safely say I don't *think* I'm harboring any inner asshole-ness."

I point at him. "You *did* quit answering my calls and texts after four dates and a kiss."

"'All right, we'll call it a draw,'" he says, in a fake British accent.

I laugh. "You can't quote Monty Python at me and think it'll win you enough points with me to get you out of this." I've long since finished my drink, but don't really want another one just yet. "Ryder, look—If you don't want to see me, that's fine. I can handle that. But at least say it to my face."

He sighs. "I apologize, Laurel. It was a childish decision and a dick move, and I'm sorry."

I wait, but he seems disinclined to say anything else. "But?"

He rolls a shoulder. "I just…I'm not there."

I nod. "I see. Well, so be it." I slide out of the booth. "Thank you for saving me from Mr. Hairy

Knuckles, for the drink, and for the explanation."

"Laurel—"

I settle my purse on my shoulder. "I'll see you around, Ryder."

I make it to my car, and then I feel a strong hand on my waist. I don't turn, because I know without looking that it's him.

"It's not that simple, Laurel," he murmurs. "Even beyond my risk-aversion, the reason I vanished like I did is because I'm so attracted to you it makes me fucking crazy."

"That's backward to me, and I don't buy it." I arch an eyebrow. "If you're attracted me, you wouldn't vanish—you'd *pursue* me."

He spins me around, presses me up against the door of my car, his forehead against mine, his nose beside mine, his lips brushing mine. "You're determined to take things slow, and with my attraction to you being at a fucking eleven, that's not an option."

"Oh," I whisper. "Why didn't you say so in the first place?"

"Would it have made a difference?"

"Maybe."

"What happened to being able to resist me pressuring you?

"Is this you pressuring me?"

"Not even close."

"To be clear, when I said I wanted to take things slow, I didn't mean we'd *never* have sex, or that it would take, like, a year of dating," I murmur. "It's just that I didn't want you to expect it right away. I wanted to have time to assess what you were like before I let you that far into my life."

"Because it wouldn't be just sex, for you."

"Is it ever?"

He nods. "Quite frequently, in my experience."

"Well, my experience has been different." My hands rest on his shoulders, roaming the mountainous curves of his heavy muscle. "I go into something telling myself it'll be just sex, and then I end up with feelings, and the guy ends up being an asshole or needy or messed up somehow, and I get stuck in the same old cycle of dealing with a guy who needs me."

"I don't need you," he murmurs.

"No?"

"But I sure as fuck want you."

"That sounds refreshing. I wonder what it's like?" I say, sounding like I'm joking when I'm not, not at all.

He laughs. "I have no idea—I've often wondered the same thing."

He's still kissing-close, but he hasn't kissed me. "What are we doing here, Ryder?"

"I'm waiting for you to change your mind."

"About what?"

"Me kissing you."

I frown. "Why would I?"

His smirk is devilish and ravenous. "Because once I kiss you, I make no guarantees that I'll be able to slow down."

"But you're not *there* yet, in an emotional sense."

"Right."

"So you'll kiss me, and probably escalate things into a more serious physical territory, but you can't promise me anything beyond that?"

"Exactly."

"Can you promise me one thing?" I trail my fingers down through his beard.

"What?"

"Instead of vanishing on me, when you get too scared of the feelings I know I'm bound to develop for you, at least give me the decency of a heads-up before you dump me."

He laughs, a quiet rumble. "I can promise you that much."

"I can live with that."

The need to kiss him has been percolating inside me since I got here, since he told me he'd ghosted me because he wanted me too much. And now, his hands on my waist, his lips brushing mine, the need boils over and I lift up onto my toes, slamming my lips against his. He grunts in surprise, and then his hands slide across my back and curl around my waist and gather me closer so my breasts flatten against his chest and our hips meet. I knot my fingers in his beard and tug him closer, opening my mouth to his.

I feel him thickening between us, feel him hard ening against my belly. My nipples ache at the feeling, and my stomach flips and my heart flutters.

I pull away just enough that I can whisper. "I should clarify something," I mutter.

"Hmmm?"

"I don't take it slow because I don't want you, Ryder. I take it slow because I *do*."

"Can we go somewhere?" he asks, his palm skating across the small of my back.

I groan, resting my forehead against his. "I wish."

"Fuck. I knew it."

I curl my fingers into his shoulders. "No, you don't understand. I *can't*—my babysitter is a high schooler. She has to go home pretty soon." I pull back to look up at him. "I *want* to go somewhere with you, Ryder. I really do."

He growls, pulling away. "I'm not calling you a cocktease, but *dammit* woman, you really know how to turn a guy on and leave him hanging."

I glare at him. "That's not fair. I really do want this as much as you do. I just have other responsibilities that have to come first."

He sighs, turning away, passing his hand through his messy tangle of red hair. "I know, I know. I'm sorry. It's just…every time we're together, I leave like this."

I follow him toward his truck. "Like what?"

He laughs, a sharp bark. "Like *this*," he growls, gesturing at his zipper. "Hard as a fucking rock and no way to relieve it."

"Till you get home, you mean," I say, smirking.

Ryder's eyebrow arches. "You think I…what? Go home and jerk off thinking about you?"

"Don't you?"

His lips curl in a wicked grin. "Wouldn't you like to know?"

"Yes, I would, actually."

He sidles over to me, and I stand my ground, staring back up at him, the challenge clear in my eyes. "No, Laurel. I do not go home and jerk off while thinking about you."

"Why not? I thought that's what all guys did."

He frowns. "Because that feels degrading and disrespectful, to me. I'd feel gross about myself for using you like that, so I just suffer the blue balls."

I laugh, a soft huff. "I hate that answer."

"Why?"

"Because it turns me on, and I really do have to

go." I hesitate, and then stroke my fingers through his beard again. "What if I gave you permission?"

"I've never even seen you in a bathing suit, Laurel."

I grin. "You'll have to use your imagination, then."

"Or…" he says, prompting me to follow it up with the logical question.

"Or what?"

He smirks. "You have my number, and you have a smartphone with a camera."

I breathe a laugh of surprise. "You're asking me to send nudes?"

He tugs on a lock of my hair as he backs away. "Just suggesting it as a possibility. Otherwise…" He keeps walking backward toward his truck. "I'll just have to suffer until we can find a way to go somewhere together."

I shake my head. "I've never taken a naked picture of myself in my life, much less sent one to anyone. You *are* crazy if you think I'm doing that."

He shrugs, hands lifted palms up. "Worth a shot."

I hesitate, and then call after him. "A week from tomorrow I'm taking Nate to Paul's for a weekend visitation." I let the silence burgeon with significance. "Which means I'll have Friday night through Sunday afternoon free."

He sighs. "I'll probably die of blue balls before then."

"That's the best I can do, Ryder."

"What time do you drop him off on Friday?"

"Five thirty."

"Dinner—six fifteen. I'll text you with a location Friday afternoon. Dress nice."

I arch an eyebrow. "I always dress nicely, Ryder."

He smirks. "Something with cleavage and a short hem, preferably." He scans my outfit, which is work-appropriate, meaning business casual and modest. "Something sexy, just for me."

"Any other demands?" I ask, laughing.

"Yeah, heels." He pauses. "And if you won't send me a nude, I wouldn't mind a shot of you in your lingerie."

"Don't push your luck, bub," I say. "You're getting a date—nothing else is a sure thing."

He smirks again. "The way you kissed me told a different story."

I just shake my head. "Don't be rude."

"I'm not, I'm just saying," he says with a laugh. "The way you kissed me just now…"

"I have to go," is my only response.

I turn back to my car and slide behind the wheel, then watch as Ryder climbs up into his truck, which

is a classic 1940s Chevy box truck—it's been beauti-
fully and lovingly restored, painted a deep, glossy
forest green with *Ryder Electrical* in white lettering on
the door, the box end is heavily customized, featur-
ing chrome-handled, wood-paneled tool and equip-
ment cabinets of varying sizes, with a rack for ladders
across the top.

He waves at me as he pulls out of the parking lot.

I head home, pay Allyson, my babysitter, and
spend a few minutes with Nate, talking about his day
as we share a bowl of ice cream.

Once he's in bed, I bustle around my small but
cozy suburban home, tidying, picking up after Nate,
vacuuming, doing dishes…

Pretty much anything to keep my mind busy.

Eventually, it's nearly midnight and I know I have
to go to bed.

Normally I sleep in a T-shirt and underwear, but
for some reason today I decide on a full set of pajamas—button-down top and baggy drawstring bottoms, white with cute little kittens.

Not at all sexy.

I remove my makeup, brush out my hair, brush
my teeth…

And then I glance at myself in the mirror. My
hair is poofy from being brushed, my face is plain
without makeup, and I have a dab of toothpaste foam

at the corner of my lip.

Yeah, not sexy at all.

Which is why I'm at a loss as to what I'm thinking when I take a selfie in the bathroom, just like that, and send it to Ryder.

He replies immediately.

Ryder: *Damn, girl, you make even kitty jammies look sexy!*

I cackle out loud as I reply.

Me: *Wow. Laying it on thick, huh?*

Ryder: *I mean, if you'd asked me thirty seconds ago if I thought kitty pajamas could be sexy, I'd have laughed at you. And then you send me this photo, and I realize how very wrong I would have been.*

Me: *I have toothpaste on my mouth and my hair looks like I stuck my finger in a socket.*

Ryder: *As a licensed electrician, I would highly recommend against ever actually doing that.*

Me: *Ha ha. No kidding.*

Ryder: *I'd send you a pic of me in my pajamas, but I'm not wearing any.*

Me: *Let me guess...you sleep naked.*

Ryder's response is a winking emoji.

And then my phone bloops again as another message comes in, and this time, it's a photo.

Of Ryder.

In his bathroom, a toothbrush in his mouth,

toothpaste dribbling down his chin, clutching a towel around his waist. It's very evident he's naked except for the towel. He has a smattering of reddish body hair on his chest and in a trail down the center of his stomach leading under the towel, which is held loose and low. He's somewhere between having abs and a belly—there's a hint of definition up near his diaphragm, but lower down near his hips he has an area that says he likes good food and beer more than he values visible abs. His arms rival my thighs for size, rippling with power and definition. His chest is equally massive—each pec is like an anvil, hard and thick and solid. He looks strong enough to carry the weight of the world on his shoulders, but the twinkle in his eye and the grin tipping his toothpaste-foamed lips says he never takes himself that seriously.

The hint of a V angling from his hipbones taunts me, as does the hint of reddish hair just below his navel.

I have no idea how to reply.

Hubba hubba?

FML?

Heart-eyes emoji?

No reply?

I dab on some moisturizer and then stare at myself in the mirror, contemplating my reply.

I eye my phone, sitting beside the sink.

"Don't do it, Laurel," I tell myself.

Who am I kidding?

I unbutton the top button of my pajama top. Then the second and third—enough to show some cleavage. Then, suppressing a grin of disbelief at my own impulsiveness, I undo the bottom button, and the next one up, and the next, until there's only one button left buttoned—the one keeping my breasts from flying free, and that poor button is straining desperately to restrain me.

There's no way I'd ever send him a photo of myself naked, or even totally topless, but maybe I could push the limits a *little*?

I slide the last button free of the buttonhole, and the weight of my breasts parts the edges of the shirt, and now I'm bare, to a degree. A wide slice of tan skin from my navel upward is visible, along with a generous amount of the inner swell of my boobs. I tug the bottoms down an inch, another, until my hip bones are visible—and then I tug a bit further, baring the V where my thighs crease against my core. Nothing is technically visible, entirely. But it *is* pretty sexy.

I grin at myself—not bad for a thirty-six-year-old single mother of a nine-year-old.

I snap a selfie, delete it, take another, adjust the edges of my top to make sure no nipple or areola is visible, and then take another—after about twenty deleted photographs, I find one I'm satisfied with, and send it before I can second-guess myself.

And then I wait on pins and needles for his reply.

Ryder: *You DID give me permission, right?*

I suck in a breath. Bite my lip. Try not to think about what he'd look like…

Me: *I did…*

Ryder: *Good, because I'm not sure I can stop myself.*

I gulp, set the phone down, and walk away. I make it three steps before I whirl back around and snatch my phone off the counter.

Me: *I didn't need to know that.*

Ryder: *No, but you wanted to.*

A minute passes…two minutes.

Curiosity burns inside me, but I fight it.

And I lose.

Me: *so…did you?*

The little gray dots jump and dance, stop, start, vanish, and start jumping again, and I huff in aggravation. Eventually, a message pops up.

Ryder: *You're seriously asking me if I just masturbated to the pictures you sent?*

Me: *no*

Me: *yes. Maybe?*

Ryder: *What do you want the answer to be? Do you want me to tell you yes, I did? Do you want to hear that I thought about ripping those stupid fucking kitten paja-mas off you and doing all sorts of dirty things you? Do you want to know that I made an awful goddamn mess of myself thinking about you?*

Ryder: *Or would you rather hear that I held out? That I couldn't bring myself to do that even with permission?*

I groan, because I don't know what I want the answer to be.

I turn back to the mirror, letting my top stay open and my breasts bare, but I press my wrists against my-self to cover the center of my breasts, and I send it.

Me: *I want to know the truth.*

Ryder: *Yes, Laurel. I did.*

I groan again, because this time, the thoughts that flashed through my mind were of Ryder, of those strong hands clutching himself, stroking, sliding, glid-ing, all while he moans my name and tries to imagine me naked.

I throw my phone across the room onto my bed before I do anything rash…like send him a photo that would have him coming to thoughts of me all over again.

All over.

Dammit. I couldn't stop an image of Ryder, of the way he'd grunt and groan my name, the way he'd have laid a hot stripe of cum up his belly…

DAMMIT.

It wasn't supposed to be like this. I wasn't supposed to want him like this. When I met him at that party, I had images of us going on sweet dates together—dancing, going to a movie, me eating his popcorn, kissing on the porch of my house.

And here I am, picturing him jerking off to thoughts of me, picturing him moaning my name and coming on his stomach.

Wishing, deep down, that it wasn't just images in my head.

Ryder: *Now who's not answering texts? What's the matter, Laurel? Cat got your tongue?*

Me: *I have to go to bed.*

Ryder: *I'll let it go...for now.*

Half a minute later, my phone dings again.

Ryder: *You are the most beautiful woman I've ever seen, Laurel. And if that's all of you I ever get to see, I'll be the luckiest man in the world for having seen it.*

I swallow hard. He wasn't supposed to make it sweet. He was supposed to leave it dirty and inappropriate, so I could tell myself all he wanted was sex. That all he cared about was getting me naked, or if not that, then at least seeing me naked.

Instead, he turned it sweet. And I couldn't tell myself any lies to keep me on my high horse.

Me: *You're making this difficult, Ryder.*

Ryder: *Making what difficult?*

Me: *Not wanting you.*

Ryder: *Can't help you there, babe. I conceded that fight back in the parking lot of Billy Bar. I want you. And I guess I'm willing to fight dirty to get you.*

Me: *Good night, Ryder. See you Friday.*

Ryder: *If I don't see more of you before then…*

Me, with an eye roll emoji: *You wish.*

Ryder: *Absolutely. I wished you'd send me a peek of what was under those jammies, and I got that wish. Now I'm wishing I'll get a peek at what's behind those hands, what's under those kitty pajama bottoms. Hoping this wish comes true, too…*

Me: *You're impossible.*

Ryder: *You know it, and you know you like it.*

Me: *Good night.*

Ryder sent a selfie of himself, obviously in bed. Smirking at the camera with tired, heavy-lidded eyes, brilliant red hair messier than ever.

Apparently that was his version of good night, because I didn't reply and neither did he.

I fell asleep quickly, but my dreams were filled with Ryder, and by thrilling, naughty, erotic images of him touching himself, of me touching him…and of me helping him find the release he was throbbing for.

FOUR

THE WEEK PASSES BY BOTH TOO QUICKLY AND NOT quickly enough. My days are busy, but the meetings drag. Nate has basketball practice every day after school, which means I have two hours every afternoon to kill. I usually end up going home, doing laundry and housework…and texting with Ryder.

Friendly banter, mostly. There are no more pictures between us, risqué or otherwise. Every once in a while, one of us will make an innuendo. Mostly, though, it's just friendly banter.

Easy.

Fun.

He asks about Nate, and I send him a photo of Nate making a layup at the end of practice. I ask about work, and he sends me a photo of himself with a screwdriver in his teeth, surrounded by a rat's nest of multicolored wires and cords and frayed copper ends.

I dread the coming of the weekend, and I also can't wait.

I dread it because Paul gets Nate every other weekend, and I worry incessantly—Paul's extreme mood swings and unpredictability never resulted in any court action that would revoke visitation privileges. While Nate is at Paul's apartment I don't get much sleep for forty-eight hours, and I spend most of the time panicking, fraught with anxiety. Paul does love Nate; I can't and won't take that away from him. They have fun together, and Nate rarely comes back upset or off-kilter…no more than any nine-year-old in a fractured family, at least.

I think.

I'm also looking forward to this weekend, because I'll get to see Ryder.

Thursday finally arrives and Nate and I have dinner and I hear all about a new friend he made at school. Once dinner is over, we clear up and Nate watches an hour of TV while I read, and then he's off to bed.

It's quiet.

Normally, this is one of my favorite parts of the day, when the house is quiet and I can do whatever I want. Which, usually, just means taking off my pants and bra, having a snack, and bingeing on Netflix in my room.

Lately, though, my mind has been wandering.

I get as far as taking off my pants and bra, and then some stupid, impetuous, horny little voice inside me starts whispering for me to send Ryder another risqué selfie. I ignored the voice all week and focused on other things: a docuseries I've been meaning to watch; emptying out the fridge, cleaning it, and throwing away moldy leftovers and expired condiments; sorting my clothes and organizing them by season and color, and getting rid of stuff I haven't worn in at least a year; deep cleaning the baseboards; scrubbing around the base of the toilets because Nate's aim is perpetually terrible.

Tonight, though, I can't think of a single project to distract myself.

I could dust, and go underneath everything instead of around like I usually do. Or I could polish my collection of leather boots. Or…um…

I groan out loud, flopping backward onto my bed, phone clutched in my hand, telling myself NOT to text Ryder a picture of my boobs.

It's stupid. It's immature. It's indecent.

But sexy and thrilling…

I'm a mother.

But not a nun…

It'd be giving something away when I should make him work for it…

Except it's just a photograph…

He might share it with the guys, or post it online.

No way would Ryder do something like that…

My phone chirps just then.

Ryder: *WYD?*

Me: *What does that mean?*

Ryder: *What you doing. I learned it from one of the apprentices at the job I'm contracting for.*

Me: *You don't work for James?*

Ryder: *I do, yes. He's my primary employer. But he doesn't always have work for me, so I take jobs as an independent contractor to fill in the gaps.*

Ryder: *So. WYD?*

Me: *Fighting with myself.*

Ryder: *LOL. About what, and who's winning?*

Me: *I probably shouldn't tell you.*

Ryder, with a smirking, mischievous, emoji: *Oh, really? Well, in that case, you HAVE to tell me.*

I groan again. Don't.

Laurel…don't. DO NOT.

Me: *it was kinda fun sending you those pix the other night. I was…um…thinking about sending another one.*

Ryder: *I think that's a fucking fantastic idea. Are you wearing the kitty jammies again?*

I look down at myself—pink knee-high socks with sloths holding a beer stein, and the top I'd worn to work, sans bra; the top was a basic white silk button-down, and I had it unbuttoned quite a ways down.

I hold the phone above me, but the angle isn't quite right—it takes some maneuvering so the photo shows my face, torso, and legs. I take the photo and do a little editing to get rid of the bruise on my thigh from where I'd banged my leg against the counter the other day, and then get ready to send it.

And then I have a better idea.

I take another photo, this one of just my legs with my funny pink drunk sloth socks and I send that one first.

Ryder: *OMG! Those socks!*

Ryder: *Are you wearing any pants? Please tell me you're not wearing any pants.*

Me: *Who wears pants at home alone after 10pm?*

Ryder: *Not me, that's for damn sure.*

He accompanied this with a photo of himself in his kitchen, wearing nothing but a pair of gym shorts. He's in a goofy pose, one knee drawn up with a finger over his pursed lips, a saucy grin on his face—it's a comical parody of a supposedly sexy pose you'd see on Instagram.

I laugh out loud.

Me: *I'm pretty sure gym shorts count as pants.*

Immediately, he sends another photo of himself in that same pose, except his shorts are around his ankles and he's wearing nothing but a pair of tight gray boxer briefs that do nothing to hide the...um...scope...of his endowment.

Ryder: *Better?*

Me, with a wide-eyed in surprise emoji: *Yeah... better is one word for it.*

Ryder: *Oh stop, you.*

Ryder: *Not really. I have a fragile male ego, so you should compliment me some more.*

Me: *My compliments are...non-verbal.*

Ryder: *Meaning?*

Me: *Meaning the fact that you're doing that stupid pose, but I can't stop looking at the pic.*

Ryder: *Looking at the pic, and...?*

I let impulse reign, and in this case the impulse is to take another photo. Me, on my back in bed, staring up at the camera with my lip caught in my teeth and a wide-eyed look of arousal on my face—not at all faked or exaggerated. The fact that I'm not wearing a bra and my shirt is mostly unbuttoned means my breasts sag downward with gravity, the edges of the shirt just barely covering my nipples. The lower edge of the photo cuts off at mid-thigh, which is more than enough to show my bright yellow underwear...

And my fingers are in the act of sneaking under the waistband.

Naughty, naughty.

I send it without touching it up or overthinking it.

Ryder: *holy fucking hell, Laurel. You're killing me.*

Me: *Killing you?*

Ryder: *how am I supposed to keep this light and fun and MOSTLY innocent when you send me a pic like that?*

Me: *Oops?*

Ryder sends another photo, this time a regular front-facing, waist-up selfie…with the gray underwear dangling from a fingertip.

Ryder: *Oops?*

I swallow hard, only just resisting the impulse to ask him to pan down.

Instead, I slip out of my shirt and take another selfie, squeezing my breasts together so I can cover my nipples with one hand while taking the selfie with the other. Which is a trick, and it takes a few tries to get right.

Me: *Oops?*

Ryder: *I'm out of oopses, and you're still in your underwear.*

I rectify this, the daring of this game making my heart pound as I snap a photo of the yellow boy short panties dangling from my finger.

Me: *Better?*

Ryder: *Yes. No. I don't know.*

Ryder: *I think I need more to be sure.*

Me: *More what?*

Ryder: *More of you. All of you.*

I swallow hard, swallow down the urge to give him what he wants—all of me, bare, in a photograph.

Me: *Not yet*

Ryder: *I'm so conflicted right now.*

Me: *Conflicted about what?*

Ryder: *My need to see you naked has me wanting to beg you for more. But another part of me respects you for holding your ground.*

Me: *You respect me for holding my ground?*

Ryder: *Absolutely. I also appreciate the continued...mystique, I guess, although that's not the right word. I'm even more crazy fucking hard for you than ever, but I've still not seen all of you. And, honestly, I'm glad, because it'll make the reality of you, bare, live and in person, that much better. Especially when I'm the one to strip you out of your clothes.*

Me: **gulp* I'm not sure whether to say thank you, ask you to show me how hard you are, or rethink my stance on sending you a nude.*

Ryder: *Now who's not making things any easier?*

I groan.

Me: *I better go.*

Ryder: *Something better to do?*

Me: *Yeah...myself.*

Ryder: *Not fair. Not fair AT ALL.*

Me: *Like you won't be doing the same thing?*

Ryder: *...*

Ryder: *while thinking of everything I can still only imagine.*

Me: *Tomorrow is Friday...*

Ryder, after a brief pause: *You have the weekend?*

Me: *yeah, why?*

Ryder: *the place we're going to for dinner is in the city. We may be dining late, and not feel like driving all the way back out this way...*

Me: *You're suggesting we get a hotel room for the weekend?*

Ryder: *Well, technically, YOU suggested it, I just implied it.*

Me, with an eye-roll emoji: *Don't split hairs with me.*

Ryder: *It's not hairs I'm dreaming of splitting...*

Me: *RYDER.*

Ryder, with a laughing emoji: *... So? Yea or nay?*

Me: *I'll have to think about that.*

Ryder: *Fair enough. Am I picking you up? Are you following me? Are we meeting somewhere?*

Me: *I'll have to think about that too. I'm sorry.*

Ryder: *No apologies. I understand.*

Me: *I'll text you tomorrow morning with my answers to both questions.*

Ryder gives me a thumbs-up, and I toss the phone aside. I sigh, rub my face with both hands, and then sit up, running my hands through my hair.

What am I thinking? What am I doing?

Am I teasing him, or myself?

He wants to get a hotel room.

A weekend in downtown Chicago with Ryder. Alone.

Since the day we met in James's backyard, I've wanted him. The first thing I wanted to do when I saw him was run my hands through his brilliant red hair, and the second was get him alone, and naked. And inside me.

When was the last time I had sex? Derek abruptly dumped me over a month ago, and he'd been acting weird and standoffish for a few weeks before that so we hadn't had been having sex, plus there was my period which had put an obvious damper on things… which means it's been over two months, almost three.

Or is it four?

Three months, almost four? Something like that—a long-ass time without sex.

Damn—no wonder I'm a horny disaster.

A weekend alone with Ryder.

Gah. How can I say no?

But how can I say yes?

I'd fall for him.

Or, rather, fall even harder. It's already bad, and I'm already only just barely holding my feelings for him at bay through a carefully choreographed process of avoidance, suppression, and just not thinking about it.

But then we have text exchanges like the one that just happened, and all that goes right out the window.

His smile, his silly, wry, goofy sense of humor, those mesmerizing hazel eyes, the thick red beard… that body, hard and heavily muscled without being intimidating or scary.

He's sexy and hysterical at the same time, and apparently that's like catnip for me.

A weekend alone in Chicago with Ryder.

A hotel room, all to ourselves, for forty-eight hours.

This is not going to go well.

Or, to be accurate, it's going to go *amazing*, and then, if history holds true, he'll turn out to be an asshole and I'll already be head over heels in love with him and I won't be able to help myself from indulging even though I know I'm only going to end up getting hurt.

Basically, I'm gonna get hurt anyway, so I may as well just have fun and enjoy myself as much as possible before the heartbreak.

I hold out for an hour, and then text him.

Me: *get us a room.*

I turn off all the lights and climb into bed, under the covers.

And try to go to sleep.

Only, the second I close my eyes, I see Ryder. Swathed in shadows, moonlight gleaming on his muscles, his fist sliding up and down his thick shaft.

I open my eyes, but the image still unfolds in my imagination.

My room is dark, with only a sliver of moonlight across my bed. I toss off the covers, groaning, over-heated for some reason.

My phone chirps.

Ryder: *I'd say you just made my day, but it's more accurate to say week…month…hell, lifetime.*

Me: *Lifetime?*

Ryder: *Too much?*

Me: *Only if it's not true.*

Ryder: *It's true.*

Me: *How do you know? All we've done is kiss.*

Ryder: *If all we've done is kiss, and those kisses were the best kisses ever, then it stands to reason…*

Me: *It stands to reason, what?*

Ryder: *It stands to reason finally having the glorious privilege of being alone with you, getting to slowly remove all your clothing piece by piece, and then getting to spend the next forty-eight hours making you feel things you didn't know were possible would be far and away the best thing I will have ever experienced.*

Shit.

My imagination takes the fuel of his words and pours it onto the raging fire of my underserved libido.

Ryder, kneeling in front of me, his mouth between my thighs, doing things that make my knees tremble and my eyes roll back in my head. His shaft throbbing in my hands, pulsing between my lips, sliding into my tight wet channel…

My fingers slide down to my core, and I try to imagine what Ryder would look like standing over me, his hands in my hair as I take him into my mouth—what he would look like as I straddle him, taking him into me, riding him to orgasm after another.

I come in seconds, whimpering.

The strip of moonlight has widened, laying across my chest, illuminating my breasts.

I snap a photo, still quaking from the aftershocks of my self-administered climax.

I send it to Ryder. All you can see is the shape of me, outlines in shadow, except for a two-inch wide strip of silver moonlight across my nipples and areolae. It is, honestly, a rather erotic piece of nude photography.

Ryder's response is a long time coming.

Which, I believe, is not a pun, but rather a double entendre.

Ryder: *Jesus, Laurel. You realize you sent that to me right as I was seconds from coming?*

Me: *Oops.*

Ryder: *you owe me so many orgasms.*

Me: *meaning I owe you orgasms you give me, or I owe you orgasms I give you?*

Ryder: *Yes.*

Me: *Pick me up at my house at 6:15.*

Me: *Wait...when you arranged this date of ours, you said dinner was at 6:15?*

Ryder: *Yeah, I know, but then I decided there was nowhere around here good enough to take you, and the only choice is to take you downtown. So, basically, change of plans.*

Ryder: *I have to go, now. I have a...mess...to clean up.*

Me: *Where is the mess?*

Ryder: *Dirty girl. You sent me that photo, and I came the instant I saw it. No time to even grab a Kleenex first. So the mess is all over my stomach.*

Me: *Want to know something dirty?*

Ryder: *Absolutely.*

Me: *I took that photo seconds after I'd finished coming.*

Me: *While thinking about you...doing exactly what you were doing.*

Ryder. *Fuck. Stop! I'm gonna need to go again in a second if you don't stop, and if I'm going to get out of work in time to shower, change, and pick you up tomorrow, then I have to be up in like, six hours.*

Me: *Good night. See you tomorrow.*

Ryder: *Good night, you seductive temptress, you.*

Me: *Lol. I'm neither seducing nor tempting. More...promising.* I include a winking emoji.

Ryder: *promising...when you're not here to make good on the promise? Seductive temptress.*

Me: *You'll see me TOMORROW! And I did just send you the exact photo I promised you and myself I wasn't going to send you.*

Ryder: *Oh. Good point. Still, it's fun to call you a seductive temptress. So...*

Me: *Good night, Ryder.*

Ryder: *Good Night, Seductive Temptress.*

I laugh softly to myself, and then, just to be sure I actually sleep, I turn my phone on "do not disturb" mode.

Tomorrow can't come soon enough.

FIVE

"**M**OM?" NATE, IN THE BACKSEAT, IS EYEING ME with intense curiosity.

"Mmm-hmm?" I ask absently, as I make a left turn into Paul's subdivision.

"Why are you all fancy?"

This jolts me to awareness. "Um. I…"

"Are you going on a date tonight?"

I smile at him in the rearview mirror. "Yes, I am."

"I thought so." Nate, my nine-year-old son, is tall for his age, with dark brown hair and light brown eyes, and an adorably earnest grin. "You only make yourself that pretty when you're going on a date."

I laugh. "So, what—I'm ugly the rest of the time?"

"No! Don't be dumb. You're pretty all the time. But when you're going on a date, you're extra special pretty." He plays with his LEGO guy for a moment, jumping him across from armrest to knee and then flying through the air—but I can tell Nate has another question percolating. "Mom?"

Ah, there it is.

"Yep?" We're on Paul's street, and I pull over to the curb a half mile away so I can finish talking to Nate—Paul has a tendency to come right out as soon as he sees me pull up.

"Is it with Derek?"

I hesitate. "No, it's not. It's someone else."

"Oh, good. He was a butthole. He only liked you 'cause you're pretty."

I shove the shifter into park and twist to look at Nate directly. "Excuse me?"

Nate shrugs, nonplussed at my outburst. "It's true. He was a big slimy butthole and I didn't like him. And I heard him on the phone one time, talking to somebody about you. We were out to dinner, and I was in the stall going poop, and he came in to pee and didn't know I was there, and I heard him talking."

"And? What did he say?"

Nate shifts. "You won't be mad?"

"At you? No? Why would I?"

"Cause I didn't tell you what he said."

I smile. "I'll answer that after you tell me what Nate said."

Nate fiddles with the gun in his LEGO guy's hand. "He said that you…" he trails off. "It wasn't appropriate. Do I have to say it?"

I frown. "I hate that you overheard this." I pat his hand. "Just tell me, and remember you don't talk like that, now or ever."

"He said the only real hot thing about were your…" He makes a dramatic, disgusted grimace, and points at his chest. "And then he said that's really the only reason he kept seeing you, because dealing with her annoying brat was almost not worth it." His expression darkens. "I peed in his shoe and blamed it on the cat."

I splutter before I can stop myself. "You did not!"

Nate holds the angry expression. "I did! I peed in his shoe, and when he found out, I blamed it on Mr. Tubbins, because Mr. Tubbins is always peeing on things."

"Nate—" I have work to hold back the laughter. "That's not okay. You can't go around—you can't go around peeing in peoples' shoes just because they say mean things about you."

He crosses his arms dramatically. "Then why do you think it's so funny? He only liked you because you're pretty! I don't know much about going on dates because I'm only nine, but even I know that makes Derek a big slimy butthole. After someone pooped— and *didn't* wipe."

I gag. "Nathaniel Paul Madison! That's disgusting."

"*He's* disgusting. He called me an annoying brat."

I sober. "Okay, serious time. Yes, that just adds to the ways that Derek was a…a not nice person. But that's not how we behave in this family, you understand me?"

"What family? It's just you and me. I think you need at least three people for a family." He points ahead. "And don't say Dad, because he doesn't count. I only see him cause the court says I have to, but when I can decide for myself, I'm not gonna. *He's* an annoying brat."

"Nate, now come on—"

"He is!"

"I thought you had fun when you spent time with Dad?"

He shrugs. "Oh, sure, *I* have fun. He takes me to laser tag and arcades and buys me stuff, and I always leave it at his house so I have something to do when I'm there."

"Laser tag and arcade games sound fun."

"Yeah, but he doesn't do it *with* me. He just watches. So, yeah, I have fun doing that stuff, but the whole point of me spending every other weekend at his house is for him to see me, but he never actually spends time with me. It feels like I go over there because he feels like he has to spend time with me, because the court says so."

I sigh. How do I navigate this? I made a promise to myself when things first went to hell that I'd never talk bad about Paul to Nate, or discourage him from seeing him.

"Nate…"

"Who's your date with?" Nate cuts in.

"You remember those times Miss Holly came over last month?"

He nods. "Yeah. They were dates, because you looked pretty and you were nervous."

I laugh. "I wasn't nervous!"

"Uh-huh! You were too! You were twirling your hair and asking me a million questions about how you look, and I'm nine, what do I know about how you're supposed to look on a date?" He makes a "duh" face. "So yeah, you were nervous."

"You're too precocious for your own good."

"For your good, you mean." He wrinkles his brow. "Does precocious mean annoying?"

I laugh. "No, it means smarter than you should be for your age." I put the car back into gear. "I'm going out with the same man I went out with those other times. His name is Ryder."

"That's a cool name. What's he like?"

I smile. "He's funny, and very nice."

"Is he a slimy poophead like Derek?"

I groan a laugh. "No, he's not. And I didn't realize

Derek was a slimy poophead until much too late." I grin at Nate in the mirror. "Next time you think a guy is a slimy poophead, you tell me right away, okay? That's your job—to tell me when a guy is no good if I don't realize it soon enough."

"Am I allowed to think Dad is a slimy poophead?"

I cough. "He's your Dad, and he loves you. He just...he's always had trouble showing that he loves people."

"Is that why you guys divorced?"

I nod. "There were a lot of reasons, but yeah, that's a big part of it." I give him a stern look. "But he's still your father, and he loves you, and you'll be respectful to him, okay?"

Nate nods. "He's just dumb and doesn't know how to have fun with a kid. I mean, it's laser tag! How do you not have fun with that? Seriously. He's lame." He perks up. "Would Ryder play laser tag with me, you think? Dad wouldn't even talk to me if he didn't have to."

I think back, and realize that Nate is right, and that Derek was fairly adept at hiding the fact that he didn't like kids, and that he was only dating me for my looks.

Shit.

I'm stupid.

"Well? Would he?" Nate asks.

I blink, realizing I never answered. "You know, I have a feeling he probably would."

"Will I meet him?"

I pull into Paul's driveway and put the car into park. "Maybe. I'm still deciding on Ryder. I want to make sure he isn't a slimy poophead, before I bring him around you."

Nate frowns. "Then how am I supposed to see if he is one before you?"

I laugh. "Good point! After this date, if it goes well, I'll let you plan a day for us to go do fun stuff, and if Ryder is willing to hang out with you, and you like him, that'll be a pretty good test for both of us, huh?"

"Paintball!" Nate shouts.

I arch an eyebrow. "We'll have to see about that one." I see Paul exit his building, and I unbuckle so I can give Nate a hug. I leave the car and meet Nate at the hood, kneeling down to give him a big hug. "Have fun, okay?"

He rolls his eyes at me. "I will," he drawls in an annoyed monotone. "You're gonna get me at four on Sunday, right?"

"Four? I usually pick you up at five thirty."

"Yeah, but I have basketball practice at five, and we have a game against a really good team next week so we'll need the practice."

I glance at Paul, who is watching us with crossed arms. "Will that work okay, Paul?"

Paul shrugs. "I guess."

A touch under six feet tall, Paul has dark hair with streaks of silver at the temples, attractive features, brown eyes that can shift from rage to joy in an instant. He used to be in decent shape, but hasn't kept up with it in recent years, so there's a bit more of a bulge around his waistline, and some sagging around the jaw that wasn't there before. He's a handsome man, but all I can see when I look at him is the mercurial moods, the narcissism, and the unpredictability.

"You're sure?" I ask.

Paul rolls his eyes. "I said so, didn't I?"

"You said you guess. Which isn't the same thing. I just don't want any mix-ups on Sunday."

"Pick him up at four. It's fine." His eyes rake over me. "Plans for the weekend?"

I resist the urge to tug my top up to hide my cleavage from him. "Um…yeah."

Nate looks up at me, and seems like he's about to say something, so I kneel down and give him another hug. "Love you, bud. Be good."

Nate hugs me back. "Love you. *You* be good," he says, winking obviously and mischievously.

And then he scampers off, shouting for Paul's enormous bullmastiff, Arnie. The first thing Paul did when we separated was to get the biggest dog he could find. Nate adores Arnie, and he's always begging me for a dog of our own. So far, I've resisted. But after Nate's latest revelations, Mom Guilt has me reconsidering.

I give Paul a short, small smile, and then head for my car.

"You look really good, by the way, Laurel," Paul says.

I blink at him. "Um. Thanks."

"I made pasta—there's plenty extra. You could stay if you wanted."

I sigh, desperately searching for a way out of this with minimal awkwardness. "Thanks, Paul, I…" I go for partial honesty. "I can't. I have plans."

"A date?"

I suppress a groan. "Paul, come on. I just…I have to go, okay?"

He gives me a look that's somewhere between a smirk and a snarl. "You know, I think you look better now than you did when we were together."

"I'm not sure how to respond to that, Paul." I open my car door. "I have to go. I'll see you Sunday at four, okay?"

He waves, and it's a quintessential Paul gesture—not quite a dismissal, but not quite a regular goodbye either. Passive aggressive, hard to read, and irritatingly vague. If Paul has a middle ground between manic and depressive, this is it.

I'm a tangled mess of annoyance, frustration, and confusion as I head back home. Because time was tight after work today I had showered, changed, gotten dressed, and put on makeup before picking Nate up from basketball and taking him to Paul's. Now I have to hustle home to pack for the weekend—and I only have five minutes before Ryder will arrive.

My overnight bag is on my bed, open, and I have a few potential outfits laid out. A skirt and a top, some pajamas—or rather, loungewear, since I don't honestly anticipate wearing much by way of pajamas—some boots, some heels, another fancy dress, several sets of sexy lingerie, a pair of jeans, and a sweater. But now that I'm looking at my selections, I'm rethinking them. The skirt is a little short, and the top is a little deeply cut, and the loungewear is a pair of yoga pants that are essentially skin tight with a with a long sleeve T-shirt, not sexy but somehow still risqué. The dress is one of my favorite items to wear so I'm happy with that one, and the lingerie I know I look good in, but they're sets I bought for myself on a sudden urge to splurge and make myself feel sexy, and I've never worn them in front of anyone, just under my work clothes as a kind of secret thrill. The jeans and sweater are fine, too.

Basically, it's the sexy stuff I'm not sure about.

My doorbell rings, and I panic.

"SHIT!"

I stare down at my pile of clothing, waffling on whether to ask Ryder to wait a few more minutes, but then I realize if I do that, I'll get stuck in a cycle of trying to decide what to bring and what not to bring, and so I end up stuffing the pile of clothing in my little hard-sided overnight bag, along with my toiletries bag and to-go makeup case. I zip it up, lug it to the front door, and then stop, sucking in a deep breath—hold it—and let it out slowly.

And then I open the door.

Ryder is leaning against the doorframe, looking devastatingly sexy. Black jeans with polished but worn black leather boots with red laces, a white button-down shirt, and a gray corduroy blazer with leather patches on the elbows. His hair is brushed casually off to the side, but it's too thick and unruly to ever truly behave, and it looks like he's been running his hands through it. His beard is neatly trimmed and groomed and brushed, and his eyes are hidden behind a pair of silver, mirrored aviation sunglasses.

"God, you look hot," I blurt.

His grin is pleased and amused. "Betcha didn't think I could clean up this well, did you?"

I roll my eyes at him. "I wasn't sure you owned

anything besides ratty old blue jeans and electrical supply company hoodies and T-shirts."

"Surprise!" He spins in a circle, arms outstretched, and then does a goofy little dance. "I have button-downs and blazers!"

I touch his elbow. "The elbow patches on the corduroy blazer? Major turn-on."

He arches an eyebrow. "Are you being sarcastic?"

I laugh. "No! I'm being dead serious. I had no idea I even thought so until I saw it on you just now, but for some reason, the patches just do it for me." I laugh again, self-consciously. "Who knew the professor look was such a turn-on?"

He shakes his head. "Well, I'll be sure to wear blazers with patches more often, in that case." His eyes rake over me, slowly, sliding from head to toe and back again. "Laurel, you look…"

I smile, huffing a laugh as he trails off. "I look what?"

He holds out his hands palms up and then drops them at his sides. "Breathtaking."

I duck my head, the compliment sending a rush of warmth through me, a thrill of excitement settling in my belly. "Thank you."

I'm wearing a dress I've had for years, but haven't had reason to wear until now. A curve-hugging bandage dress, it's a pale green that makes my eyes pop even more brightly, showing off my naturally tan skin, and emphasizing my assets to an almost indecent degree. Paired with a push-up bra, the effect is, honestly, pretty jaw-dropping.

I turn in a slow circle, because the back of the dress is racerback, showing off my shoulders, which I work hard to make sure look amazing.

He whistles. "Seriously, Laurel. I didn't think you could get any sexier, and then you put on that dress."

I grin. "Thanks. I've had this for years, but haven't had a chance to wear it until now"

Ryder frowns. "Well that's a goddamn shame." He grins, then. "I'll have to make sure to take you out to a lot of fancy dinners in that case, so you can wear that dress for me again."

I smirk. "Or I could wear another one."

He widens his eyes. "You have more like that?"

My smirk turns mischievous. "You'll have to take me on more nice dates so you can find out."

His expression is heated, then. Deadly serious. "Am I allowed to claim you every weekend Nate is with his dad?"

I want to shout "YES!" but instead I just shrug. "Let's see how this weekend goes first, shall we?"

He just snickers. "Playing it cool, I see. That's fine. I can play it cool too." He takes my bag and gestures to the curb. "Shall we?"

I check my purse for keys and phone and other essentials, make sure I've turned off all the lights, and then lock my door behind me. Turning to follow Ryder, I glance at my phone to make sure I don't have any last minute work emails, and then silence it and put it in the pocket inside my purse. When I look up, I'm startled to see a bright orange classic BMW instead of his antique box truck.

I look over the car. "Wow. This is awesome!"

He grins proudly. "It's a 1965 BMW 700. Once I finished my truck, I needed a new weekend project, and restoring cars has been my hobby since I was a teenager. My uncle was a classic car restoration expert, and I spent every weekend during the school year and most of my summers in his shop, helping him and learning." He pats the roof of the car. "This baby was a hell of a lot of work, and more money than I'd like to admit, but she turned out pretty slick, if I do say so myself."

I nod admiringly. "I'd have to agree. I don't know anything about cars, but this thing is really cool."

"It's got the original flat six in it, the original radio, and all the hardware and upholstery is vintage BMW as well, just not original to this car."

"So, do you own any cars newer than this one?" I ask, joking, as he opens the passenger door for me.

I buckle up and admire the clean, classic interior

as he rounds the hood and slides in.

"Nope." He chuckles. "Actually, that's not true. I do have an old beater pickup in my barn. It's from… ahh…eighty-eight? Eighty-six? Somewhere around there. A big old monster of a thing with a rusted bed and wheel wells, but it's a four-by-four and pretty much unstoppable. I drive it in the worst of the winter weather. I tinker with it now and then, now that the Beemer is pretty much done, but I'm leaving it as a beater."

I laugh. "So nothing actually new."

He snorts, derisive and dismissive. "Nah. New cars aren't my thing. There's no fun in 'em. I like to buy a junked-out old piece of shit and turn it into something beautiful." He pats the steering wheel. "This, for example, was basically just the body when I bought it. The engine had been parted out, the upholstery was in shreds, the glass was gone, but the body and frame were in amazing condition. I spent months looking for the right motor to put in this thing, and once that was done, the rest was fairly easy."

"So now that this is done, are you gonna find a new project?"

We're heading for downtown Chicago, a drive of a little over half an hour. He shrugs. "I don't know. Probably, eventually. I only really finished the last few touches on this over the summer, so I'll probably just enjoy driving her for a while. Eventually I'll need a new project, though."

"What do you think it'll be?"

"Ehhh? I don't know. I've done a muscle car; I've done a truck, and now this. I think I'd like to work on something a little obscure or different. One of those old seventies or eighties Toyotas or Land Rovers like you see in the documentaries about Africa or Australia, or an Austin Healy, or a Fiat, or a Rolls or something."

As we continue down I-294, we chat about his passion for restoring old cars for a while, and then he asks about how I ended up working for a nonprofit.

"Honestly, it was mostly just chance," I say. "I'd been working dead-end jobs for years—waitressing, hostessing, answering phones, crap like that. I have a degree in business, but when Paul and I got married, I got pregnant with Nate pretty much right away, and we decided I'd be a stay-at-home mom. But then Paul couldn't hold down a steady job, and I didn't have the time to really go job hunting properly, I just had to find something to pay the bills. And this was when the market was in the tank and there were no jobs anyway, so finding a job as a waitress was pretty much the best I could do at the time. I had the degree and the internship, but no experience, so I couldn't just go and get a career-trajectory sort of job even in a good economy. Then Paul and I divorced, and I was…" I shake my head and shrug. "I was miserable. I was overweight and out of shape, working two jobs as a single mother, and getting basically nothing from Paul in alimony or child support. I decided the first thing I had to fix was my body, because that was the one thing I felt like I could control. So, I hired Audra to kick my ass into shape, because I was seriously at least fifty pounds overweight, probably more."

Ryder eyes me. "I have trouble picturing that."

I snort. "You don't *want* to picture that, Ryder. It wasn't good. At *all*. I'm not sure there are any photographs of me from that period, now that I think about it. Working and taking care of Nate was all I could do…it was just raw survival. But I'd gotten so fat and out of shape that I was ashamed of myself and refused to take pictures. And, really, it was just Nate and me for the first couple years. I had no friends, my parents are retired and live in Arizona, and my sister and her husband have five kids and live in Oregon. I moved here with Paul after we got married because he'd gotten a job of some kind. I don't remember what, but it was a bullshit job that paid crap and he got fired after six months, leaving us with three grand a month in bills and no income, and a one-year-old son."

"Ouch. So you went to work."

I nod. "I went to work. I had no time to think about trying to transition from dead-end restaurant jobs to a career, because it was all I could do just to keep a roof over our heads and food on the table. But I was just...honestly, at the end of my rope. Something had to change. It *had* to. And I figured the one thing that was in my control was what I ate and whether or not I was in shape. So I took extra shifts, saved my money, and paid Audra up front for six months of personal training. I told her I wanted to feel pretty again."

Ryder's smile is understanding. "I can empathize. After my divorce, I started drinking a lot and eating garbage. It was Franco who ended up kicking my ass into shape." He laughs. "That about ended our friendship, though, because he was a real bastard about it. You've seen him—he's so shredded it's embarrassing. But, he got me to eat a bit more cleanly, made me do burpees and push sleds and barbell cleans and all that shit until I legitimately hated him."

I laugh. "Oh god, I feel you there. I loathed and craved going to the gym in equal measure. I loathed it because burpees are from Satan and cleans are a close second, but I craved it because I started feeling strong again, and my clothes started getting looser and the scale finally started going to a number I wasn't embarrassed by."

"So how does getting into shape lead you to managing a nonprofit?"

We're nearing downtown, now—the skyline is in front of us and getting closer by the mile.

"I was in shape, eating clean, feeling good... and still making crap for money. I'd managed to get promoted to assistant manager of a restaurant, so at least I was on a salary, but it was only nominally more money—it was steady, predictable money instead of the unpredictability of waitress tips. But I hated it. I hated the hours, I hated the food, I hated everything about it. And once I'd taken back control over what I looked like and felt like, the next logical step was improving my living situation. So, I started putting in applications. With no real business experience, I got zero offers from anything that wasn't just a step sideways. I went from assistant manager to general manager, and actually sort of turned the restaurant around a bit. It had been floundering pretty badly, and when the GM quit, the owner put me in charge. So, I did things my way. Fired people and hired new ones, adjusted the menu, did some minor updates to the decor, streamlined the finances. It got business on the uptick, and I think that year or so of turning the restaurant around was what got me the job. One of my regulars was a woman named Mary-Jo. She was older, retired, a widow, and very well-off. The restaurant was walking distance to her condo, so she ate breakfast there every morning, and we got to be friends, because I always worked the opening shift. One day, she called me over to sit down with her after the breakfast rush."

Ryder grins knowingly. "She offered you a job."

"Not right away, actually. She'd watched me take over as manager, had seen the improvements I'd made, and the effect it had on business, and for a few weeks, she just asked me a lot of questions—about me, my son, my divorce, my finances, my dreams… everything, really. I had few friends, and it honestly was cathartic to unload all that on someone. And then, yes, out of the blue, she offered me a job."

We're downtown, now, stuck in the last dregs of rush hour traffic. "Mary-Jo's passion project, after her husband died and she retired, was animal rescue. She and her husband owned a farm outside Chicago, and they rescued all sorts of animals—horses, cows, dogs, cats, pigs, even an ostrich. When her husband passed away suddenly, she had to sort of rethink things. She ended up selling the farm and sending all the animals to other farms and shelters, liquidated most of her assets, and bought a little condo downtown. Her husband had a hell of a life insurance policy, and when that kicked in, she was suddenly faced with having more money than she knew what to do with, but no purpose and no husband. The logical step for her was to start another animal rescue, but the thought of another farm without her husband was too much for her, so she opened a more traditional nonprofit dog and cat rescue. But she quickly realized she was passionate about animals, not running a business, and was looking for someone to take over the business aspect of things. She'd done several rounds of interviews with all sorts of people, and none of them fit what she was looking for." I shrug. "For whatever reason, I fit."

"The reason, obviously, is that you're amazing." He winks at me.

"Oh." I laugh. "Clearly."

He pulls up outside a restaurant, and a valet scurries over to take the car. Ryder waits as I round the hood, and then offers me his arm in a gesture of classical gallantry. "M'lady?"

I laugh, because his faux arch accent is funny, but the feel of his strong arm under my hand makes my stomach flip.

Our table isn't quite ready yet, so we find seats at the bar and Ryder orders us a bottle of red wine. We sip wine and chat—and the conversation is easy, a loose and rambling series of rabbit trails, from movies and music to funny college drinking stories, worst dates, best dates, and everything in between. Then a hostess takes us to our table and we order steaks and more wine, and the conversation continues. It deepens during dinner, as we tell stories of the things from our childhoods that have scarred us, more meandering discussions of our respective exes, and a more lighthearted exchange about how neither of us really enjoy celebrating birthdays. Talking to Ryder is the easiest thing in the world. Even talking about Paul and raising Nate by myself is easy—and somehow not awkward or tense. Usually, talking about exes and single parenting is a no-no on dates, because it's kind of a turn-off for most guys, I guess. But Ryder initiates the discussions and asks probing questions and listens with an attentiveness that tells me he's really, truly interested.

He truly listens, and that's just hot. A sexy man who can stare at you with expressive, attentive eyes and make you feel like you're the only woman in the world while he's hanging on your every word? It's intoxicating. Arousing.

God, I was an idiot for trying to find reasons not to like him—it's pretty much impossible not to, I'm realizing. He's a good man, a decent man, and I'm screwed.

Finally, we've had dinner, finished the second bottle of wine, and spent another hour talking over a slice of cheesecake.

"You want to take a walk?" Ryder asks, once the

bill is paid and we've lingered over coffee. "It's a nice night, and I'm enjoying talking to you."

I expected him to want to take this immediately to the hotel, and so this is an unexpected question.

"Sure," I say. "A walk sounds good."

I wore my most comfortable heels, and I did bring a sweater, and after all that food and wine and dessert, a walk along Chicago's streets actually does sound wonderful.

We wander around the Golden Mile area for another hour at least, strolling casually, continuing our discussion of anything and everything. There are lots of people out doing the same thing we are, and the people watching is entertaining. At some point, his hand finds mine and our fingers tangle. Never has holding someone's hand ever felt so amazing. It's simple, nonsexual, and…intoxicating.

Yes, we've shared two bottles of wine, but that was over several hours and lots of food, so I know neither of us is even really buzzed. The intoxication is…emotional. Psychological. Neurochemical. Libidinal.

Eventually, even with my comfy heels and sweater, my feet start to hurt and I get chilly.

Ryder notices, and we stop walking. "Done walking?"

I shrug. "I'm enjoying the conversation, but

heels aren't made for extended walking, and it's getting a little cold out here." I smile at him. "Shall we go somewhere for a nightcap?"

He doesn't smile back; his eyes meet mine, intense, wild. "We could." He has both my hands in his, and his thumbs brush over my knuckles.

"You have a better idea?"

His smirk is suggestive. "I might."

"Do tell," I say, giving him a coy grin.

"This is us," he says, gesturing to an adorable boutique hotel right in front of us. It's small, trendy, and inviting. I frown at him. "What about your car?"

He smirks. "While you were in the bathroom at the restaurant, I spoke to the valet attendant. For a few extra bucks, I had them bring my car here and leave it with the hotel valet."

I laugh. "So this whole walk wasn't just random wandering, was it?"

He shrugs. "I wanted to keep talking to you." His gaze is earnest. "I'm really enjoying getting to know you, Laurel. But no, it wasn't random. I chose the restaurant and hotel because they were within walking distance of each other...just so we could do this." He gestures at the sidewalk. "Just walk, and talk, and get to know each other."

I melt just a little more. "I like getting to know you too, Ryder." I trace a finger across his shoulder, my eyes on his. "I wouldn't mind going in now, though."

He brushes a thumb over my cheekbone, leans close, a touches a ghost of a kiss to my lips. "Thank god." Another slide of his lips over mine, a tease of a kiss. "I'm dying to get to know you in a whole different sort of way."

I squeeze his hand hard, teasing him with my lips, darting away from his kiss and then closing in to nip his lip. "You want to know me Biblically?"

He rumbles an amused laugh. "Nothing Biblical about what I want, Laurel."

"It's an expression—" I start.

He laughs, pressing closer to me, and kisses me to shut me up. "I know," he says, whispering against my lips. "But what I want with you sure as hell ain't the kind of thing you'd read about in a Bible."

"Take me to our room and show me what you mean," I murmur back. "Please?"

He growls as he backs away, his eyes blazing. "Don't have to ask me twice, babe."

He takes my hands again, leading me into the hotel. He signs a slip to acknowledge that they have his car in valet parking, takes the ticket from them, goes through the process of getting our room key.

The entire time, I'm leaning against him, my hand in his, fingers twined. I can't help touching him, teasing his fingers with mine, running my finger between his, rubbing the back of his hand with my thumb, gripping his massive bicep over his blazer sleeve, resting my head against his shoulder, gazing at him as he accepts our room keys and listens to the usual spiel from the desk clerk.

Finally, we're on the elevator. Ryder backs me into a corner, pins me against the wall, his palms on my cheeks, thumbs brushing my skin, lips slanting against mine. My heart pounds, my eyes slide closed, and my hands roam his shoulders, up into his hair, mussing it further. I feel his hand burying into my long, loose black hair, while the other roams down my waist to my hip. His kiss is wild and hungry.

All too soon, the elevator dings as we arrive at our floor, and Ryder backs away, dragging a wrist across his mouth. "Damn, girl. You kiss like you've never been kissed before, and I mean that in the best possible sense."

I follow him as he backs out of the elevator, and I touch his mouth with my fingers. "I haven't—not in the way you kiss me."

"And how is that?"

"Like…like you want me so bad kissing me is the only way to even start expressing it."

"That'd be an understatement." He looks at the envelope containing our key cards, which has our room number scrawled on the outside. "I wasn't listening when he told me the room number." He glances at me with an amused smirk. "Somebody was playing handsies and distracting me."

I lift my eyebrows and endeavor to look innocent. "I haven't just held anyone's hand in a long time. I was enjoying it, that's all."

He examines the signs on the wall, and leads us toward our room. "A likely story."

I laugh. "What? You think I was intentionally trying to distract you?"

"That thing you were doing with your finger on the back of my hand? Yeah, distracting." We reach the correct room, and Ryder slides a card through the reader, but it blinks red. "Dammit. The card's not working."

"Try the other one," I suggest.

He does, but he has it facing the wrong way, and it blinks red again. "This is stupid."

I laugh. "I don't have to try to distract you—you do that all on your own."

He tries the first card again. "You in that dress… that's distracting enough."

Another red flash from the door. He's getting frustrated, and I decide to lighten the mood a little. I lean up and kiss the back of his neck. Then the side of his neck. And then I lean up against his back and run my hands over his stomach and kiss along his jaw by his earlobe.

"Is that distracting?" I breathe.

"Nope," he growls. "Not at all."

He tries the card again, and swears as it flashes red yet again. "Fucker must've programmed it wrong."

"I think you're just doing it wrong," I say, suppressing laughter. "You're *distracted*."

"I'm *not* distracted." He flips the card, but still gets the same reaction.

"No?" I unbutton his shirt, button by button, starting at the top and working my way down until it's hanging open, and I untuck it, and then slide my hands under his T-shirt, palming his stomach and caressing his hot bare skin. "Not at all?"

He thunks his head against the door, switching cards. "This fucking thing better work."

I laugh. "Let me try." I take the card from him; swipe it, and immediately the light turns green.

Ryder laughs, both annoyed and amused. "Of course it works for you."

I follow him in, stumbling after him, not letting go of his skin, roaming his chest and stomach, tracing his belly just above his belt buckle. "I just have the magic touch."

He lets the door slam closed, stops just inside, and then spins around. He grabs both of my hands in one of his and pins them against the door over my head. "You don't play fair, woman."

I suck in a sharp breath. "No, but that's why you like me."

He kisses me, and I forget that he has my hands pinned over my head, I just sink into the kiss, into him, letting him take all of my weight, letting him pin me against the door with his big hard body, letting his lips scour and search mine, letting his tongue find mine and demand it and demand more, letting him press both of my hands against the door. His other hand slides down my waist to my hip, hugged by the skin-tight green dress. His touch dares further down as we kiss, to the hem, just above my knee.

Abruptly, he backs away, once more dragging the back of his wrist across his lips. "That fucking dress, Laurel." His tone says more than his words—heavy and thick with desire, ragged with need.

"What about it, Ryder?" I ask.

"I can't fucking handle the way you look in it," he says, his voice a deep bass snarl.

"Then take it off."

SIX

RYDER STEPS UP CLOSE TO ME, HIS EYES BORING INTO mine. "I like the way you think."

He reaches for me, his hands closing over my hips, fingers digging into my flesh. With a quick jerk, he tugs me away from the door and up against him; I squeak in surprise, and then the squeak turns to a moan as he dips and slashes his lips over mine. Both hands slide up my body, bury in my hair, tilt my face up so he can deepen the kiss. His body is hard, powerful, and warm. The kiss heats, morphing from a single extended crush of mouth against mouth into a breathless tangle of lips and tongues. His hands scrape down my back and stop, hesitating at the small of my back. I arch into him, raking my hands under his shirt. In a swift, complicated maneuver, he shrugs out of his blazer and button-down at the same time and I shove his undershirt off, and then his whole mammoth, muscular upper body is bare and hot under my hands, his chest bulging with power, his arms thick and corded, his stomach hard and flat. I slam my lips against his the moment his shirt is free of his head, and scour his body with my hands, my touch as eager as my mouth.

I arch against him again, and he takes the hint for what it is: his palms splay open and carve down over my butt, and I feel more than hear the rumble in his chest as he explores the curves and weight of my ass. His hands glide down to the hem, and then whisper up the backs of my thighs, bringing my dress up with it.

I laugh. "Down," I tell him, pushing down on his hands.

He pulls back, frowning at me. "What? I thought you wanted—"

I laugh again, putting my hands on his and guiding them to the straps of my dress, helping him tug them off my shoulders. "The dress. It goes down to take it off, not up."

He huffs a laugh, resting his forehead against mine. "Oh. For a second I thought you'd—"

"Changed my mind?" I ask, tangling my fingers in his beard and tugging his mouth back down to mine. "No way," I murmur, my lips moving against his.

"Oh. I hadn't noticed a zipper, so I thought it

would just go up and off like a shirt."

I snicker. "Not a chance. It's way too tight for that. It'd get stuck…" I arch an eyebrow suggestively, "in certain places."

"I could try. That might be fun."

I smirk, suppressing a laugh. "More funny than fun if you think watching me struggling awkwardly to get out of the world's tightest dress is funny." I bite my lip. "When I tried this on earlier, to make sure it was what I wanted to wear before taking a shower, I tried taking it off over my head." I laugh, then. "It was…*not* sexy. I got it halfway off over my head, and then it got stuck at my boobs. I was legitimately stuck in my dress for five minutes. I had to work one arm out underneath and then yank it off the rest of the way. And thank god I hadn't done my hair yet because it would've been totally ruined."

"Ah. Well…" He tugs the strap down one shoulder, then the other. "As much as I love a good laugh… let's go with down, this time."

"This time?"

"No guarantees I won't try it the other way at some point, just to watch you get stuck. It seems like it'd be the perfect combination of sexy and funny."

"You'd just stand there, watching and laughing, wouldn't you?"

His eyes go to my chest as he slowly peels the

dress down. "Absolutely." He guides my arms out of the straps. "And then I'd help you out of it."

"Good to know." I laugh, but the humor is hard to hold on to when Ryder's eyes blaze with lust as he slowly, carefully peels my dress down over my bra. "If I ever get stuck, I'll have to wait for you to help me."

"Hey, I'm helping you right now. You looked stuck in this thing. I mean, god, it looked awfully uncomfortable. So tight, so constricting. I figured you needed help getting it off."

I can't help laughing. "Oh yeah, for sure. Thank you, Ryder, for such a selfless act. You must be a saint."

He has the dress past my breasts and continues to peel and tug it downward. It's bunched, now, though, and stuck. I don't help him. He sinks to his knees in front of me, and my heart leaps into my throat. Anticipation sears through me, pulsing in my blood. I tingle, his touch electric; I gasp, his gaze ravenous.

With a yank that has me stumbling and inhaling in surprise, he jerks the dress past my hips, and now I'm standing in front of him wearing nothing but the lingerie I chose for this precise moment.

Red lace…completely sheer. Racerback, push-up. It hides nothing, shows everything. Emphasizes, teases. Taunts. Promises.

The thong is a barely there slip of red lace over my core and a string around my waist.

"*Fuck*," Ryder growls, sinking backward to sit on his heels. "Fucking hell, Laurel."

My breath catches at the utter worship in his gaze. "What, Ryder?"

He lurches to his feet and clasps me in a swift, sudden, fierce embrace, his arms wrapping around me, curling me into him, cradling me against him. His hand claws into my ass, the other grips python-strong around my shoulders, and I'm bent backward and dipped, my head in the crook of his arm. I'm utterly helpless, off balance, off my feet completely, dangling in the air, held up only by the strength in his arms. He's over me, his lips hungrily grazing mine, teasing, touching, and then smashing in for a searing kiss.

I'm dizzy, giddy. Utterly enthralled.

I've never in my life been dipped backward for a kiss. It looks romantic in the movies, but I always thought the reality would be frightening. In truth, it is, because I'm so helpless. I can only cling to his shoulders and palm his jaw and whimper into the kiss and let him hold me, losing myself in the hunger of his kiss. I can only trust him to keep me cradled safely in his arms.

The kiss becomes a conflagration, swiftly igniting into more than just a kiss.

He stands me up and presses me up against the door and palms my cheek, and his hand slides up my hip and cups my breast over the lace.

"This one goes up," I murmur.

The kiss broken, he drags his lips down, nuzzling into the side of my neck. I exhale softly, his beard tickling and scratching, his lips warm and wet, his tongue licking at my skin. A kiss to my shoulder. My breastbone, at the peak of the valley of my cleavage. Down, down, kissing and kissing his way to my left breast. Over the lace. My nipple hardens as his mouth nears it, and then throbs and aches as his mouth closes over it, the lace between his lips and tongue and my flesh. Another kiss, dancing across and kissing the inside of the left, then the right, and now my right nipple is aching as well, his hot breath huffing against it, searing through the lace, pressing the scratchy material against my nipple. And then his tongue flicks against the lace, and I gasp.

He pulls back from the kiss, gazing at me as he tugs the bra upward—slowly, gently, inexorably. I bite my lip and stop breathing, waiting. My breasts rise, bulge against the lace, and then begin to slip and squish out underneath. And then with a single smooth tug, Ryder rips the bra up and off, his eyes never leaving my breasts as they bounce free.

He drops the bra at our feet, his hands lifting, cupping. His breath catches as my breasts fill his hands. I'm not breathing, his hands hard and huge and scratchy with callused power, yet soft and gentle and reverent.

My hands tangle in his hair as he drops to his knees. He cradles my breasts around his face, clutching and cupping, nuzzling.

I can't help a laugh. "Did you just die and go to heaven?"

He turns his eyes up to mine as he covers my nipple with his mouth. "Uh-huh."

One breast, then the other, both—I caress his hair as he kisses and licks and squeezes and kneads my breasts, the attention of his hands and mouth sending an aching thrill shooting down to my core.

He lets go, then. "Actually, no. I haven't gone to heaven just yet."

I frown quizzically. "No?"

He sinks to sit on his heels, scraping his hands down my sides, his hooked fingers catching in the string of my thong and dragging it down and off as he settles onto his heels. His eyes stay fixed on mine as he wraps his hands around my ass, kissing my stomach, my navel, my hipbones, the fronts of my thighs.

"Now I'm getting closer to heaven," he murmurs.

"Oh…" I breathe, lack of oxygen and the pounding heat of arousal sapping me of witty comebacks. "That's heaven for you, huh?"

"I need a taste of heaven, I think," he whispers,

kissing the inside of my thigh.

"Oh…oh god." I gulp, gasp for air. "Ryder…"

He kisses, nips, licks the tender silk of my inner thigh, and I automatically widen my stance, arousal and need overriding anything else and everything else. His palms skate up my body and cup my breasts again as he touches kiss after kiss to my inner thighs, each one a millimeter closer to my core.

He pauses. "Can I taste you, Laurel?"

I can't answer in words. I've lost all sense, all capability of intelligibility. I'm dizzy, fraught with need, aching. Instead, I knot my fingers in his hair and guide his mouth to my core—that's my answer.

He growls a laugh, which I feel as he nuzzles between my legs. His beard—god, it tickles, scratches. It adds to the assault of sensation as his lips brush against me, his tongue sliding over my seam. I whimper, flex my hips forward. He slides his tongue against my core, lapping into me, delving it between my lips and upward. I moan, then, and shift my legs farther apart and tighten my fingers in his hair and pull him against me, aching for the high I'm anticipating.

He doesn't disappoint, doesn't drag it out. No teasing, no playing. His mouth closes over me and suckles, and I whimper, whine in my throat, flex my hips forward harder, and then sag as he pulls away. His eyes go up to mine, watching my reaction as he drags a middle finger against my damp core, and then slides it into me. Just the one finger, his knuckles mashing against my lips as he delves into me, curling his finger inside me. I gasp as he finds that perfect, magical place, that touch which has my knees giving out and my thighs trembling and my breath catching, and his mouth slants against my core and his tongue flicks and circles and swipes and laps. I feel him add a finger, and now he's gathering them forward, sliding them out, curling them back in, matching the rhythm of his touch to the lapping of his tongue, and my hips are bucking, and I'm gasping-moaning-whimpering in synch with his touch and tongue. I want it faster, but he holds his pace, and I'm clawing at his scalp and knotting my fingers hard in his hair, pulling him against me, grinding my hips wantonly against him.

"Ryder! Oh god—oh god, oh fuck…Ryder…"

His response is, finally, to speed up just a hint. Enough to make my gasps and whimpers intensify. Fingers curl and thrust, tongue lashes. I thrash and flex, crying out as a blast of ecstasy slams through me, a precursor to the orgasm. Another wave hard on the heels of the last, and then another, and I'm lost in this, wailing and screaming without thought, with utter abandon as his tongue and fingers crush me into climax. The waves of crashing, scything heat and pressure have exploded, united into a detonation of climactic intensity so powerful I'm unable to even scream, can only let my mouth hang open, lungs spasming, legs giving out, curling forward over him as he lashes me with his tongue and fucks me with his fingers in an unrelenting assault.

When I catch my breath, it's only because the orgasm has finally faded to mere earthquakes of bliss, and I can move again so I resume thrusting against his face to milk every last shred of this experience.

And then, abruptly, my legs give out.

Ryder catches me, standing up with me so I have no choice but to wrap my legs around his waist and cling to his broad hard shoulders and gasp for air and whimper as the last throes of orgasm rack me. I feel him walking with me, effortlessly carrying me across what feels like a suite, and then he's setting me carefully on the bed, laying me backward and moving to kneel above me.

His beard is damp as he brushes his mouth over my belly and up between my breasts. I giggle, getting him to pause with my hand on his shoulder.

"Your beard…" I breathe. "It has…me…on it." I wipe my hand over his mouth and down his chin, wiping at the dampness until his beard feels drier.

He smirks, an eyebrow arched. "What if I was saving that for later?"

"Eeew, gross."

"Hey, I happen to like the smell of you on my beard." He slides the fingers that had been inside me into his mouth. "Mmmm. Tastes like sugar."

I laugh, but the way he licks his fingers clean tells me he's not joking.

He's kneeling between my thighs, hands fisted into the mattress just above my shoulders. "I feel like maybe I've said this already, but seriously, Laurel— that was the hottest thing I've ever fucking seen."

"Which part?"

"You, coming apart for me."

I don't hide or restrain my pleased grin. "Feel free to give me orgasms like that anytime you want."

"Yeah? It was pretty good, then, I take it." His self-satisfied smirk tells me he knows exactly how good it was for me.

I run my hands over his shoulders and over his chest, fingers pointing down, aiming for his belt. "It was okay." I try to keep a straight face, because that's such an understatement. "I feel like maybe you could have done a little better."

"Is that a challenge?" He sounds absolutely serious.

I bite my lip and nod, letting my hands continue to slide slowly down his torso toward his belt line. "Yep. I don't think that was your best. Not quite your A-game."

He lowers his brows and growls. "So what you're saying is, I need more practice."

I nod, endeavoring to keep my face straight and serious as I reach his belt. "Yep. You definitely need practice."

"I'll need a willing subject to practice on, in that case. Someone with a pretty strong appetite for orgasms."

I shrug a shoulder, nonchalant. "I may know someone who fits that description."

I free the end of his belt from the buckle, remove the prong from the hole, and then the belt is loose and I strip it off of him in a loud whipping motion. I toss it aside, and then twist the button of his jeans free and tug down the zipper. I feel him bulge against the opening, a hard presence straining against the stretchy cotton of his underwear nudging my knuckles as I lower the zipper.

"You may know someone," he says, watching my hands. "Tell me about her."

I wiggle his jeans past his hips and down over his butt; he makes no move to help as he kneels over me, letting me undress him. "Well, she's somewhat out of practice herself. She hasn't received that kind attention in…oh, well, a very long time. She's a quick learner though, and if you get good enough, she may be willing to spend a little time practicing…" I pause, bite my lip, focusing on shoving his jeans down his thighs and then tugging them off. "Well, see, she just needs practice. All around. Receiving orgasms, and giving them."

"Hmmm. So this person you're thinking of… you're saying she's interested in giving orgasms? Any particular kind of practice you think she has in mind?" He lifts off his knees as I push his underwear down, letting me tug them past his knees, and then he's naked.

I shrug again. "Oh, I don't know. She's really out of practice in just about everything, you see. Manual, oral…everything."

He nods. "Well, I suppose I would be willing to help her out."

I take my eyes off of his, finally, and lower them to take in the full glory of Ryder naked for me. And god, is he gorgeous.

I reach for him, my breath catching as I close my fingers around him. He's thick, *so* thick, and so heavy. Every vein straining, dripping a bead of pre-cum. He's hot in my hands, hard as steel yet so soft. His jaw flexes and tenses as I slide my fingers down his length in a slow exploration. Touching him is…well, he used the word already: Heaven.

I smile to myself, watching him go through a series of expressions while I explore his cock with my hands. His brows lower, tighten, his jaw clenches and releases, he sucks in a deep breath, holds it, lets it out slowly; his eyes slide closed when I wrap my other hand around him and clutch him, then glide my hands around him in a slow caress.

"I think maybe I need to practice right now," I say. "What was it you said? Oh yeah—I think I need to taste a little bit of heaven."

He shakes his head. "No—no fucking way."

I stroke him, watching him tense, watching his belly go taut with each touch. "No? Really? No?"

He growls, dropping his head, sucking his belly in and arching his back as I stroke and caress him with both hands in a rhythmless exploration of him. "No. You put your mouth on me, I won't last five goddamn seconds, and there's no way I'm wasting this time I have with you on that."

"I wouldn't think of it as wasting time." I squeeze, release, stroke. "You made me come so hard I couldn't stand up. I just want to return the favor."

"You will," he growls. "When I'm inside you."

I blink, suck in a breath. "Oh. I—I see."

He shifts forward, braces his weight on one fist, palming my cheek with the other, and bends down to kiss me. It begins as just a kiss, lips and tongues in an expression of affection and desire. But then, the moment I taste his tongue and my essence on his lips and the smell of me on his beard, I need more. I moan, opening my mouth to him, arching up to meet him. His hot hard cock throbs in my hand, and I stroke him, caress him, run my thumb over the tip, smearing that droplet of pre-cum and eliciting more with every touch. God, I want him. I want all of him, in every way there is. I want him inside me. I want him above me. I want him beneath me. Behind me. I want to wrap my legs around his waist and ride him. I want to roll him onto his back and taste that pre-cum on my tongue, and I want to feel him slide between my lips and stretch my jaw with his thick shaft and feel those veins ripple over my tongue, and I want to feel him grunt and hear him groan and feel him thrust and move and lose all restraint. I want to taste the smoke and musk of his cum and feel it slide thick and viscous and hot onto my tongue.

I want to feel him driving into me, wild and furious as he pulses and pounds and comes, shouting my name.

Problem is, I want it all, and I want it now, and I don't know which I want first.

All these thoughts and images of him coming has me aching. Needing. Throbbing and rising toward climax without him even touching me, except for his mouth on mine and his tongue slashing against mine.

"Ryder," I whisper. "I need you. Right now."

He rocks backward, up onto his knees. "I have condoms in my bag. Hold on." He rolls off the bed, pointing back at me. "Stay there."

I laugh. "Did you think I was going to go downstairs and get a drink instead?"

"Smart-ass."

He yanks his duffel bag off the floor, sets it on the dresser, and rips it open, finding a new, unopened box of condoms. He brings the box over to the bed, ripping it open quickly.

I smile at him. "There's no hurry, Ryder. I'm not going anywhere."

He glares at me. "You're wrong about that. I fucking need you. I've never needed anything so bad as I need to be inside you right fucking now."

He finally gets the box open, fumbling free an entire string of condoms. He's facing the bed as he tosses the box onto the bedside table and then goes to rip one of the squares free of the strip. Only, it doesn't rip free cleanly, and two of the foil packets tear open. He curses, grumbling under his breath.

I move to the edge of the bed and reach for him, laughing. "Relax, Ryder. We'll use both of them." I smile up at him as I clutch him. "You're awful tense about this."

He separates the two packets and withdraws one of the rings. "I don't usually fumble or mess up like that." He tenses as I lean forward, toward him. "You just…I want you in a way I've never wanted anything, and I want this to be perfect."

I toss my hair over one shoulder, wrap a hand around his ass and hold on to him for balance as I lean partly off the bed, stroking him with my other hand. "It is perfect, Ryder. And trust me, I want you just as bad. You make me crazy. I want you so bad I don't even know how to deal with it."

"Laurel…"

I sink my mouth onto him, tasting him as I swirl my tongue around him. I back away and glance up at him. "I can't help it. I just…need you."

I taste him again, caressing him with one hand as I sink my mouth around him, stroking my fist up to my lips, pumping, gliding, tonguing him.

He jerks away with a grunt. "Fuck! That feels too good, Laurel."

I stand up, following him, taking the condom from him. "Good. That means I'm doing something right."

"Yeah, a little too well. You do that again, and this will be over before it starts."

I fit the condom over him, and then roll it down his shaft with both hands. "That would be okay with me. We have the whole weekend."

"I know, but Laurel…" He palms my face, moving

in for a kiss. "That's not how this is going to go. That's not how I want you. Not right now."

I smile. "No? Then how do you want me?"

He sits on the edge of the bed and pulls me toward him. "Like this." He guides my knees up onto the bed beside his hips. "For now, at least."

I climb up onto the bed, straddling him. He gazes up into my eyes, his hazel gaze intense and wild and fraught with lust and need and something deeper, something wilder, something more. I grip him, and I feel his fingers at my opening, and together we guide him to my entrance. He takes over, moving my hand aside, fitting himself just inside me. He thrusts in a slow, shallow, gentle, rolling movement, so just the very head slides in and out of me, splitting the lips apart but not quite entering. Teasing. I'm up on my knees, over him. Mouth open, eyes wide at the delicious, burning stretch from this little bit of him.

I touch myself, and his eyes go to my slowly circling fingers. "God, Ryder. I'm already close."

He rumbles. "Good. Let me watch you come."

His mouth goes to my breast, nuzzling, and then his teeth saw gently at my nipple—he cups my breast, lifting it to his mouth, and laves attention on it, then both of them, his hips flexing in that same slow, shallow rhythm that's nowhere near enough.

But it's somehow perfect, just enough, almost too much, as I smear my two middle fingers around my aching center, his mouth on my breasts ratcheting the intensity a millionfold, the tease of him being almost inside me taking it further yet.

I whimper as the first wave hits.

Sob as the second rolls over me.

My hips flex on their own and a loud cry escapes me as the third and strongest wave yet crashes through me.

He's still pushing and receding in that same maddening shallow thrust—just barely moving into me, barely penetrating my lips. I'm gasping nonstop, now, as the orgasm rises, rises.

"Oh fuck—Ryder."

He moans wordlessly around a mouthful of my breast—he's worshipping them, kissing and devouring and licking, cupping and squeezing and kneading, flicking and pinching and rubbing.

"I—oh god. Ryder, I'm—oh, oh, oh *god*, oh *god*—I'm coming!" I cry this, raggedly, as the orgasm smashes through me.

And now I have no choice but to take him, all of him, all at once.

He bellows a feral, bull-like roar as I slam down, my ass slapping loudly against his thighs as he speared up into me, filling me. I scream as I take him, aching as he stretches me beyond capacity, so much of him it's almost too much, and I can't breathe for the ache, the burn, the eye-watering fullness. It almost hurts, but the orgasm is still smashing through me, wave after wave as my fingers fly around my clit, and the climax spurs me to move.

I cry out, a burst of shrill, breathless ecstasy. I curl forward, his face buried between my breasts, my nose in his hair, my arms around him, my fingers clawing desperately at the hard muscle sheathed in soft skin. He drives up, and I'm filled further. I lift up, emptied of him, crying at the lack, the loss, and then sob as I sink down to meet his thrust.

"Laurel—" His voice is ragged, guttural. "Jesus, Laurel."

"I know."

He shakes his head. "No, you don't." He releases my breasts and cups my face instead; eyes closed, I still somehow unerringly know where his mouth will be, that he's seeking mine, and we meet, tongues slashing and spearing, breath tangling in ragged gasps, huffing and groaning into each other's trembling mouths as we sink and rise in perfect rhythm.

I cling to him, only my hips, thighs, and ass moving as I ride him through my orgasm.

He groans, grunts, his movements growing

staccato, losing his so-far flawless rhythm.

My own climax fades, but another is hard on its heels; I peer down at him and see the tight, contorted expression on his face, recognize instinctively the rictus of intensity, the contortion of concentration as he holds himself back.

Oh, no.

Oh no, no, no. That won't do at all.

I lean hard against him, pushing on his chest, and he falls backward. Pulling out of me briefly, he shifts further onto the bed, and then I move up astride him again. He moves, lifting up, seeking to change to a different position, but I push him back down.

"No," I whisper, straddling him, lifting up. "Let me."

"Let you what?" he grunts.

I slide him into me, and now, accustomed to him, loosened by orgasm, still racked with the shivering pressure of another waiting to be drawn out of me, I take him fully into me in a single smooth glide. "Let me take you there."

He sinks down, relaxing. His eyes soak up my whole body, roaming my face, my loose, wild, ink-black hair, my breasts, my hips, then focuses on where we're joined, watching as I lift up, watching himself sink into me as I lower myself onto him. His hands rest on my hips, and I lift up on my knees. I cup my breasts, lift them, and let them bounce as I fall onto him. I feel him throb inside me.

"Oh god, Laurel."

"Yeah?"

He nods, his hands tightening on my hips. "God, yes. So good."

I rise, fall, rise…fall—a slow stutter at the end of the rhythm. It's all me—he's still, so far, holding himself taut and tense, his eyes on my body as I move on him.

"God, Laurel." His voice is ragged with need.

I see the need in him; I see it in every taut, tense line of his body. "What, Ryder? Tell me. What do you need?"

His hands claw into the generous swell of my ass and he pulls me down onto him. "You said to let you, but…I—I can't."

"Are you close?" I murmur, keeping the rhythm, the quick-quick-slow pattern.

He nods. "Yeah—god, god you feel so good, Laurel."

"How close?"

He groans, his hands beginning to control my movements, lifting me up and yanking me down. "So fucking close."

I lean forward; bracing my hands on his chest,

I curl my legs beneath me, resting my ankles on his shins so all my weight is on him, on the place where we are joined.

"Don't move, Ryder," I whisper. "Let me take you there."

He groans in something like agony. "I—fuck, I can't. I need to—"

I lower my torso against his, draping my breasts on his chest, I feel him gliding against me, hitting me just right, and the climax waiting pent up deep inside starts to rise, and my hands clench into the mattress above his head—I'm writhing on top of him, now, my whole body stretching and contracting and thrashing harder and faster and harder and faster.

"Fuck, Laurel—Fuck, oh god—*fuck*, you feel so perfect, so hot, so tight, so wet." His voice is breathless, guttural, a ragged whisper. "I have to move. I can't hold still anymore."

I bite his lip, bury my face in his neck. "Show me," I whisper. "Show me."

He snarls like a predator, one big, strong hand spearing into my hair and palming my cheek, ear, and jaw all at once—his other arm wraps like an iron bar around my ass, his hand seizing me with wild need. And just like that, I realized—

I never had control.

He was giving it to me.

And now, he takes it back.

Beneath me, he shows me how completely I am his. He kisses me, but it's no longer just a kiss, no longer just an expression of desire and affection—it's a claiming. His tongue spears into my mouth, searching my mouth and tongue and lips. His hips slam up into mine, driving himself into me, my ass slapping against his thighs. I cry out, the sudden ferocity of his powerful thrust sending me spiraling into a mad helter-skelter rush of orgasm—not a gradual falling over the edge or rising into it, but just *there*, immediate and nova-hot. I want to move, and my hips flex and push, but his arm keeps me in place and refuses to allow me the slightest amount of movement. He holds me against him and drives into me, snarling in my ear, thrusting hard and growling gutturally, wordless and crazed.

"Ryder—" I gasp.

He won't let me speak, either. His kiss demands I breathe only him, take only his tongue, swallow his grunts and devour his snarls and taste the furious passion of his lips. The thrusting of his hips demands I accept him, demands that I writhe with him, that I whimper against his kiss and roll my hips and try to find his rhythm.

His hand slides through my hair and cups the back of my head and crushes our lips together, but it's not a kiss or anything like it, just our mouths fused and our mutual moans merging and tangling. My breath comes in ragged gasps between torn whimpers and shrill shrieks of agonized ecstasy—the kind of pleasure that is so furious and wild and deep and powerful that it almost hurts. I feel myself clenching around him, squeezing him so tightly every vein ripples through my spasming channel, so I feel every inch of him as he drives in with a resounding clap of flesh, the slaps growing faster and our cries and grunts and curses and whimpers and snarls louder and faster.

I come, then.

Like never before, with a white-hot shattering intensity—I come, and I weep with the fury of it.

I'm not screaming, not shrieking or gasping—I am flat-out sobbing as I come around him.

He pulls back. "Look at me, Laurel," he commands.

My eyes fly open, and I have to fight to keep them open.

"Don't look away, beautiful," he murmurs.

"I—I—Ryder...oh god oh god oh god, Ryder!"

He is lost to the onrushing detonation of his orgasm, and I'm still clenching around him and he's so thick inside me that I feel him pulsing as he unleashes inside me—I feel every last pulse and rush as he thrusts, and I come all the harder, feeling him like this. Instead of slamming into me harder as he comes, he gentles; it is a conscious thing, his eyes on mine. He trembles, shakes, his whole body shivering with exquisite control in the midst of utter release.

"Laurel..." he gasps.

Each slow, sliding thrust is a meeting of souls—I feel this. Our eyes are locked, hazel on green, each of us trembling. Shivering, he pushes deep into me, holding me against him and thrusting slowly but *hard*, so his thick spasming cock fills me to the brim, my channel clenching around him. Even his hips and thighs shake with his control, both of his hands claw into my ass cheeks, pulling them apart so he can thrust more deeply yet, and I'm rolling on him, grinding my hips, working myself around him to take every last shred of this mutual climax.

Not once do either of us blink or look away—to do so is impossible.

Finally, he sinks with shuddering relief to the mattress, wrapping me in his arms as I shake and quake with the aftershocks of my subsiding orgasm. He pulls out of me, and then I lie on top of him, heedless of the mess smearing against me, needing only the comfort of his arms.

Needing momentary relief from the intensity of the moment, I lift up on an elbow and grin down at him. "Well. That definitely exceeded my expectations."

Ryder bursts into laughter, cradling me against him. "Oh god, Laurel. You are just…" He pulls my face to his for a brief, hot kiss. "You're absolutely perfect."

SEVEN

THE FACT THAT WE NEED TO GET UP AND GET CLEANED up can't be ignored any longer. We've lain drowsing in the afterglow for I don't know how long. Periods of silence and then chatting about random things have kept us occupied for at least half an hour.

But the sticky mess between us has grown cold. Ryder sighs. "I need to clean us up."

I look up into eyes. "I was trying to think of a sexy way to say that."

He slips his arm out from under me and rolls away, chuckling. "How about we skip to the part of things where not everything has to be sexy?"

He goes to the bathroom and closes the door, and I hear water running. When he comes back out, he's discarded the condom and has cleaned himself up, and has a washcloth in his hand. He comes around to my side of the bed, perches on the edge and leans over me, using the warm washcloth to clean my belly and everywhere else, and then I take it from him and wipe myself, getting everything clean.

I hand him the washcloth. "I'd say we've pretty well skipped to that point, Ryder. Nothing about cleaning up like this is terribly sexy."

"I'm glad," he says, tossing the washcloth into the corner of the bathroom near the tub. "I like it like this."

"I'm not peeing in front of you yet," I tell him as he climbs back onto the bed. "We're not there."

"Yeah, I'm okay with that." He glances at me. "That is a pretty big step in a relationship."

"Would it be weird or ruin the moment if I asked how long it took you and your ex to get there?" I say.

He shrugs. "Not at all. We never really did, to be honest. Amy was always weird about that."

"I thought I was alone in that," I admit. "Paul and I never did either. Paul was always very…private, about that stuff."

"What's weird to me is how it feels to talk about our exes together," Ryder says crossing his arms under his head. "It should be a turn-off, or tense or awkward, but it's just not. And that's a little unusual."

"You know, I feel the same! It's nice, because I've never really had anyone who understood what I dealt with." I sigh, turning to my side to look at him, tracing lines on his chest with a finger. "I think the reason it's weird is because we're kind of skipping the golden phase, the honeymoon phase or whatever you want to call it, where the other person is perfect and everything is amazing and it feels like a movie. We're kind of skipping forward to things being…" I trail off, shrugging, unsure how to finish it.

"Just…real?" Ryder says.

I nod. "Yeah, just real." He shifts closer, extends an arm, and I immediately snuggle into the crook of his arm and I find the perfect spot. "You give good nook, Ryder."

His arms tighten, wrapping me closer, twisting toward me so we're partially facing each other, and his free hand slides to rest on the bell of my hip. "It takes two to nook. You're pretty great at it yourself."

"Would you be mad if I fell asleep right now?" I say, drowsily. "Because I totally could."

"I'd be offended if you didn't. That's what nooking is for, obviously."

I let my hands wander his chest and stomach as I drift off. "Good. Because I'm not sure I can stop myself, at this point."

"I won't be far behind you."

Silence ensues as each of us begins to drowse.

"Ryder?"

"Hmmm?"

"Thank you."

I feel his attention, sudden and sharp. "For what?"

I smile against his skin. "For making me feel so beautiful."

His only response is to twist his head, press his lips to my temple, and kiss me.

And that simple, sweet gesture…is my undoing.

I've fallen. That kiss to my temple—for better or worse, it's the tipping point of me accepting and embracing having fallen head over heels for Ryder McCann.

I fall asleep smiling about it.

***

We never closed the curtains in our room, so city light shines in, waking me.

It's still night—without twisting out of his arms, I can't see the clock, but the sky beyond the window tells me it's nearing dawn, because the blackness between the glassy pillars of skyscrapers is smudged with gray.

I drowse, wanting to sink back into sleep, but I can't quite fall back under the veil. And honestly, just lying here in Ryder's arms is almost better, in some ways. He's asleep, deeply, snoring softly, cutely. His arm is draped around me, resting on my hip. The blankets are up around my shoulders, lying across his chest, cocooning us in warmth.

I've never felt so safe, so protected, so wanted.

My chest aches with a feeling, a swelling, a soaring joy, a deep, abiding sense of peace and serenity that is at once comforting and energizing.

My hand rests on his chest, and I give in to the need to just touch him, to express even to myself how pleasing it is to simply touch this man. I let my hand roam his chest, and he stirs but doesn't wake. I explore the heavy muscle of his chest, the solid strength of his abs hidden under that slight layer of softness. The ridge of his hipbone. The firm breadth of his thigh.

My hand brushes, quite by accident, his flaccid cock, and I grin to myself. It's not often, at this stage of things, that you get to see a man like this, and I lift the blanket to get a peek.

Ryder shifts, making a small soft sound in his throat and, as I watch, he hardens. I smile, realizing this has nothing to do with me—it's just the nature of male biology…although the way he's moving and shifting in his sleep makes me wonder if it's got something do with his dreams. A smile touches the corners of his lips, and then vanishes, and he's back under the veil of deep sleep again. Only now, he's completely hard.

I should let him sleep.

It'd be selfish to wake up him up now.

And then I laugh to myself, because if I know anything about men and male psychology, it's that no man would ever, ever complain about being woken up for sex unless he was sick or so exhausted it was like being sick.

Leaving the blanket pulled up around my shoulders, I rest my hand on his stomach, biting my lip as I argue with myself about giving in to the desire to just touch him.

Who am I kidding? There's no argument.

Just a feeble attempt to make myself think my will is stronger than my libido.

And it's not.

And honestly, why should I resist this? I've fallen for him, and I'm going to enjoy every moment of it for as long as I can. If it doesn't work out, I'll deal with that. I'll lean on my friends and probably drink a little too much for a few weeks, and then I'll pull myself out of it and carry on with my life.

I shy away from trying to envision what it would look like and feel like if things "worked out," whatever that would even mean.

Instead, I just dive into the moment. Live in the present. Right now, I'm not going to fall back asleep. Right now, I'm consumed with desire. I want to touch him—I need to feel him. Where that goes, I don't know. I don't care. Sex, or something else, I don't care.

I just want him in my hand. I just want to touch him.

I gather him in my hand, biting my lip in sheer enjoyment of the feel of his hardness, the thick, heavy girth. He lets out a sigh in his sleep, some part of his subconscious is responding to my touch. I'm tempted to just crawl under the blankets right now, but I resist.

And then, once again, I ask myself why I'm holding back, what am I resisting? Why draw it out? Why hold back from what I want? I want to taste him, I want to feel him in my mouth and in my hands—I want to make him feel good, wake him up by making him feel better than he's ever felt.

I ask myself why.

The answer? I want to erase everything that's gone before. I want to be all he can think of, all he remembers. I want to make him feel better than he's ever felt—for a lot of reasons. To know that I'm capable of that, that I can be that for a man. That he doesn't need me in the way that Paul needed me, but that he wants me and wants how I make him feel so badly that he can't live without the way I make him feel. I want to know what it's like to be desired just for who I am—and I get that from Ryder. He makes me feel beautiful. Wanted. Needed. Appreciated.

Which in turn makes me want to do things for him—make him feel wanted and appreciated and desired and needed.

During my whole relationship with Paul, sex was about him—keeping him sated, keeping him happy, keeping him sane. It was about keeping up with his demands in a desperate attempt to establish some kind of equilibrium, and I had this stupid idea that if I kept up with his sexual needs while he was in that needy, low-swing state, that maybe he'd think more about me and be more approachable and reasonable when he was in the upswing. Only, it never worked that way. And the sex was never...mutual. I worked hard to make sure I felt some kind of release from it, but it was never about me.

Ryder makes it about *me*.

Even when I showed him that my desire was for him, that I wanted something that would make him feel good, he turned it back on me, brought it back to me. Made me come more than I've ever come in my life in a single night—more in terms of both volume and intensity. He kissed me through it all. Looked me in the eye and never shied away or acted afraid of how intense it was. He demanded I keep eye contact as we came together, and I think he knew damn well the effect that would have on both of us, emotionally.

I think he knew going into this weekend what would happen.

Is that why I have his erection in my hand, contemplating crawling under the covers and taking him in my mouth?

Is it for him? Or for me?

Both.

I want to know how I can make him feel by doing this. And I want him to know I *want* to make him feel that way.

I look at his handsome face, younger-looking and vulnerable in repose. There are care lines at the corners of his mouth and eyes. A slackness to his mouth, which can utter such sweet, funny, and sexy things. His beard is messy, tangled.

He stirs, shifting, pushing his hips upward, the tense strain of his erection making him seek relief, even unconsciously. I slide my fist down his length, and he makes a sound in his throat, a soft, boyish murmur. I remain quiet; keeping my touch light and soft, I stroke him slowly. He huffs, sighs, and his hips flex upward.

I'm aroused and amused by how reflexive and expressive he is in his need, even asleep. I lift the blanket and slide down his body, ducking under the blankets and leaving them over my head. It's stuffy under here, though, so I lift the covers near his feet to create a little ventilation hole. Why don't I just toss back the blankets? Because I have this dumb idea that it's sexier if he wakes up and I'm under the blankets, sucking him off.

you think less of me if I said I didn't think I could go again if I tried?

"God, no! I'm so sore right now, I think I'll need at least a week to recover." I cover myself with one hand. "I'm going to be walking funny for a few days, I think."

He blows out a sigh. "Thank god we're on the same page. My poor balls need a break."

I cup the body part in question. "Awww. The poor babies. They've done a lot of work the last thirty-six hours, or whatever it's been."

Ryder hauls me up against his chest and cradles my head in the nook of his arm. "I need a quick nap, and then we can actually shower, and actually put on clothes, and actually have lunch before you have to go pick up your kid."

I nuzzle closer, wrapping an arm over his waist. "Sounds good to me. I don't think we slept more than four or five hours last night."

I feel myself slipping under into sleep almost immediately. As I do, I murmur the truth that's been bubbling inside me since Friday night. "Ryder? If I wasn't already falling for you, I am now for sure."

He doesn't answer, and I figure he's asleep already. But then, as I drift and twist and flutter deeper into sleep, I hear him rumble in a drowsy, sleepy voice.

"I started to fall for you the first time I laid eyes on

you, Laurel. I just didn't want to admit it to myself."

The only response I'm capable of is a tightening of my fingers into his waist, letting him know I heard him. And then, happy and sated and exhausted, I tumble the rest of the way into sleep.

———

I wake abruptly and sit bolt upright. "SHIT! What time is it?"

Panic slams through me as I twist to look at the clock on the table beside the hotel bed: 3:36.

"Whass'mater?" Ryder mumbles.

"It's three thirty and I have to pick Nate up at four." I scramble out of bed. "I have to go. Like *now*."

Ryder sits up, blinking blearily. "Hey, relax. It's gonna be okay. You'll be fine."

I can't go pick him up stinking and sticky, so I have to at least rinse off. I twist the shower on and jump in while it's still cold, gasping as I scrub the essentials with a bar of soap, and then hop out and dry off, twisting my hair into a messy bun while ripping my clean clothes out of my bag.

I glance at Ryder, who has taken my place in the shower. "No, you don't understand," I tell him. "I've never been late picking him up—Paul is almost always late, and it's been a constant problem for us in our co-parenting. If I'm late, I'll never hear the end of it. It'll be basically giving him free rein to be late as much as he wants."

Ryder spends no more time in the shower than I do, cleaning off, rinsing, and jumping out, and he's finished getting dressed before I am. "Well, that's bullshit," he says.

I laugh bitterly. "Yeah, but that's Paul."

He frowns at me. "Laurel, I'm taking you to get Nate. It'll save time."

I shove my feet into the flats. "Um…thanks, but no. Just drop me off at home."

"You'll be even later, in that case." He shrugs. "I really don't mind, and I've got nothing else going on today. Plus, it means more time with you."

I hesitate over my answer, stuffing my dirty clothes and heels into my bag. "Ryder, I appreciate the offer, but…"

He sighs. "You're not ready for me to meet Nate."

"It's not that, honestly, it's not." I shoulder my bag and take his hand. "It's more about Paul. I'm not quite ready to answer his questions about who I'm dating. He was acting weird when I dropped Nate off, and if I'm with you when I pick him up, I'm worried it'll escalate."

"Weird how?"

I glance at the clock: 3:46. "Shit!" I pinch the bridge of my nose. I hang my head, groaning. "I feel so irresponsible. Even if I left right now, I'd be super late."

"Call him," Ryder says. "Explain that you're running late—not his business why—and that you'll be there at four thirty."

"That's still pushing the schedule, though. Nate has basketball practice at five, and I still have to get him home to change into his practice clothes and then get him to the school."

Ryder brushes his thumb over my lips, cupping my jaw. "Let me help, Laurel. Please?"

I bite my lip and unexpected tears begin to form. "It's too soon. For him, for me, for Paul. It's too soon."

He wraps me up in his arms. "Laurel, listen." He pulls back and meets my eyes. "You're a single mother. I knew that going in. I accept that as part of you. I understand that it's complicated, and that you have to put Nate first. I get all that. I'm okay with it."

"I heard what you said just before we fell asleep earlier," I tell him.

He nods. "What this is, where it's going to go, what it'll look like, I don't know." He squeezes my hand. "But I'm willing to explore it with you."

"Me too." I sniff. "I just…I'm scared. For Nate."

I sigh. "And myself."

"Hey, I get that too. I can't say I'm not a little nervous or scared of this whole thing myself. It's all happening super fast and I wasn't expecting any of it. But we can just...take it one step at a time, okay?" He grabs my phone out of my purse. "Step one, right here and right now, is to call Paul. Then we'll go get your kid and take him to basketball. I won't even get out of the car, okay?"

I sigh. "This isn't how I planned for you to meet him, much less Paul."

"How did you have it planned?"

"You and I would take Nate out for a fun afternoon—a movie, or laser tag." I eye him. "Although Nate was asking for paintball. Either way, it wouldn't involve my ex, or being late picking up my son."

Ryder just shrugs. "Yeah, well, in my experience, life rarely goes as planned."

"No kidding." I dial Paul, and it rings half a dozen times before he picks up, seconds before voicemail kicks in.

"Laurel, hi." Paul's voice is distant, as if I'm on speakerphone. "I hope you're not calling to tell me you're early, because we're just leaving the mall."

"Actually, no," I say. "I'm calling because I'm actually running a little late myself."

A brief silence. "You are? Why?"

I suppress a sigh of irritation. "How often have I questioned you about why you're running late?" He just mutters something unintelligible, his usual response when I'm right and he hates it. "Exactly."

"Yeah, well, you don't get to give me shit for being late if you're going to be late."

I can't restrain the sigh, this time. "Paul, you're late more often than you're on time. This is the first time since we started co-parenting that I've ever been late. So yeah, unfortunately for you, I do still get to give you shit for being late."

"Nate is having a panic attack about being late for basketball practice."

"He'll be on time." I gesture at the door, and Ryder and I head for the elevator as I try to wrap this stupid conversation up. "We'll be there at four thirty."

Shit.

"We?"

"Paul—"

"Who's we?"

"Don't worry about it. I'll see you at four thirty."

"Laurel, who's we?" I hear the tinge of suspicion in his voice, the edge of anger—Paul working himself into a jealous rage.

"Don't worry about it. I'm hanging up now."

"Laurel, you don't get to just—"

I cut in. "You lost the right to tell me what I can or can't do a *very* long time ago."

"Laurel—"

"I'm hanging up now, Paul. I'll see you at four thirty."

I end the call, toss the phone into my purse, and ignore it as it begins ringing. I manage to hold it together as Ryder checks us out, and then the valet brings Ryder's car around, and I slide in. Ryder tosses both of our bags into the trunk, and then we're roaring off, away from the hotel. Within minutes, we're outside of downtown Chicago and flying down the freeway toward the suburbs.

"Shit." I swallow hard, but the knot in my throat is too thick and hot to swallow.

Ryder takes my hand. "Hey, just breathe, okay?"

I shake my head. "You don't know Paul."

"What's he going to do?"

I shrug. "Who knows? When I started dating Derek, Paul lost his damn mind. Got jealous, tried to tell me I wasn't allowed to date anyone, wasn't allowed to bring other guys around Nate without his permission, all sorts of crazy bullshit. Really, it only ended when Derek and I broke up—the entire time we were dating, Paul was a mess." I sigh and rub my face. "And now it's going to start all over again."

"He's still possessive of you? And you've been

divorced how long?"

"Rationality has never been Paul's strong suit."

Ryder squeezes my hand. "It'll be okay."

I laugh weakly. "Well, at least one of us thinks so."

EIGHT

W E PULL TO A STOP ALONG THE CURB IN FRONT OF
Paul's house. I exit the car and head for the
front door, but before I'm halfway there, Nate bursts
out the door at a run.

"Mom!" He slams into me. "You're finally here!
Come on! We gotta go!" He glances past me. "Wait—
where's your car?"

I hesitate. "Um. I'll explain later. For now, we're
riding in this, okay?"

Nate peers across the lawn. "Is that the guy you
went on a date with?"

"Can we talk about this in the car?"

"Are you sure that's a safe vehicle for our son to
be in?" I hear Paul from behind me. "Some of those
old cars don't even have seatbelts."

I work at remaining calm. "I need your booster."

Paul eyes the shiny orange classic BMW. "We
talked about this. You have to tell me when you're

dating someone new."

I groan. *"You* talked about this—*I* don't have to do anything. We are *divorced,* Paul. I can do what I want with my life, see who I want, when I want, and I don't owe you anything." Nate is watching very carefully, listening to every word. "We have to go. May I please borrow your booster seat?"

"I should meet him, at least."

I grind my teeth together. "Sure. When we're not running late."

"Yeah, well…whose fault is that?"

"Mine. I admit it. Now quit being difficult, please. Just get me your booster so I can get Nate to practice on time."

Paul eyes me. "I never liked the last guy you dated. He was sleazy."

"If I want your opinion on who I date, I'll ask."

"Mom, Dad, can you quit arguing, please?" Nate glares at Paul. "I *have* to be on time for practice, Dad. Can you please just get my booster seat?"

Paul grumbles under his breath, but he heads for his garage and returns with Nate's booster. He hands it to me, and his eyes as he does so are troubled—and troubling. "This isn't how this was supposed to go," he mutters.

I move toward Ryder's car, pulling open the rear passenger door and lever the booster seat into position. Nate climbs in and buckles up. I can tell he's tense and unhappy.

Straightening, I move to slide into the front seat, but Paul's hand on my arm stops me.

"Laurel."

I pull away from him. "What, Paul?"

"We need to talk."

I shake my head. "No, we don't. There's nothing to talk about."

He grinds his jaw, frowning. "It doesn't have to be now." He glances into the car, at Ryder. "Next time you bring Nate over."

I sigh. "We'll see."

He growls angrily. "Laurel, come on. I'm asking for a few minutes of your time."

"We have to go. Nate is going to be late." I sink into the deep bucket seat and buckle up. "Next time I drop Nate off, we can talk, okay?"

He backs away. "That's all I'm asking for."

I close my door, and Ryder glances at me, then at Nate.

"Everyone buckled?" he asks.

"Yes," I bite out. "Let's go, please."

Ryder just nods, once. "You got it."

He doesn't say a word after that, and the next few minutes are tensely silent.

Nate is the one to break it. "This is a cool car."

Pulling to a stop at a red light, Ryder twists to face Nate. "Thanks, man." He extends a hand. "I'm Ryder."

Nate takes Ryder's hand and shakes it—I can tell by the focused grimace on Nate's face that he's squeezing as hard as he can. "I'm Nate."

Ryder laughs, playfully shaking his hand when Nate lets go. "Quite a grip you got there, dude."

Nate shrugs. "My dad told me to always use a good strong grip."

Ryder laughs again. "I don't know man, it kinda felt like you were trying to break my hand." He shakes it out again. "Seriously. That's my shifting hand."

"What kind of car is this?" Nate asks—he's non-plussed by Ryder's attempts to charm him, it seems.

"It's a BMW."

"Did you build it yourself?"

Ryder nods. "Yeah. Well, I didn't build it, per se, I restored it."

"Did it take you a long time?"

"About a year."

Nate is eying Ryder closely. "So, what do you do?"

"For work?" Ryder glances at him in the rearview mirror. "I'm an electrician. What about you?"

Nate frowns. "I'm nine—I go to school."

Ryder grins. "I know. I was messing with you. I don't like asking people what they do, because I've always felt like a person is a lot more than what they do for work. I mean, you're more than just a kid who goes to school, right?"

Nate nods. "Right."

"Well, I'm more than just a guy who does electrical work."

"I guess I get that. So, what else are you, then?"

"I restore classic cars. I help my friends build houses." He hums in thought. "But all that is still just things I *do*. I guess I would say I'm a person who likes to build things with my hands." He eyes Nate in the rearview mirror again. "What about you?"

"Dude, I'm nine. How am I supposed to know?"

Ryder laughs. "Good answer! You don't have to know. What kinds of things do you like doing?"

I'm watching the exchange with intense interest; Nate rarely gets this involved in conversations with adults, and wouldn't even give Derek the time of day. Which, I realize now, was a reaction to how Derek treated him—I feel guilty about that, and hope desperately that I'm not making a similar mistake with Ryder. But then, Ryder is a one-hundred-and-eighty-degree difference from Derek, in every way. Where Derek worked hard to be cool and smooth, Ryder is goofy, effortlessly cool, and rarely smooth. Ryder is who he is, take it or leave it, and he makes no apologies for the rough edges and quirks in his personality.

"I dunno. I like sports. I like video games—not as much as my friend Brian, though. He's, like, literally addicted to Fortnite, and I think it's stupid. He called me a loser and now I'm not sure we're friends anymore."

Ryder pulls into my subdivision. "If he's gonna treat you that way about a video game, he wasn't really your friend to begin with. True friends don't give a shi—a crap about that stuff. You can like different things and still be friends."

Nate doesn't answer right away. "I thought that liking the same stuff was what made you friends."

Ryder shakes his head. "No way, man. Liking the same stuff is what brings you together, what starts the friendship, but if you don't like all the same stuff, that's fine. Like, my three best friends: Jesse, Franco, and James—we all like building stuff. But Jesse hates working on cars and I love it. James hates dealing with fiddly, precise stuff like electrical currents and voltages and stuff, and I love it. Franco loves working with wood and carving things and all that, and I just end up with splinters. But we all like building things in our own way, and that's what bonds us. We're friends because we like who the other person is, and we have fun together, no matter what we do."

"Huh. Brian and I both like sports and watching YouTube. I just think Fortnite is dumb."

"And if he's really your friend, he won't care. You just don't have to do that particular thing when you hang out."

We pull into my driveway, and I glance at Ryder. "We just have to go get him changed into basketball stuff. You want to come in or wait?"

"I'll come in." He hesitates. "If it's cool."

I climb out and let Nate out. "It's cool."

"You're sure?"

I nod. "It's cool."

Nate lets out an annoyed groan. "God, you guys are weird. Let's go, already. I'm a team captain. I have to be on time."

He hustles ahead of me, his overnight backpack bouncing on his back. I reach the door just after him, unlock it, and Nate tears off through the house, dropping his bag and shedding clothes as he goes.

"Nate—god," I huff. "You could at least put your clothes in the hamper!"

"No time, Mom!" he calls from his bedroom.

I sigh. "It takes literally the same amount of time to take all your clothes off in your room and throw them in the hamper as it does to strip on the way to your room, leaving clothes all over my living room." Ryder is snickering, and I shoot him a glare. "What are you laughing at?"

"Just that I tend to take my clothes off the same

way—especially if I'm in a hurry."

I roll my eyes. "Boys are so messy. I don't get it. You're not saving any time, and actually just making more work for yourself later." I frown at him. "Unless you never bother to pick up after yourself."

Ryder pulls a face. "I do." He snickers again. "Just not…you know. A lot."

"So you're saying your house is a pigsty."

"Um, somewhere between a little messy and a pigsty? I *do* clean up. Every once in a while."

I shake my head. "Gross."

Ryder is looking around at our house—mismatched furniture, a dozen photos of Nate by himself and Nate and me together, a 40-gallon tote bin full of LEGOs on the floor, with a handful of pieces scattered around it. Stacks of DVDs on the entertainment center, next to the TV, mostly Ninjago and Ninja Turtles, as well as my collection of vintage 80s cartoon DVDs—*She-Ra*, *He-Man*, *ThunderCats*, *GI Joe*, *Voltron*, *Transformers*.

Ryder immediately goes to the vintage DVDs. "Dude, you have my entire childhood right here."

I laugh. "Nate and I were trying to agree on something to watch together one Saturday morning, and I happened across an episode of *He-Man* on some cable channel, and we ended up watching that, which sent me on a mission to find collections of all the cartoons my sister and I used to watch together."

"You watched this stuff? Not, like, *Strawberry Shortcake* or *Rainbow Brite*? Every Saturday morning Franco and Jesse and I would go over to Jesse's, and his sister and her friends would be watching *Rainbow Brite*. We'd always pretend we didn't like it, but we always ended up sitting on the floor watching it until it was time for *Transformers* or whatever."

I shrug. "My parents both worked on Saturdays, so Leah and I would stay home alone all morning eating cereal and watching TV." I laugh. "It was the eighties—you could do that back then. I'd never leave Nate home alone at this age, even though Leah and I were younger when Mom and Dad left us to go to work."

"MOM!" Nate shouts. "I have a knot in my shoelace, and I can't get it out, and we're gonna be late!"

He hops into the living room, one shoe on and tied, the other dangling by the knotted laces from his finger. I reach for it, but Ryder takes it first.

"Look, knots are easy. You just gotta figure out where it's going and work backwards." He examines the knot, and then points at a particular part of the knot. "See this? Pull on it."

He hands it back to Nate, who wiggles the indicated section free, which loosens the knot enough that he can untie it himself. "Wow. How'd you do that?"

"My uncle was a sailor. And I don't mean he was in the Navy, I mean he sailed on an old antique schooner with sails and all that. He and a bunch of other guys from his Vietnam unit met every weekend to build this full-scale, working replica of an old Great Lakes merchant schooner. When they finished it, they'd go sailing on it every weekend. He was a master with knots, and he was always teaching me different knots and stuff."

"That's the coolest thing ever," Nate says.

"Is that the same uncle who taught you how to restore classic cars?" I ask.

Ryder nods. "Sure is. Uncle Pete. He basically raised me."

Nate has his shoe tied, and hops up. "Okay. Let's go."

Ryder laughs. "You're really serious about this, aren't you?"

Nate is out the front door already, leaving it swinging, and I just laugh. "He's *the most* serious about it. He was chosen as a team captain this season, and ever since he's taken the whole thing so seriously I don't even know how to deal with it."

"It's good he takes the responsibility seriously, though."

I nod. "He's a good kid." I can't help a sigh. "I just hate that he's caught between Paul and me when things like today happen."

He squeezes my shoulder. "You're doing an amazing job. Don't second-guess yourself."

As we climb into his car—Nate is already buckled up and bouncing impatiently—I ask, "How do you know I'm doing a great job?"

Ryder starts the car and with a throaty roar he pulls away, squealing the tires—to Nate's immense delight. He accelerates so fast we're pushed back into the seat, but he slows to the speed limit almost immediately.

"Because he's a cool kid. You don't raise cool kids if you're doing a crappy job as a parent. That's how you end up with self-centered little assholes."

I frown at him. "Ryder!"

"It's true, Mom," Nate says. "There's this kid in my grade, and he's always being super mean to people on the playground, and I heard him saying his parents hate each other and his mom is always sending him to stay with other people so she can go out with her boyfriend, and he said his mom has a new boyfriend like every week. I feel bad for him, but he's a jerk." He glances at me. "He's a slimy poophead."

"Well, we still have to be nice to slimy poopheads, Nate," I tell him. "He's probably mean because he's lonely and sad."

"Slimy poophead, huh?" Ryder says, laughing. He slides his phone from his pocket and hits a speed dial. It rings three times, and I hear someone pick up, construction noises in the background. "Hey, Jesse—you're a slimy poophead!"

Jesse doesn't answer right away, and then he cackles. "Yeah? Well…you're a…a…a moldy turdface!"

Nate laughs at that. "That's lame! Slimy poophead is better!"

"Who said that?" Jesse asks.

"Nate," Ryder answers. "Laurel's kid."

"Laurel's kid, huh?" I hear questions in Jesse's voice, but knowing he's on speakerphone, he's wise enough to keep them to himself. "Moldy turdface is better, so there."

I groan in annoyance. "You're both as bad as he is, and you're grown men!" I can't help a laugh, though. "You do realize I've been trying to get him *not* to talk like that, right? And then you two come along and encourage him!"

"News flash for you, Laurel," Jesse says. "The four of us never really grew up. Inside, we're still all essentially ten-year-olds."

"Wonderful," I drawl. "Juuuust great."

"I gotta go," Jesse says. "James and I are in the

middle of putting up a six-foot load-bearing beam."

"Billy Bar later!" I hear James call. "I've got questions!"

"Hello?" Ryder makes fake static sounds. "You're breaking up…can't hear you…" and then he hangs up, shoving the phone under his thigh.

"Wow, that was…not subtle," I remark. "Avoiding them, are you?"

He shrugs. "I'm not quite ready to answer a bunch of questions just yet."

"That I understand. I'm gonna get questioned by the gossip gestapo myself—especially now that Jesse and James both know you're with me and Nate."

"The gossip gestapo?" Ryder asks, laughing.

"Yeah, Audra. She's absolutely merciless when she wants to know something."

"Now that Jesse and Franco are dating Imogen and Audra, we have our own little circle of gossip," Ryder says. "Anything that happens to any of us, everyone else knows instantly. Jesse and Franco are just as bad as the women when it comes to spreading shit." He winces. "I mean, crap."

We make it to the elementary school with two minutes to spare, and Nate jumps out, shouting over his shoulder. "I'll be done in an hour and a half, then we get pizza! Okay, see you later, love you, bye!" He pauses, halfway through the door into the school. "I meant I love you Mom, not you, Ryder—that'd be weird!"

Ryder laughs. "I like that kid. He's funny."

I grin. "I'm pretty fond of him myself."

"So. Now what?"

I shrug. "I could've just taken Nate to practice myself, but I wasn't thinking clearly." A moment of silence between us—kind of awkward, a little strained, neither of us knowing exactly how we're supposed to say goodbye after the weekend we shared. "We always get pizza for dinner on Sunday." I hesitate. "I'd invite you to have dinner with us, but I kinda feel like I need to spend some time with Nate. We usually talk about what he did with his dad."

"It's fine," Ryder assures me. "The guys and I almost never miss a Sunday night at Billy Bar, so if I skip, I'll just get questioned worse later." He laughs, running his hand through his hair. "I, uh…I'm not sure how this is supposed to work. Like, what we do next, or what to say…"

"Me neither."

He puts the car into drive. "How about this—I take you back to your place, and we figure out how to say goodbye to each other."

I snort. "I know what *that* means."

He snickers. "Hey, what can I say—I can't get enough."

"I thought we agreed we needed a break." I eye him with an arched eyebrow.

He shrugs. "We've *had* a break. Like, two whole hours."

"Not even," I say. "We left Chicago at ten to four. It's just now five thirty."

"Close enough."

I sigh, pat his hand. "I can't. I'll lose track of time again." I shift in the seat. "Plus, I honestly just don't think I physically can. I'm *really* sore." I lean close to him and whisper in his ear. "You're a *lot* to take that many times, Ryder. You're gonna have to give my poor little vagina some time to recover."

His laugh is a low rasp. "You really know how to...*stroke* a man's ego, Laurel."

I groan, resting my head against his shoulder. "Don't say things like that, dammit. You'll turn me on."

"It doesn't seem like it's all that hard, babe," he teases.

"It's mostly just you," I tell him. "There's just something about you."

"Is it the hair?" He runs his hand through his hair with dramatic flair. "You probably just have a thing for gingers."

I kiss the edge of his jaw. "Nope. Just you."

He smiles at me as we pull back into my driveway.

"Seriously. Being around you is *amazing* for my ego."

"I could say the same thing." I don't want to go; I sigh, reluctantly unbuckling. "That was the best weekend of my life, Ryder."

"Mine too." He gets out of the car, circles around and opens my door.

I climb out, close the door, and he presses me up against the side of his car, cupping my face in both hands. He kisses me, and it's a kiss meant to remind me of everything we did, everything we shared. As if I could ever, ever forget.

"When will I see you again?" Ryder asks, when he finally lets the kiss subside.

"You can't kiss me like that and then leave," I whisper. "Not fair."

His grin is a little cocky and a lot amused, and even more aroused. "That's the point."

I tug on his beard. "You realize there's absolutely no chance I'll be able to sleep tonight? That I'll be dreaming about you the entire time?"

He wiggles his eyebrows. "Dreaming about me, huh?"

"It'll probably be interminably sexy. I'll likely end up calling you."

"Have I mentioned yet that I love the way you think?"

"It may have come up once or twice."

He sighs, letting me go. "You probably should go now, while I have the resolve to actually let you leave unscathed."

"Unscathed?" I say, incredulous. "I'm very much scathed, Ryder."

"Is scathed even a word?" he asks.

I laugh. "I don't know. If unscathed is a word, then scathed has to be."

"Oh, right. Like, a scathing remark."

"Stop distracting me with grammar," I say.

"I'm trying to diffuse the sexiness of the situation so it's easier for you to leave."

"Why, how kind of you, Ryder. You're so thoughtful!"

He brushes imaginary lint off of his shoulder. "Tis my nature to but think of you before all else, m'lady," he says in an arch, formal tone.

I kiss him, once, quickly, softly. "Thank you, Ryder."

"For what?" He sounds genuinely puzzled.

"For making me feel so safe, beautiful, and wanted. It's been a very long time since I've felt that way."

His expression melts. "Laurel, if I did anything, it was to point out the obvious. And as far as you feeling safe, well...I hope that you always feel safe with me. Because you *are*."

"I'm still scared of this, Ryder."

"You and me both, honey." He takes my hands and kisses the backs of both. "We can be scared together?"

The thump and pitter-patter of my heart is so loud I'm sure he can hear it. "Yeah."

He juts his chin at my house. "Get, while the gettin's good."

"Trying to get rid of me?" I tease.

He groans. "I'm getting turned on, and it's making my balls hurt."

"Go home and ice the poor babies."

He laughs, ever so gingerly patting his crotch. "Gotta get 'em back in fighting shape so we can see if the pattern continues."

I climb out of the car—it's so low-slung it's kind of a struggle. "I'll talk to you later, okay?"

"You never answered me—when will I see you again?"

"See me again? Or get me naked again?"

He groans a laugh. "Don't talk about me getting you naked! Oh god, it hurts!"

"Do you think we overdid the sex?" I ask, leaning against the open door.

He immediately goes serious, pointing an accusatory finger at me. "You quit that blasphemy, woman." He reaches for my sleeve. "Hey—do I seriously have to wait all the way until the weekend after next to go out with you?"

I sigh. "Honestly, I don't know." I shrug. "We'll have to figure things out one day at a time."

He nods. "One day at a time I can do, babe."

Nate and I are sitting across from each other at our favorite local pizzeria, eating gluten-free pepperoni pizza. He's chowing down, ravenous after a practice that left him dripping in sweat and breathing hard for several minutes after I picked him up. I can tell something is percolating in his head, though—he always gets a focused look on his face when he's trying to figure out what to say and how.

When he's eaten about half his pizza, he finally stops eating and looks at me. "So. Ryder's definitely not a slimy poophead."

I nod seriously. "You determined this during the ten-minute car ride from Dad's to our house and then to school?"

"Yep." He takes a monster bite and talks around it. "It's pretty easy to tell. Ryder's cool."

"I'm glad you think so," I say, my voice quiet.

He picks up on something in my voice. "You like him, huh?"

I smile. "I think he's pretty cool."

"So. When are we going paintballing?"

I sigh. "I don't know. I've never been paintballing, and I don't know if Ryder even wants to do that with us."

"Well, ask him. Paintball is awesome!"

"How do you know? When did you go paintballing?"

He rolls his eyes. "It's shooting people with paint guns, Mom. Of *course* it's awesome."

"Can't argue with that logic, I suppose." I steal a piece of his pizza. "I'll talk to him. But, Nate, I don't know what's going on with Ryder and me, so don't…"

He slows his chewing, sensing the seriousness in my voice. "Don't what, Mom?"

I shrug. "Don't get too attached, I guess."

He frowns. "But if you like him and you're going out on dates with him, doesn't that mean *you're* getting attached?"

"I mean, yeah, but—"

"So why can't I get attached? If I like him, why would I pretend I don't?"

"I don't mean pretend you don't like him." I set my pizza down on my plate and wipe my fingers on a napkin. "Nate, look, it's…complicated."

He rolls his eyes at me. "You only ever say that

when you don't *want* to explain it. To adults, complicated just means something you don't want to tell a
kid."

I can't help but laugh. "Fair enough. You want
the adult version, then?"

"For real?" he asks, his eyes bugging out.

"For real. But I warn you, it *is* complicated."

"I'm *nine*, Mom. I'm not a little kid anymore."

"Mmmm, I see." I suppress a smirk. "The thing
is, I honestly don't know what is happening with
Ryder and me. We like each other and we're going to
go on dates and stuff, but—"

"Are you gonna marry him? If you do, will that
make him my dad? Or no, that'll make him my stepdad. Do I call him stepdad? That's a lot to say. Can I
just call him Ryder?" He breaks off with a sigh. "That
is complicated."

"Nate, slow down." I laugh. "But yeah, that's why
it's complicated. I like him, but getting married again
is a big deal. And after what happened with Derek,
I'm even more scared of making a mistake that will
hurt you."

He frowns. "Mom, Derek was an asshole. I knew
he was an asshole the first time you brought him
around me."

"You're not supposed to talk like that, mister." I
groan. "Why didn't you say anything?"

"I didn't know I could—I didn't know I was supposed to."

I play with a loose lock of my hair. "It's not fair of me to put that on you," I say. "Listen, buddy—I want you to always be honest with me. Always, about everything. But it's not your job to tell me when I'm dating a—a butthole. I just…" I take a bite of pizza to buy myself time to figure out what else I need to say to my son. "I know Derek was a mistake. He didn't treat you right, and that should have been my first clue that he was a jerk. I was being selfish, and I'm sorry."

"I forgive you, Mama." He brightens. "I like Ryder, though. And not just because he has a cool car."

"Why else, then, if not for his cool car?"

Which, admittedly, is seriously cool.

He shrugs. "He *talked* to me. Like a normal person. I mean, I'm a kid and he's an adult, but he talked to me like I'm just another person. Like you do." He glances at me, dipping the crescent of his crust into a cup of ranch. "Dad doesn't talk to me like that."

"Baby, no one will ever replace your father. I hope you understand that."

He shifts. "But Mom, I—what if I *want* someone to?" He looks at me almost fearfully, as if he's saying something terrible. "I don't really *like* Dad. He's my dad and I love him, but I don't always…*like* him.

I guess I don't want someone to replace him, like I'd never see him again, I just…I don't know." He sighs deeply. "You're right—this is really complicated."

"Nate…my point about Ryder is that I don't want you to get super attached to Ryder being around and then him and I stop seeing each other and you get hurt." I take his hand. "I get what you're saying about your father, though. He can be…difficult, sometimes. There are reasons he and I got divorced, none of which have anything to do with you."

"Is it because Dad is a slimy poophead?"

I groan. "Nate, you can't say that about your father. It's not okay."

"Fine. But I think I like Ryder better."

I laugh at that. "Are you trying to barter with me?"

"I don't know what barter means."

"It means—never mind what it means."

"So you'll talk to Ryder about going paintballing?"

I lean across the table and ruffle his hair. "We'll see. I'll talk to him, and that's all I can promise."

He grins at me. "We're totally going paintballing."

I sigh, because he knows he has me. "Like I said— I'll talk to him and we'll see what happens."

I give up trying to go to sleep a few minutes before midnight. I've tossed and turned and counted sheep *and* my blessings, but blessings end up meaning the number of orgasms I had with Ryder over the weekend, which leaves me worked up and flushed and missing him. I pull my cell phone out of the bedside table drawer, turn off the "do not disturb" mode, and send Ryder a text.

Me: *I really had a great time this weekend. Thank you. :-)*

Ryder: *I'm really glad you came to Billy Bar and called me on my shit. Because thanks to that, I had the most epic and incredible weekend of my life. I'm looking forward to a lot more of them with you.*

Me: *I'm glad I did, too.*

Ryder: *I wish I could text you all night, but I have to get up early.*

Me: *Same. Talk in the morning?*

Ryder: *For sure. Sleep well.*

Me: *You too.*

Ryder: *Don't text me back, this time! If we're both trying to get the last word in we'll never stop texting.*

I'm tempted to text him a winking emoji or something just to troll him, but I don't, simply in the interest of actually getting some sleep tonight.

And so, thus ends the text conversation. I plug my phone back in, put it on "do not disturb," and drift off, smiling to myself.

Only to be woken what feels like a few minutes later to a soft but insistent knocking on my front door. I moan in annoyance, but squirm out of bed and tug on my robe.

Wondering if it's Ryder standing on the other side of the door—and hoping it is—I leave the robe untied over my T-shirt and underwear, loosely grasping the edges closed.

"Just couldn't help yourself, could you?" I say, opening the door.

"No, I couldn't," Paul says, as he takes a good look at me. "But it looks as if you were expecting someone else."

NINE

I YANK MY ROBE CLOSED, TIE IT HURRIEDLY, AND CLOSE THE door to a thin crack. "What the hell are you doing here at this hour, Paul?" I hiss.

"I had to talk to you."

"It's one o'clock in the fucking morning, and I told you we'd talk next time I dropped Nate off."

"That's in two weeks, and I can't wait that long."

I close my eyes and work furiously to batten down my temper. "Well, regardless of what it is you so desperately need to talk to me about, please understand this: you absolutely cannot ever show up at my house unannounced, especially at one o'clock in the goddamn morning."

"It's important, Laurel."

"Are you dying or something?"

He frowns, rearing back as if struck. "What? No!"

"Then it's not important enough to show up at my front door at one in the morning. Or at my front door *ever*, regardless of the time."

He grinds his molars together, a sure sign of his burgeoning temper. "I have every right to insist we talk, Laurel."

"No, you don't. I owe you nothing. *You* owe me, in fact—because you don't pay me shit for child support or alimony, and instead of reporting that to the court I let it slide because I don't want or need your money, but have you ever stopped to think about your son and what he needs? God knows you've never been able to hold down a job for more than six months..." I realize my voice is rising, and I force my voice back to a whisper. "Go home, Paul. We'll talk next time I drop Nate off for his visitation."

"Why are you being so cruel, Laurel?"

I flinch. "Cruel? *I'm* being cruel? I put up with your unpredictability and jealousy for *years*, Paul. I did everything I could to take care of you, but it was never enough. Nothing I could ever do would ever be enough for you, and I eventually realized that. *We... are...DIVORCED!* I am the mother of your child, and that's *it*! I am not your friend; I do not owe you anything—and certainly not explanations of where I go, or what I do or with whom. My life is my business, not yours. I don't know what you do with your life, and frankly, I don't care, as long you treat our son with love, and protect him when you're with him." I sigh, rubbing my face. "I'm not doing this with you right now, Paul. I'm tired, I was just about to fall asleep, and you're pissing me off. And if you wake Nate up, I swear to god you'll regret it forever."

He breathes out slowly. "Just…give me five minutes, Laurel. What I have to say I can say in five minutes."

"Now? At one a.m.?"

"Yes."

I tug my robe closed tighter, retie the knot, make sure the front door is unlocked, and step out onto the porch. I put my back to the door and cross my arms. "Okay. I'm listening."

Paul closes his eyes and lets out a slow breath, relief on his features. "I know I wasn't always the best husband to you." He pauses, and I have to stifle the urge to make a nasty retort. "And I don't think I've ever truly apologized for that. So…I'm sorry, Laurel."

"Apology accepted." I make to open the door, but he keeps speaking.

"The thing is, us divorcing was, in a weird way, the thing I needed most. It showed me that I…that I was a disaster. That I had problems I'd never resolved, issues I was ignoring."

I again stifle the urge to snap at him. "I'm glad you're coming to these realizations, Paul."

"I've actually been seeing someone."

I blink. "Wow, um. Okay. Good for you."

He pales, stammers. "NO! Not—I don't—I didn't mean like that. I meant as in a therapist. A psychologist." He searches my face. "It's been life changing, to be honest."

I sigh—I can't stifle that one. "I'm really happy for you, Paul. For real."

He shakes his head. "Laurel, I don't think you're hearing what I'm saying."

I frown. "You're finally getting the help you've always needed—I'm hearing you, Paul."

He shakes his head again. "I'm on medication—staying level. I know it's something I need, and that it's not something I'll ever fix, that I'll always need it." His eyes turn to mine, sincere, pleading, and my heart thumps, pounds with the realization of where he's going with this.

"Paul…"

"I'm not—I'm not saying I'm fixed, but…I'm better."

I count to ten, eyes closed, breath held tight in my lungs. Then, as calmly as I can manage: "Paul… don't. Please don't."

"Don't what, Laurel?"

I flick a finger between him and myself. "This. What you're about to do. What you're doing."

He hesitates. "Laurel, I…"

"I'm going inside now, Paul," I say, turning to the door.

"I'm still in love with you."

I whirl, eyes blazing. "You were *never* in love with me, Paul! You *needed* me, but you never gave a shit about what I wanted, or what I needed! You used me every single day of our marriage." I stab a finger in his direction. "And if you weren't using me, you were flat-out ignoring me. So, no—sorry, Paul. Not buying it."

He looks genuinely hurt. "Laurel, come on—"

"No, not another word." I shake my head. "That has to be the saddest expression of jealousy yet."

"It's not jealousy—"

"Go home, Paul."

"Laurel—"

I hold up a hand. "Go—*home*. This doesn't happen again, okay? I'll get a restraining order, if I have to."

"Now come on—that's a little extreme, don't you think?"

"You're one to talk about extremes?" I groan in aggravation. "Go home."

He backs away. "Fine. But I'll prove it to you. Just wait."

I rub my palms over my face. "Don't. Please don't."

"Why not? Is it this other guy? You're in love with him?"

I stare at him balefully, doing my utter damnedest to stay calm. "This is the last time I'm going to say this kindly and calmly, Paul—go home. Leave me alone. Don't prove anything to me—there's nothing to prove. Stay out of my life, okay? You're Nate's father, and that's all you will be to me ever again, no matter what you say, no matter what you do, no matter how healthy you become. Anything that was ever between us is long since gone, Paul, and there's nothing there to revive. So just…don't. For yourself, if nothing else."

He just blinks at me. Backs away another step. "You'll see. I'll show you."

"It's one in the morning and you're standing on my doorstep professing your love for me—and you expect me to believe you when you say you're better, that you're medicating? Don't you see how this makes that a little hard to believe, even if I wanted to, even if I cared?" I stomp my foot, anger finally slipping through the cracks of my control. "Go…*home*, Paul. Please."

He turns away and climbs into his car, drives away, forgetting to turn his headlights on for at least a block. Typical—he's so lost in his own head that he forgets basic things like buckling up, turning on headlights, all sorts of things, other reasons I worry about leaving Nate with him.

I wait, watching, until he's out of sight and actually gone before I go back inside. I deadbolt the door and then, in a panic, rush around the house making sure the rest of the doors are locked. And then, finally, I sink down into one of my kitchen chairs, shaking.

A hiccup slips out of me.

Another.

And then the hiccups turn into a sob, and a second. A third.

He's in love with me? He's *still* in love with me? I laugh, and it turns into a sob, too.

He's going to prove it to me? That sounds…scary. Worrisome. He's never frightened me before, but…

I can't breathe. I'm fighting the tears and the anxiety, but it's a crushing pressure on my chest, in my head.

I stumble into my bedroom, struggling to breathe.

I have no thoughts except one: to seek comfort. And there's only one place in my life right now that I know where to find it.

I dial the number and hold the phone to my ear, trembling all over.

"H…h'lo? Laurel? Z'at you?" Ryder sounds so sleepy, so disoriented. I feel terrible, now.

"God, Ryder, I'm sorry. I—I didn't want to call you. I just..."

He's instantly more awake. "Hey, no. No. It's fine. I'm here. What's going on? You sound upset."

"He—I heard a knock on my door and I—I thought it was you. And it wasn't—it was Paul. And he was talking crazy, and I just wanted him to leave, and I was worried he'd wake up Nate, and—and then he told me he was still in love with me and how he was going to prove it to me, and I—I—"

"I'll be there in five minutes."

"You don't have to, Ryder. You have to be up early, and it's so late."

"Five minutes. Don't open the door unless you know it's me."

"Ryder..." I have to force my lungs to suck in air. "I'm sorry. I just—I can't breathe."

"It's okay—it's going to be okay. I'll be there in five minutes." I hear a motor start. "I'm coming, Laurel. Just breathe."

"Don't hang up, Ryder. Please. I'm sorry."

I hear the motor sound grow fainter as he backs out, and then tires squeal and the motor roars. "I'm not hanging up, Laurel. I'm here. Talk to me."

"I—I can't breathe. Paul, he just...he just showed up. He's never done that before." I try to breathe, but now that Paul is gone I'm experiencing a delayed reaction. I'm terrified. "I'm sorry I woke you up, I...I didn't know what else to do."

I hear his motor roar again, more squealing tires, a downshift and the change in the tone of the engine. "Don't apologize, Laurel. That's what I'm here for." He laughs. "That, and as many orgasms as you can physically tolerate, plus one extra."

I'm shaking with fear and anxiety, but a small laugh escapes through the tears. "Not tonight, though. Tonight I just need—"

"To be held," he cuts in. "I know. Tonight, I'll hold you until you fall asleep."

I hear him pull into the driveway and shut off his engine, and then the quiet thunk of his door closing. I go to the front door, and this time I peer out of the peephole to make sure it's him.

I open the door and before he's even halfway to it, I throw myself into his arms. "Ryder."

He wraps me in his arms, easily scooping me up off my feet. I curl my legs around his waist and inhale him, shuddering and shaking. He carries me inside, pausing to deadbolt my front door. My bedroom door is the only one in the short hallway that's open, so he carries me in there and around to my side of the bed. He sits down, kicks off his shoes, and rotates his legs onto the bed, all without letting go of me. Sliding downward, he props a pillow up behind his head, tucks me against his chest, and cradles me in his big, strong arms.

Immediately, I can breathe again, and he hasn't said a single word since arriving.

"Ryder," I breathe again.

"I'm here. I've got you. It's okay." He's shirtless, clad in a pair of gym shorts and nothing else.

I snuggle against his warm, bare skin. "You didn't even put a shirt on?"

He chuckles. "You were upset. I took off without stopping to think about anything. I'm not sure I even grabbed my wallet." He smooths my hair back. "My only thought was to get here."

I inhale deeply, hold it, and let it out slowly. "Thank you, Ryder."

"Hey, what are boyfriends for?"

I tense. I twist my head on his chest to look up at him. "Boyfriend?"

He just grins. "Yep. I figure 'beau' is too old-fashioned, 'lover' is a little…dramatic, and I'm hoping I'm a lot more than a fuck-buddy."

I tangle my fingers in his beard. "A lot more." I touch my lips to his. "Boyfriend. I like that."

"Me too."

"And, you know what? I'm not upset anymore."

"No?"

"Nope. The second you got here and put your

arms around me, I was fine."

"Makes me feel like I have a superpower or something." He laughs, deepening his voice. "I am… *comfort-man!*"

I giggle. "You're such a dork."

"You know it."

"Yes, I do, and I like it."

"Well, that's good, because it's kind of in my DNA." He tucks more flyaway hair behind my ear. "Just relax. Rest, okay? I'm here."

I nod, and suddenly I'm overcome with fatigue.

Then, suddenly, a thought occurs to me. "Nate… if you're here when he wakes up, he may be confused."

"I've got it covered, babe. Sleep. I've got you. No more worries, okay?"

I nod. "He likes you, you know."

"Nate?"

"Uh-huh," I murmur sleepily. "He wants to play paintball with you."

"That sounds like fun."

"Really?" I peer up at him with one eye open.

He rumbles a laugh. "Fuck yeah! I haven't gone paintballing in forever."

"You don't have to."

"I *want* to, Laurel." He huffs another laugh. "In fact, I'm thinking…what about a Dad Bod Contracting paintball party extravaganza. We all take the day off,

James brings his girls, and we have a big ol' blow out. Followed by a pool party and a barbecue at my place."

I open both eyes and gaze up at him. "That's a lot to unpack."

He arches an eyebrow. "What do you mean, a lot to unpack?"

"First, I tell you Nate wants to play paintball with you, and you immediately think, let's go play with everyone? Also, you have a pool?"

He shrugs. "Yeah, I have a pool. It was a summer project for the guys and me. And as far as paintball goes? Paintball is a ton of fun, and I know all the others will be down with the idea. We're all due for a good time, and I know from experience that paintball is best experienced with a bunch of people. We'll rent out a place just for us. It'll be great."

My voice catches. "Oh."

I sense his puzzlement even as I hear it in his voice. "What's wrong?"

I shake my head. "Nothing. I just…" I exhale, toss my hair, and glance up at him. "You're just amazing, that's all. Finding someone who doesn't just tolerate my son—"

He cuts me off. "Tolerate? What kind of bullshit is that? He's a cool kid—who in their right mind *tolerates* a cool-ass kid like Nate?"

"His own father?" I blurt, and then immediately

regret it. "That's not true, and not fair of me to say. Paul loves his son. He just…he's not the type to have fun with him. Nate was telling me the other day that Paul took Nate to play laser tag, but didn't actually go in and play with him."

Ryder growls. "That's horseshit." He hesitates. "Look, it ain't my place to get into any of that, but your boy deserves to have fun. He's a kid. I won't say anything about anyone, 'cause like I said, it's not my place." He touches my chin. "What time does he get out of school?"

I blink. "I—um. What? Why?"

"What time?"

"Three forty-five. But, Ryder—"

"You trust me with him?"

I suck in a sharp breath—there's the ten-million-dollar question right there. "I…Ryder, I…"

"I want to take him to play laser tag, but if you're not comfortable with it, just say so."

"What about work?" I ask. "Don't you have to work?"

"I can take off a couple hours early. I'll just go in early tomorrow and stay late. It'll be fine, I promise."

I close my eyes and consult my feelings—and not just the ones that are deliriously happy to be back in Ryder's embrace. Do I trust my son with Ryder McCann?

It doesn't require much by way of consultation.

"Yes, Ryder. I trust you." He starts to talk, but I touch his lips with my fingers to quiet him. "I'm not sure you understand what a huge deal this is for me, though. It's brutally hard for me to leave him with Paul, and I've never left him alone with anyone else, ever."

"Laurel, I wasn't trying to—"

"But you're different. Nate already said he likes you. He wants to hang out with you because you're cool—and not just for your car, according to him. There are two kinds of people in the world for Nate: Slimy poopheads, and everyone else."

"So I made the cut, huh?"

I nod. "You did. But making Nate's cut is one thing. For me to feel comfortable letting you go anywhere with my son?"

He kisses my forehead. "It's a big deal."

I nod. "The biggest."

"I just want him, and you, to know I like him for him. I like kids, and as you may be aware, I'm not afraid to be goofy and have fun." He meets my eyes. "But Laurel, this is your choice. I'm not going to push anything. I just want to have fun with Nate."

"I'm not sure I'm ready for it to be *today*, though," I say hesitantly. "How about Next week? Monday?"

He nods. "That makes sense."

"I just need a bit more time. And I need to talk to Nate about you—about us, a bit more first, too."

He smiles. "Totally understandable. This Monday it is."

"Be at the elementary school at quarter to four."

"Are you sure?" He glances at me quizzically. "It was just an idea. It can wait if you need more time."

I nod, closing my eyes again. "I'm sure," I murmur wordlessly as I wiggle to get comfortable. "I'll probably have a minor anxiety attack when it's time to actually let him go with you, but I'll work through it."

"Laurel—"

I touch his lips. "Shushy-time."

He rumbles a laugh. "Yes, dear."

"Mmmm," I hum, too sleepy to make sense any more. "Good boy."

I feel him laugh again, but then I'm tumbling down into a deep, deep sleep.

TEN

I WAKE UP ALONE IN MY BED AND IT'S EARLY. MY ALARM clock is buzzing—the only reason I woke up at all. I already miss Ryder's presence, his warmth, his soothing strength, and I've only been awake fifteen seconds. But…

I smell coffee.

And…pancakes, and…bacon?

I shuffle out of bed, and to my door, but then pause before leaving my room, realizing I'm still in my robe, T-shirt, and underwear. I head out to the kitchen where I find Nate sitting at the kitchen table, shirtless and wearing pajama pants, a mind-bogglingly enormous stack of pancakes in front of him, absolutely drowned in butter and my sugar-free xylitol syrup.

Ryder is fully dressed, a beanie covering his messy red hair; he's at the stove, frying bacon with tongs in one hand, and flipping pancakes on my griddle with the other hand. His phone is on the counter beside the stove, playing country music.

Nate sees me. "MOM! Look who came over extra special early to make me pancakes?"

"Wow," I mumble, not quite awake enough to handle Nate's energy level. "It's really early."

Ryder turns and winks at me. "I was awake early, and figured you guys would enjoy some pancakes and bacon." He pulls a mug from the cabinet and pours a cup of coffee, which he places on the table near Nate. "And coffee, of course. I hope you don't mind, but I brought my own coffee. I'm kind of a coffee snob."

I shuffle to the table and sit down, taking a tentative sip. "Wow. This is…incredible."

He nods. "Sure is. Single origin organic beans from a family-owned farm in Columbia."

I snort. "Let me guess—you know a guy? Or is this your uncle, too?"

He chuckles. "Nah, I get it from a subscription service. They send me a new batch of single origin, freshly roasted beans every two weeks."

"You take your coffee very seriously."

"The only things I take more seriously are my work, my cars…" He grins at me. "And pancakes and bacon."

"These pancakes are amazing," Nate says, around a mouthful of food.

"Nate, don't talk with your mouth full."

He rolls his eyes, but chews and swallows. "Where'd you learn to make pancakes like this, Ryder?"

"I taught myself. I eat breakfast for dinner a lot, so I perfected the art of making pancakes a long time ago."

"You can do that? Just…have breakfast for dinner like…*all the time*?"

Ryder laughs. "That's one of the perks of adulthood, kiddo."

I see Nate's wheels turning, and narrow my eyes at him. "Don't get any ideas, bud. We won't be having pancakes and waffles for dinner every night."

"Darn. You're always crushing my dreams, Mom."

"That's me—Evil Mom, the Destroyer of Dreams," I say, deadpan.

"Yup. Just like when I had the idea to crumble up my cupcake in my ice cream and you said no."

Ryder turns, an expression of admiration on his face. "DUDE. That's genius."

Nate turns to me, triumphant. "See? Ryder thinks it's a good idea."

"It was a chocolate cupcake and Superman ice cream."

Ryder fakes a gag. "You didn't mention that

part—that'd have been nasty."

I roll my eyes at him. "You're not supposed to encourage his antics, you know."

Ryder just grins, turning back to the griddle; he flips the pancakes deftly from the griddle onto a plate, tongs the bacon onto another plate lined with paper towel, and brings both plates to the table. He sits down at the table, with Nate on one side and me on the other. My stomach flips and twists at the intimate moment—the three of us, having breakfast together.

Like a fam—

No.

Nope.

No.

A few good dates and some earth-shattering sex are not grounds to let my heart start tossing that word around. Shut it down, Laurel. One day at a time—take it slow.

Ryder slides three thick, fluffy, perfectly golden brown pancakes on the plate in front of me along with a few pieces of bacon, and then nudges the butter and syrup toward me. I drench my pancakes in butter and syrup and dig in, moaning in delight.

"These really are incredible," I say.

Ryder grins. "My own special recipe. Mostly oat flour mixed with a little almond flour—none of that bleached bull…um, crap. Good, and good for you."

I wash down a bite with a mouthful of hot, black coffee and nibble on some bacon.

I could really get used to this.

"Me too," Nate says.

I blush, realizing I said that out loud.

Ryder just chuckles. "Me three. I've been eating alone for a long time, and it's kinda nice having company." He stabs a forkful of pancake. "Plus, it's nice having people appreciate my pancake recipe. I've been tweaking it for years."

"I didn't mean to say that out loud," I mumble.

"But you did," Ryder says.

"Well, thank you, Ryder. Nate and I are super grateful for bacon and pancakes and amazing coffee."

Nate makes a face. "I don't like coffee," he says. "Mom let me try it one time, and it tasted like poopy dirt mixed with barf."

Ryder cackles. "You've really got a way with words, you know that?"

I roll my eyes. "Not everything has to be potty talk, Nate."

"You won't let me swear, so how else am I supposed to express myself?" he argues. "You're always telling me to be myself, and maybe that's just how I express myself."

"You can't find a way to express yourself that isn't nasty?"

"No, probably not. I'm nine—it's what we do."

Ryder is desperately trying to suppress laughter, and I point at him with my fork. "You are *not* helping."

He blows out a breath, calming himself. "I'm sorry, I'm sorry—he's just funny."

Nate grins, and it's clear he's over the moon from Ryder's praise. Now, having eaten all his food, he gets up from the table.

"Hey, now, mister. Clear your plate." I arch an eyebrow at him. "Having a guest over doesn't change the rules."

He makes a dramatic show of clearing his place, rinsing the plate and putting it in the dishwasher, along with his fork and cup.

"Good, thank you." I gesture toward his room with my fork. "Now, brush your teeth and get ready for school, please."

When Nate is in the bathroom with the water running, I glance at Ryder. "You still want your plan for next week to be a surprise?"

He nods. "I think it'll make it more fun."

I shrug. "Like I said last night, I'll probably have a minor anxiety attack when it comes time to let you actually drive away with him, but I'll get through it."

"I don't want you to have an anxiety attack, Laurel."

"No way around it. It's part of being a mom— letting your kid out of your sight at all is grounds for a minor anxiety attack. Letting him leave with someone else—even someone you trust—is the most difficult thing in the world. I sobbed like a baby his first day of school. I still get teary-eyed, honestly, and he's in third grade."

"I'm not taking it lightly, Laurel. I know what it means to you."

I laugh. "No, I don't think you do. You can't— you're not a parent." I sigh, and smile at him. "But I appreciate that you're making the effort for me."

He shakes his head. "You don't get it, do you? I'm not making an effort for you, or for him. I mean, I am, partly, but mostly, I'm doing this for myself."

I tilt my head to one side, leaning back from my plate—I've just about eaten myself into a coma. "How so?"

He grins. "Well, for one, it's an excuse to play laser tag. Being a kid in a grown man's body, I'm just excited. Two, I want to show you that I'm serious about this—you, and Nate. I say I'm doing it for myself, because if you understand that I'm for real…" he trails off, shrugging.

I smirk at him, checking to make sure Nate isn't secretly listening. "Then you get more sex?" I say, in a voice just above a whisper.

"Well, yeah. But also it means you're more invested in me, and that's a win on its own."

I hesitate over the truth. "Ryder...I'm not sure I can get any more invested, at this point." I gesture at the table. "This? This was a dangerous move, my friend."

He frowns, puzzled. "How do you mean?"

"I've been trying to convince myself to take this slowly, to not get in over my head too fast. And then you make breakfast for my son and I?" I shrug. "You're making it hard to stay objective."

He laughs. "What if I don't want you to be objective?"

"Then you're doing a good job." I meet his eyes. "Because I'm not. I'm very much in over my head," I whisper.

Ryder leans across the table and takes my hand. "Laurel...I'm not objective either. I'm in over my head as much as you are." He pauses. "This whole thing has shifted so fucking fast, you know? Like, before you showed up at Billy Bar, I was like, no way, I can't do anything serious with her. And now...? All of a sudden we're having weekends away together and I'm taking your kid out to play laser tag next week. It's a lot really fast, and I have no idea what I'm doing. I just know I really like you, and that I'm definitely falling for you."

I blink hard. "Ryder…"

"Okay! I'm ready!" Nate says, bounding out of his room. He's wearing blue camouflage pants with a red-and-black checked shirt.

I laugh. "Whoa, there. You may need a little fashion help, buddy."

"Gotcha covered," Ryder says, rising. He puts his hand on Nate's shoulder, guiding him back into his room. "Okay, there's basically one really important fashion rule. Follow this one rule, and you'll be fine: Never mix your patterns."

"What's that mean?" Nate asks.

"It means if you're wearing camo pants, wear a plain shirt, like a solid color. If you're wearing a checkered or flannel shirt, wear jeans or khakis or something."

"Oh." I hear the confusion in Nate's voice. "I thought this looked cool."

"You know, I think it looks cool, too. But here's another little secret for you: we don't dress to look cool for ourselves, we dress to look cool for the people we like."

"Why?"

"Well, you don't have to look at yourself all the time, right?"

"Right."

"Your mom does, and your friends do, and your

teacher does. Right?"

"Right."

"So you pick clothes to look cool for them."

"But Mom always says that those who matter don't mind, and those who mind don't matter. Or something like that."

"You got it right. And that's what I'm saying. You and I may think camo and plaid go together just fine, but your mom doesn't, and I guarantee you the cool girls at school won't either."

"I'm still confused."

I'm laughing to myself, listening to this. Oh Ryder. So sweet.

"All right, put it this way—if you're anything like me, you're never gonna quite get the hang of fashion. So, the simplest and easiest thing to do is just let your mom tell you what looks cool and what doesn't."

There you go—Momma knows best.

"But Mom always wants me to dress like a dork."

Ryder chokes on a laugh. "Yeah, that's tricky. But here's the thing to remember—it's never been cooler to be a nerd, my man. Think about all the superhero comic book movies that are out, right? Nerds are in!"

"Yeah, sure, but that doesn't mean I'm not gonna get made fun of for wearing collared shirts and button-downs all the time."

I wince, because I didn't realize he was getting

made fun of—I make a mental note to let him pick some of his own clothes…with guidance.

"That's when you remember what your mom told you—if they're making fun of you, then their opinion doesn't matter. Screw 'em." I hear him gulp. "I—I mean. Um. Crap. I just mean…shoot. Don't tell your mom I said that."

Nate laughs. "Dude, you know she can hear us, right? She's got mom hearing—you say anything bad, she'll know. I said a bad word at school once, and I swear there were no teachers or recess monitors around, and she *still* knew."

I laugh out loud at that—he said the bad word with his teacher standing literally right behind him, and I got an email about it later that day.

I check the time, and curse under my breath— Nate's bus will be here in less than five minutes and I'm still in my robe. I hustle into my room, lock my door, and get dressed for work in record time. I'll have to do my makeup in the car on the way, but at least I'm clothed. When I leave my room, Ryder is watching Nate struggle with his shoelaces.

Eventually Nate gets frustrated, and Ryder kneels down. "Try it this way. Make a loop, wrap the other lace around it, slide the pointy end under the bridge, and pull it tight."

Nate tries Ryder's method and gets it the first

time. "That's a lot easier."

"Wanna know a secret? I had Velcro shoes until I was in fourth grade because I couldn't figure out how to tie my laces. I spent an entire summer trying to figure it out." He laughs. "And you know, I still hate tying my shoes." He points down at his feet, which are shoved into pull-on style work boots.

Damn him—he's making this really hard for me. I want to take it slow, be cool, make sure this whole thing makes sense, and that I'm not making a mistake with Ryder, but then he does things like this, and proves how great he is with Nate, and my stupid heart melts and melts and melts, and all I want to do is kiss him until neither of us can breathe.

I check the time, and again have to spring into action. I toss Nate's lunch into his backpack, snag his hoodie from the hook by the front door, and hand it to him.

"Bus is going to be here in a second, buddy," I tell him, shoving the hoodie over his head. "Time to go!"

Nate pokes his arms through, shrugs into it, and shoulders his backpack on one shoulder; he leans into me for a hug, and then hesitates in front of Ryder.

Ryder extends his fist, the two tap knuckles. "See later, Nate," Ryder says. "Be cool."

"You too!" He hesitates, and then grins at me shyly. "Love you, Mom."

"Love you too." I kiss his cheek. "Be good. Make good choices."

"Okay! The bus is here. Gotta go, bye!"

He bolts out the door and jogs to the end of the driveway; I follow him out onto the porch, as the bus squeals to a stop. He hops up the first two steps, pauses on the third to wave, and then vanishes inside. I watch as the bus disappears out of sight, before going back inside.

Ryder is in the kitchen, scrubbing the griddle. He glances at me. "I woke up at five out of habit, ran home, showered, changed, and came back." He shrugs. "I just...I wasn't quite ready to leave, but I know you said you didn't want Nate to wake up with me here like I stayed here, so I pretended like I just showed up randomly—"

He's rambling, and I realize he's nervous, wondering what my reaction to his breakfast surprise will be, now that we're alone.

I take the griddle out of his hand and toss it into the sink with a clatter; he has a sponge in one hand, and he's soapy to his forearms. I tangle my fingers with his wet, soapy ones, splaying his arms out to the sides to keep them away from my clothing.

And then, with a sly smirk, I lean in and kiss him.

It starts out slow, but builds quickly. My heart thunders in my chest, and my heart swells at the hunger in his kiss. I can't help leaning against him, pressing him back against the edge of the sink. Rising on my tiptoes to deepen the kiss, I keep his arms out to the sides.

He growls, pulling away from the kiss just enough to move his lips against mine. "You better quit kissing me like that or this break of ours will be over before it gets started."

"I can't help it," I murmur. "You showed up when I needed you, no questions asked. You held me. You let me fall asleep. You got up early and left out of consideration for Nate, and then you came back and cooked us breakfast. You helped Nate get dressed, and tie his shoes…and you made him feel cool doing it. And *then* I come in here and find you doing the dishes?"

He grins crookedly. "I was worried I'd over-stepped my boundaries."

"What boundaries?" I whisper. "I'm so turned on right now, I'm tempted to do something rash."

"Like what?"

"Like screw the break." I bite my lower lip. "I can be a few minutes late for work."

My hand, operating of its own will, descends to his belt, and I fumble with it one-handed.

Ryder gently takes my wrist. "Laurel…stop."

I frown up at him. "Why?"

"We agreed we'd take a break."

"Do you really want that?" I murmur.

"I don't want to get carried away. You said you were sore."

I have his belt undone, and then his jeans—and now I have him in my hand, all of him, thick and hard and hot. "Ryder…" I keep my eyes on his. "Are you really going to tell me no?"

He hisses, his eyes ripping away from mine to watch my hand as I glide it up and down his erection. His jeans sag open, and I push them down around his ankles. "Shit…Laurel—you know I can't say no."

"Can't?"

He shakes his head. "Can't. Incapable." He dips at the knees as I caress him. "Shit, honey. What's your plan, here?"

I shrug. "I dunno. I just know I want you."

He tilts his head backward. "I left my bag at home—I don't have any protection with me."

I frown. "You don't keep a condom in your wallet?"

He laughs. "God, no. What am I, nineteen and desperate?"

"I don't have any here either," I murmur, not slowing my touch. "Come to think of it, I've never done anything in this house. I moved in here with Nate a year and a half ago, and you're the only man to ever be alone here with me."

His jaw flexes. "I'm—I'm honored, honey. For real. But we don't have any condoms."

I grin up at him. "That's quite a conundrum, isn't it?" I watch him struggle to maintain his balance, locking his knees even as they dip helplessly as his hips quest forward into my touch. "Whatever shall we do? It seems you're losing the battle to hold out, Ryder."

He throws his head forward, his eyes narrow, jaw grinding. He speaks through gritted teeth. "Laurel... seriously."

I drop to my knees and grin up at him. "You do things like you did this morning, and I just can't help myself."

"Not—not why I did it, Laurel."

"I know," I murmur, stroking him. "Part of why I'm doing *this*."

He groans. "God, Laurel. I do *not* fucking deserve you, babe. For real."

I sink my mouth around him, stroking him with my fists, and then, when I feel him losing the effort to hold back, I palm the hard, tensed globes of his ass and pull him toward me. My hair is loose, draping in front of my face, tangling in front of my eyes and sticking to my lips and to him—he pulls it back, holding it away as he clutches my head with shaking fingers.

"Laurel…fuck."

It's mere moments, and then he's growling through his release, and I taste him, take everything he has to give and more. When he's done, his legs are shaking and he's gasping. I stand up, wipe my lips, and tug his underwear and jeans up, zip and buckle him, and back away.

He blinks at me. "Where—where are you going?"

I smirk. "Well, I need to brush my teeth again."

He seems a little stunned, and it's cute. I go into my bathroom, smear a dab of toothpaste on my toothbrush, and start brushing. I'm only a few seconds in when I see Ryder in the mirror, entering the bathroom. The look on his face is predatory.

"You really think you can do that and get away with it?" he murmurs.

"Geh away wi'ih?" I say around the toothbrush and foam.

He palms my hips and spins me around. "Keep brushing."

I go back to scrubbing my teeth, and he stands in front of me, gathering the skirt of my dress in his hands—it's a loose, flowing cotton dress, snug around my chest, a line of small buttons marching down between my breasts. He lifts the dress up around my hips, hooks his fingers into my underwear and drags them down, going to his knees as he does so.

I spit toothpaste.

"Ryder…" I breathe.

"No arguments from you, huh?"

"Hell no." I widen my stance, taking the bunched material of my dress from him and hold it in one hand.

My electric toothbrush buzzes in my hand, vibrating against my teeth as he laps my core. I remember I'm supposed to be brushing, and give my teeth a few desultory swipes, before forgetting again as his tongue drives against me.

I gasp, bucking against him. "God, Ryder—"

He laughs. "So eager. You're already almost there." He slips two fingers inside me, and then, when his lips suction and his fingers curl inside me, I come apart, gasping.

My toothbrush rattles against the sink.

I have toothpaste dribbling down my chin.

My legs won't work.

When my climax subsides, Ryder moves to his feet, sees the state I'm in, and chuckles. He takes a washcloth and wipes at my mouth, reaches into the sink and turns off my toothbrush, rinsing it and putting it back on the charger.

I'm still holding my dress up near my navel, and my underwear is still around my ankles, but I'm still too weak and limp and racked with aftershocks to do anything about it just yet.

Ryder to the rescue.

He slides my underwear into place, and I force my hand to release my dress; he fills the cup I keep by my sink and hands it to me. "Rinse, honey."

I shake myself, and take the cup, grinning at him. "Yum—cum and toothpaste."

He licks his lips. "I'll be tasting you all day."

I bend to rifle through a container I keep under my sink, and find an unopened toothbrush. "Here."

I rinse my mouth a few times, and then rinse it again with mouthwash while he brushes his teeth—and even this feels strangely comfortable and familiar. Like getting ready for bed together—except it's almost nine and I'm going to be late for work.

Ryder rinses and swishes mouthwash, and then grins at me in the mirror. "We're hopeless, Laurel, you do realize that, right?"

"I'm not sure I was this horny as a teenager."

He laughs. "Oh, I know I was. Not that I got anywhere near this much sex." He wipes at his beard, making sure it's clean. "Honestly, I'm pretty sure you've given me more blowjobs in the last three days than I've gotten in the last ten years combined."

"Funny, because I've given you more blowjobs in the last three days than I've given…well…ever, actually."

He makes a face. "Really?"

I nod. "Until you, it wasn't really my thing."

"It doesn't show—you're amazing at it."

"Well, that's good…I think?" I laugh. "Is there such a thing as a bad blowjob?"

He nods. "Too much teeth." He fakes a shudder. "No good."

"Ah. Well, I'll be sure to keep my teeth off the goods. Don't want to damage anything." I lean against his chest, sighing as his arms go around him. "I have to go to work now."

"Same."

I twist my head to grin up at him. "I'll stop and get some condoms to keep here." He opens his mouth, and I say what I know he's about to say. "Yes, Ryder, I know—you love the way I think."

He leans down and kisses me. "Let's go." He pats my bottom. "We both have to get to work."

I head for the door to the garage, Ryder behind me. He opens my garage door for me, and then my car door. I sigh as I slide into my car. "I really could get used to this."

"Used to what?" Ryder asks.

I grin mischievously. "Sucking your big hard cock…followed by you eating me out. I'm not gonna say it's better than actual sex, but it's close." I laugh. "Or, alternatively, you cooking breakfast and opening doors for me."

"How about you get used to both?" he suggests. "Sucking my cock, getting eaten out, breakfast, me opening doors, taking Nate on fun afternoons out, weekends away together, surprise dates. All of it."

"Surprise dates?"

"I've got an idea."

"Does it involve us getting naked?"

He laughs. "You are insatiable, woman."

I start my car. "I told you, Ryder. You've woken the beast."

"Can't say I'm sorry," he says, laughing. "Starting the day with your mouth around me is pretty much my favorite thing in the world."

"I take back what I said about it being creepy if you were to sneak into my house and eat me out," I mumble. "You totally have my permission."

He growls. "Don't tease me, woman."

I arch an eyebrow. "I wasn't kidding. I have a spare key hidden."

"So I can sneak in in the middle of the night and go down on you?"

"So we can have ninja sex," I say. "Among other things."

"Ninja sex?"

"Super quiet, so as to not alert the child down the hall," I clarify.

"Isn't it a little soon to be giving me a key?" he asks.

I shrug. "Maybe. But I don't care. I know what I want, and I want you, as often as possible. Eventually, I'll let you stay the night, once I'm sure Nate will be okay with it."

"So I'll have to sneak out until then?"

"I don't want you to think I'm hiding you or ashamed of us, I just—"

He leans down and kisses me. "I totally get it." He grins. "Besides, it'll make it kinda fun, sneaking around like I'm sixteen with a girlfriend I'm not supposed to have."

"I'm too old and not flexible enough for car sex," I tell him.

He shudders. "God, me either." His laugh is lecherous. "Although, the bed of my old pickup is big enough to fit a mattress in it. Sex outside under the stars sounds pretty amazing."

I widen my eyes excitedly. "With a picnic? And champagne, and strawberries, and cheese, and chocolate?"

He kisses me again. "Hell, yes, baby. That sounds perfect. Consider it done."

I sigh, happily. "I like it when you call me baby."

He backs away. "Go. Before I drag you inside and neither of us makes it to work."

"Sure thing...baby." I grin at him as I close my door and back out.

I drive to work basically floating on a cloud of joy.

Have I ever been so happy?

No, I don't think I have.

ELEVEN

A WEEK LATER, ON MONDAY AFTERNOON, I PULL INTO Nate's school's parking lot; I normally pull through the pick-up line to get Nate after school, but today I park in the visitor lot in front of the entrance and go in to walk him out. He's a little perplexed when he sees me waiting in the hallway outside his classroom.

"Hi, Mom." He frowns. "Is everything okay?"

"Yeah, everything's great."

"Then…why are you inside? You normally just get me in the pick-up line."

"I know, but today things are happening a little differently."

He's immediately wary. "Different how?"

I take his hand and walk outside with him. "You'll see."

"I don't have to go anywhere with Dad, do I? I just saw him last weekend."

I feel sad that he looks at it as something he "has" to do. That's not how it's supposed to be. "No, buddy."

"Then what?"

I scan the visitor lot and see Ryder pulling into a spot next to my car, driving his big antique Chevy truck. I glance down at Nate, grinning. "Look who's here to see you."

Nate's eyes light up. "Ryder's here? Awesome!"

Hooooo boy. I know exactly how you feel. We haven't seen each other since last week; he had to get caught up on work, and I was swamped myself with a new rescue center opening in Vernon Hills. We've texted a lot, and FaceTimed a few times, and once we actually talked on the phone until we were falling asleep, as if we were infatuated teenagers all over again. I've talked to him, I've seen his face, heard his voice, flirted with him, sexted with him, but none of that even remotely assuages my desire to see him in person.

So yeah, I'm just as excited to see Ryder today as Nate is, if not more.

Ryder climbs down from the driver's seat, waving at Nate as we approach. "Yo, buddy. You ready for an adventure?"

Nate glances at me, curious now. "What's going on?"

Pulling him aside, I kneel in front of him. "Ryder

wants to take you out for some fun. Just you and him for a couple hours." I examine Nate's face, watching his reactions carefully. "Is that okay with you?"

Nate glances up at Ryder, then back to me. "Just me and Ryder?"

I nod. "Yup. Just you and him."

He frowns. "You never let Derek take me anywhere."

"I never trusted him, I guess—which should have been a major hint that he was a slimy poophead." I smile at my son. "I feel differently about Ryder. I trust him in a way I never did Derek."

Nate is clearly thinking hard. "Do I have to?"

I hold my expression in neutral. "No, you don't."

He looks at Ryder again, briefly. "Why?"

"Why what, buddy?"

"Why do you want to take me wherever you're taking me?" This is addressed to Ryder.

Ryder takes a knee, and I move aside for him. "Because I think you're cool." He holds up a hand to forestall Nate's protest. "I wouldn't BS you, kid."

"BS?" Nate asks; Ryder just arches an eyebrow, and Nate giggles. "Oh. Bull-crap, but the S word."

"Right-o."

Nate's eyes narrow. "Adults like to tell kids things they'd don't really mean, but when an adult does it and says it's for the kid's own good, it's not really lying. Is that what this is?"

Ryder snorts. "News flash, buckeroo, that's still lying. I don't make a lot of promises, but the one promise I can make, right now, is that I'll never lie to you, not even that kind of lie."

"Okay, so...for real. What's this about?"

Ryder takes a moment before answering, and when he does, he looks Nate in the eyes, a hand on his shoulder. "The real, honest truth...I want to take you out for two reasons. One, because I really do think you're cool, and I want to have some fun with you. I'm a boring old adult, and I don't get a chance to have very much fun."

I cough, suppressing laughter as an inappropriate response to that statement pops into my head.

Ryder eyes me sideways, obviously correctly interpreting what I was thinking. "Hush, you. We're having serious guy talk."

"Sorry, sorry."

He turns back to Nate. "The other reason is because I like your mom, a lot."

Nate frowns. "What does that have to do with me?" He pauses, and then his face lights up. "You're trying to impress her!"

Ryder laughs. "Sort of, yes." He taps Nate on the chest. "You are the most important person in her life, as I'm sure you're aware. That makes you important to me, because your mom is important to me. So, I want to get to know you. I want us to be friends."

Nate nods, understanding. "Got it." He looks away, thinking, and then back at Ryder. "Are you gonna marry my mom?"

"Nate—" I splutter.

Ryder holds up his hand to me. "I can answer, Laurel."

I have to literally bite my tongue, but I let Ryder answer for himself—and I hang on every word.

"Maybe someday," Ryder says. "Right now, your mom and I are sort of just figuring things out, but I do care a lot about your mom, and there may come a day when she and I start thinking about that. I'll make you one other promise, Nate: if and when that day comes, you and I will sit down and talk about it, man to man."

My heart is slamming so hard in my chest I worry it's going to crack my ribs open. This is too much, too soon. Talking about falling for each other, talking about the future, talking about being open and real and invested…that's one thing. But this? The way Ryder is talking to Nate? This makes it way, way, *way* too real.

Here comes that anxiety attack I promised Ryder.

I tell myself to keep it together. Breathe. Stay calm.

"So, what are we gonna do?" Nate asks.

Ryder stands up. "I was thinking laser tag."

Nate seems stuck between excitement and suspicion. "Are you going to actually play?"

Ryder grins, pointing a finger-gun at Nate. "A better question to ask is do you think you can beat me."

Nate's grin is so broad and brilliant I wonder if it hurts his cheeks, and he's letting his excitement show, little by little. "Beat you? I bet I can score ten times as many points as you!"

"Is that a bet?" Ryder asks.

Nate frowns. "I don't know what a bet actually is."

"It's kind of like a dare, but with money or something." He takes out his wallet and hands a ten-dollar bill to Nate. "We're putting this ten-dollar bill up for the bet—if you beat me in laser tag, you keep the ten bucks. If I win, I keep it."

Nate rolls his eyes. "That's dumb. What am I gonna do with ten dollars? Any time I get any money, I have to give it to Mom for safekeeping, and then I never see it again."

"Okay, well…" Ryder pauses to think. "Okay, how about this—"

"How about you don't teach my son to gamble," I say, trying hard to keep a stern expression on my face.

"Knowing how and when to take a bet is an important skill to learn on the road to becoming a man, Laurel."

"Well then, at least teach him right." I take a ten out of my purse and hand it to Nate. "A real bet works a little differently than what Ryder is telling you. If you're betting ten bucks that you can beat him, it means if you win, you keep your ten dollars *and* you take his, but if you lose, he keeps your ten bucks and his."

Ryder snorts. "I was trying to keep it simple."

"It *is* simple. But if he comes back talking about poker, we're gonna have issues."

"What's poker?" Nate asks.

I sigh. "A dumb card game."

Ryder arches an eyebrow at me. "Is this a bad time to mention that the guys and I have poker night at my house once a month, and that it's this Friday?"

I laugh. "Of course you do. So you have standing nights at Billy Bar, poker night once a month...any other Dad Bod traditions I should know about?"

"Poker night is every Friday, we just rotate between James's, Jesse's, Franco's, and my house." He taps his chin, thinking. "Um...we usually go to Cedar Point every summer."

I boggle. "Four grown men go to Cedar Point together every summer?"

He frowns at me in disbelief. "Hell—I mean, heck yeah! You're never too old for roller coasters. Plus, watching James try to cram his giant butt into those things is hysterical."

I shake my head. "You guys are ridiculous."

Ryder glances at my car. "Do I need one of those seat things for him?"

I grab Nate's booster from the back of my car and hand it to him, and Ryder examines it curiously. "What's it for, anyway?"

"So when the seatbelt buckles across him, the strap lays against his chest instead of his neck. It's safer."

Ryder nods. "Ah, makes sense."

I frown at his truck. "That thing *does* have seatbelts, right?"

He nods, handing the booster to Nate. "Oh yeah. It didn't originally, because it was made before the federal seatbelt requirement in 1968, but since I'm using it as a daily driver, I installed them as part of the restoration."

I have a million things I want to say, but I just sigh. "Please be careful."

He smiles at me, takes me by the shoulders. "Deep breath, babe. I've got this."

I smile back, a little teary. "I know. Whether *I've* got it is the real question."

He leans in and kisses me, a quick peck. "You've got it." He taps me on the nose. "Call up your girls. Go have a glass of wine and relax."

"You'll call me if anything comes up?"

"Of course."

I take a deep breath, hold it, and let it out. "Okay. I'm good. I'm good!" I circle around to the passenger side of Ryder's truck where Nate has already climbed up and buckled himself in. "I love you, Nate. Be good, okay? And have fun!"

He's on cloud nine. "This is gonna be awesome!" He looks down at me. "Are you gonna cry when we leave?"

I nod. "Probably."

Nate just rolls his eyes. "So emotional."

I cackle. "Where did you learn that?"

"TV. Dad lets me watch stuff I probably shouldn't see."

I sigh. "Great."

Nate looks at Ryder, and then at me. "You know, if you guys want to make out, I can look the other way."

"Nathaniel Paul Madison! Where in the world are you getting this stuff? Do I have to talk to your father about what is and isn't appropriate television for you?"

Nate shrugs. "Nah, that one I learned from

Sheila. She's a sixth grader, and she was talking about making out with her boyfriend."

"In sixth grade?"

"She makes a lot of stuff up, so I don't think it's true. I don't even know what it means, but I think it's like kissing or something."

I palm the side of his face and give him a playful, gentle shove. "You're too smart for your own good, buster." I lean up and kiss his cheek. "Have fun."

Nate waves me off with both hands. "Quit dragging it out, Mom! I'll be fine. We'll have fun." He points at me. "No crying!"

I roll my eyes at him as I back away. "No promises."

Ryder checks Nate's seat belt, waves at me, and then his truck grumbles to life with a throaty chuckle, and he backs out. I keep it together as he drives slowly and carefully out of the parking lot, and I keep it together as they vanish around the corner. I even manage to keep it together as I get in my car and leave the school.

I only start to lose it once I'm on the main road and heading—well, I'm not sure where I'm going. A weekday afternoon alone is something I rarely get.

I'm biting down on my lip to keep from crying as I dial Audra. She answers, out of breath. "Hello? What's up, Laurel?"

"Are—are you working?" I ask, fighting to keep the emotion out of my voice.

"Yeah, but I'm almost done." She sighs. "What did he do now?"

"No, it's not like that."

"But you're upset. I can tell."

"I need the girls."

"Do I get a preview?"

"Nate and Ryder are out, together...alone."

"Ohhhhh shit." She's known me long enough to know that's no small thing. "Okay. Tacos and margs in fifteen."

Fifteen minutes later, I've been sitting at a table alone for five minutes, and I'm halfway through a giant margarita, and only suffering a minor panic attack. The tequila is doing a pretty decent job at keeping the bulk of the panic at bay. The rest of the girls all file in at once, Audra first, then Imogen, then Nova. They sit, and the server brings three more margaritas—without having to be asked, because we're here frequently.

Audra waits until we all have drinks, and then pounds her fist on the table, once, hard. "I hereby declare a quorum. Let the counsel proceed."

I laugh, and then hiccup. "Remember when I called you in a panic because I'd fallen for Ryder?"

Audra nods. "He ghosted on you, as I recall.

Seems there's been some excitement since then."

"I let Ryder take Nate to play laser tag."

Imogen's eyes widen. "Oh, wow. That's a big step."

Nova nods. "My sister is a single mom, and she'd never ever let a boyfriend take her son anywhere. I believe her words to me once were, 'not even if he was Jesus.'" Nova's vivid blue eyes go to mine. "How'd you go from 'convince me to not like him' to this so fast?"

A tear slips down my cheek, and I hiccup again. "I—I don't know. That's the issue."

Imogen pats my hand. "If it's any consolation, all four of them are really great guys, and I'd trust each of them." She shrugs. "I *do* trust all of them."

Audra snickers. "I mean, I wouldn't leave a baby with any of them, except maybe James, since he's had experience with them."

I glare at her. "Not helping."

Audra's snicker turns to a laugh. "Oh come on, Laurel—you try to picture Jesse with a baby."

I can't help a laugh at the image of big, burly Jesse with a tiny baby. "That is a funny thought."

Imogen isn't laughing. "It's…it's not *that* funny."

We all zero in on her.

Imogen is pale, eyes wide, lip caught between her teeth.

Audra gasps. "No. Uh-uh. No way. You fucking are *not*!"

Imogen nods. "I am," she whispers.

"NO." Audra shakes her head, grabbing her best friend's hands in a death grip. "You tried for *years* with Nick!"

"I know."

"You've been with him, what…a year?"

"Barely."

I blink. "Wait…Imogen, you're *pregnant*?"

She nods. "Six weeks."

Nova eyes the water Imogen has been sipping on, and the untouched drink in front of her. "Does Jesse know?"

Imogen shakes her head, and then drops her eyes. "I'm forty-one years old. I'd given up on having kids. We're not even engaged, and we've never even talked about kids!" She looks at me, tears boiling in her eyes, as yet unshed. "I'm sorry, Laurel. I'm totally hijacking your panic attack."

She's sitting beside me, with Audra and Nova across from us, and I wrap an arm around her. "No, no, no. This is way more important."

She leans into the hug. "I just don't know what to do."

"Um, tell him?" Audra says. "The man loves you like crazy. He'll be happy, once he gets over his shock."

"Did you guys not use condoms or something?" Nova asks.

Imogen's grin is shy, and small. "Yeah, we sort of stopped, since I thought I couldn't get pregnant. I mean, Nick and I literally tried for years—literally everything, including IVF."

Nova snickers. "You and your ex fuck for years—no baby. Jesse fucks you a couple times—BAM... baby." She laughs, and it's contagious. "He must have super swimmers."

"I mean, it *has* been more than a couple times," Imogen says, trying not to laugh. "Jesse and I have had more sex in the last sixty days than I think Nick and I ever had in our entire marriage."

"Still, some guys just have super-potent sperm, and that man is a picture of vitality and virility." Nova shrugs. "But then, all four of those guys are."

We all turn to look at Nova, then.

"If anyone is a picture of virility, it's James," Audra says, wiggling her eyebrows comically. "Have you tested his virility yet?"

Nova shuts down, right on cue. "Nice try. The counsel has not been called into session to discuss *my* life."

Audra huffs. "You are seriously *no* fun." She pokes Nova in the arm. "One of these days, Nova, you're going to talk to us."

Nova narrows her eyes at Audra. "Don't poke me," she says. "And I talk to you guys all the time. I'm talking to you now."

"I mean about *you*," Audra clarifies. "You're, like, Fort Knox. You give nothing away."

Nova shrugs. "I'm private. And there's nothing to know, anyway. James and I are acquaintances at best. He's handsome, he's interesting, and I'm physically attracted to him, but that's all there is and all there ever will be. The end, amen, and let it be."

Audra snorts derisively. "*Aaaand* I call bullshit on that, but we'll let it go for now." She points at me. "So, Laurel—you're finally realizing you're head over heels stupid in love with Ryder, to the degree that you allowed him to abscond with your one and only son. Smart move—the guy is awesome, funny, hard-working, cool, and sexy as hell. You have a well-fucked flush going on, by the way, so I'll expect details in a moment." Next, she points at Imogen. "You, my lovely dumpling—you're pregnant, and I couldn't be happier for you. I know you're scared, but you don't need to be. Jesse will probably faint dead away when you tell him, but when you wake him up, he'll be excited. Give him time to process it, and then watch as he turns into the most ridiculously over-protective grizzly bear of a papa you could possibly imagine."

Imogen pales, hand over her mouth. "Oh…my…
god. He's going to literally carry me everywhere,"
she breathes. "He'll wrap me in bubble wrap! He'll
make me quit working—he'll probably try to hand
feed me."

We're all laughing now, because Jesse is already
insanely protective of Imogen—insane being the key
word, here. He walks her across parking lots as if
waiting for thugs to jump out at any minute. If she
so much as stumbles, he tries to pick her up and carry
her the rest of the way. It's adorable, and Imogen eats
it up. I think she humors his protectiveness because it
makes her feel so loved, and because it's so novel for
her. But the thought of Jesse in overprotective new
father mode? Oh my.

"Don't laugh!" Imogen insists. "He'll never let
me leave the house!"

"He knows you're not actually that delicate,"
Nova says. "He just loves you, and it's new for him."

"He's going to be impossible," Imogen moans.

We can't help snickering, but then the eyes all
turn to me, and I shift uncomfortably. "What?" I ask.

"You—Ryder—spill." Audra points at me, stealing Imogen's untouched margarita.

I shrug. "It just kind of happened. I gave him a
chance to explain, and that turned into a date—"

"And then he fucked you six ways to Sunday?"

Audra suggests.

"More like he fucked me six ways *on* Sunday," I say, giggling.

"Holy shit, no wonder you're glowing," Audra breathes. "Was it as amazing as I'd like to think it would be?"

I frown at her. "What does that mean?"

She shrugs. "I mean if I hadn't met Jesse first, I'd probably have wanted to fuck Ryder. He's hot, and I've always had a thing for gingers."

"Do I need to be jealous?" I ask, eyes narrowed.

"God no!" She waves a hand. "I've got all the sexy times I can handle, honey-buns. Franco gives it to me all night and all day, and then some. He literally followed me into the shower this morning. I was late for work, so all I had time for was a kiss and a handjob, but still. He's insatiable."

I roll my eyes at her. "A handjob? Really?"

She shrugs. "What? The handjob is underrated." She makes her voice sound like an old-timey radio commercial. "If your guy is hounding you for sexy times and you just ain't got the time, the trusty, quick, reliable handjob is ready for action."

Imogen groans, slapping her forehead with her palm. "Oh my god, Audra. You are *so wrong*!"

Audra just raises her eyebrows, arch, prim, and self-assured. "So *right*, you mean. Have you tried it?"

Imogen blushes. "Well, no. Not since I was a teenager."

"Do you blow him?"

"Sometimes."

"Next time he's all 'me so horny' and you're just super not in the mood for the energy expenditure of sex *or* the jaw ache and aftertaste of a blowjob, try a handjob and thank me later."

"And do what with the...um...mess?" Imogen asks.

Audra shrugs. "Depends. If you're at home, just lead him into the bathroom and have him finish into the toilet. Or the sink." She winks.

Imogen fakes a gag. "The *sink*? That's so gross!"

"Or, just let him go on your titties and make him clean you up with a washcloth." Audra waves a hand. "The options are endless—limited only by your imagination, my dear." She gestures at Imogen's belly. "And honestly, you'll probably be thanking me in a few months—when that baby is near term and you're big as a whale and can barely move and he's going crazy 'cause you're too pregnant for anything fun, the ol' handjob will get him off your case for a few days. Or...hours, at the very least."

"Or..." Nova raises a finger. "And I'm just spit-balling here—but he could just, you know, suck it up and deal with it for a while?"

Audra looks at Nova like she's sprouted a second head. "Are you crazy? Men are *so* impossible to deal with when they're horny. Get them off, and they're so much more…pliable."

Nova snorts and then coughs, trying not to spew margarita over the table. "*Pliable*?" she asks.

Audra nods, serious. "Pliable. Meaning, pliable to your will. Man-management one-oh-one, babe—he'll do anything you ask if you promise him sex…he'll do whatever you want before you even have to ask if he thinks there's a BJ in the offing, and once he's gotten sex, a BJ, or a handy, he'll be so grateful that he'll basically follow you around like a puppy, hoping to do something else for you just so you'll reward him again."

Nova narrows her eyes. "That sounds like manipulation."

Audra laughs. "Um, yeah. Absolutely." She holds up a finger, pulls her phone from her purse and calls Franco, with it on speakerphone. It rings three times, and then he answers.

"Hey, babe."

"Hi, lovey," Audra says. "Full disclosure: You're on speakerphone, and I've got the girls with me. I need you to answer a question, to prove a point I'm trying to make."

He hesitates. "Ummm…okay. I'll do my best."

"Just be honest, babe."

"Will this come back to bite me in the ass later if I don't answer correctly?"

Audra laughs. "Quit being so suspicious, you looney toon." She leans over the phone, and we all move closer. "Would you agree that I manipulate you with sex?"

He's quiet a moment, thinking. "Um. Yes, absolutely."

"And you're aware of this."

"Yes."

"Do you resent me for it?"

"Hell no."

"Why not?"

"Because for one, it gets me sex. For another, you're not doing it out of anything negative, mean, or, like, self-serving. You love me, and I know it—you just sometimes use sex to get around the fact that I'm stubborn, obtuse, and sometimes flat-out stupid."

We're all laughing now, and Audra holds up a hand to quiet us. "One last question. How do you feel about handjobs?"

He snorts. "I'll take them and gladly, but only if it's all I can get—other stuff is better." There's noise in the background, voices and power tools. "Gotta go, babe—I have work to finish so I can get home and claim my reward for answering your questions."

We cackle and giggle at that.

"Reward, huh?" Audra asks.

"Yup. You had to know that if you're having me answer personal questions like that in front of all the girls, you're gonna have to give me something for it later."

"My period just started, sadly, so sex is out of the question."

"Damn. Okay, well, we'll negotiate when you get home."

"Okay. See you later. Love you!"

"Love you too, babe. See you later, ladies!"

"Bye, Franco!" we all chorus.

Audra taps the red "hang-up" icon at the bottom of her screen to end the call, and then holds out her hands in a gesture of victory. "See?"

Nova is frowning. "Well, that works for you guys. I'm still not sure I'd be cool using that technique in my own relationship, though."

Audra shakes her head. "You know it's all in good fun, right? I do what I do because I love him, because I enjoy making him feel good, and because I just like doing that stuff. He'd do anything I asked without ever asking for anything in return, and I know it, and he knows the same goes for me. Throwing sexual stuff into the mix is just fun—it keeps things spicy and unpredictable. It's not actual manipulation—that'd be shitty and horrible. If you were really using sex solely to get him to do things he didn't want to do? Yuck. No way."

Nova laughs. "Okay, okay. I see your point." She waves a hand. "It's all moot anyway, because I'm not in a relationship, and not having sex."

"You could be," Audra says.

Nova glares. "Audra—don't. We're not getting into that." She sighs. "You are seriously like a dog with a bone about that."

"I just think you're in denial or something. You're flat-out refusing to even think about or talk about something that could be really great for you."

Nova groans, thunking her head on the table. "You are so impossible, Audra. God." She takes a long sip of margarita. "I have my reasons."

"Let me guess—something horrible and tragic lurks in your past, leading you to be isolated and cold, refusing to allow love into your life out of fear that you'll be hurt again, and so you self-sabotage any budding relationships." Audra arches an eyebrow at Nova, sipping her drink demurely.

Nova snorts. "Yes, Audra, you're exactly right— my life is the plot of a cheesy romance novel. Let me rip off my bodice and throw myself on James's turgid member."

"Shows how many romance novels *you've* read,"

I say. "He rips your bodice open, you don't rip it off yourself."

Audra giggles into her goblet. "Although, I'm pretty certain James's member is plenty turgid whenever you're around." She gestures with a swipe of her finger at Nova's chest—I've got an ample amount of silicone in my chest, and Nova's tits make mine look like mosquito bites. "Those monster honkers of yours make sure of that."

Nova glances down self-consciously—she's in her scrub pants, as usual, with just a ribbed tank-top underneath an unzipped hoodie, which means her, um, ridiculous, all-natural endowment is prominently displayed. "Oh, shut up. They're not *that* big."

Audra reaches over and cups one of Nova's tits, shaking it. "Um, hello? You've got Jell-O filled watermelons attached to your sternum, babe." She kisses Nova's cheek, making the other woman cringe away, batting at Audra. "I'm just teasing you, Nova, chill. I love you, and I only make fun of you for your tits because I'm a little jealous. Until you came along, mine were the biggest, and you've usurped my place as the biggest-titty bitch of the bunch."

Nova sighs in resignation. "Story of my life. Men only see me for my tits, and women are jealous of me for them. I've thought about getting a reduction just to make my life easier." She cups herself with both hands. "But I never do, because at the end of the day, I love my girls."

"James sees you for more than your chest, Nova," I say. "I saw that much at the party."

Nova growls in wordless frustration, bending forward to thunk her head on the table. "CAN WE PLEASE STOP TALKING ABOUT JAMES?" she shouts.

Imogen grabs my hand and Audra's. "Enough, you two. Leave her alone about it. She clearly is not willing to talk about this and we shouldn't try to force the issue." She lets go of Audra's hand and takes my other in hers. "We're here to talk about you and Ryder."

I shrug. "I just...it's a lot, really fast, and I don't know what to do."

"There's only one thing *to* do," Audra says.

"What's that?" I ask.

"Hang on tight, and accept the fact that you've fallen into something real." She pats my hand. "Trust me, I know exactly how scary it is. Falling in love with Franco was fucking terrifying. But if you just let go and accept that you're in love and he's worth it, everything will work out fine."

"Wait, do I let go or hold on?" I ask, my expression somewhere between a confused frown and amused smirk.

"Both. That's why it's so hard," Imogen answers. "You let go of expectations and doubts and fears, and hold on to—"

"His giant cock," Audra cuts in.

Imogen backhands Audra's arm. "No, you slut— not everything needs to come back to giant cocks." She rolls her eyes, and then goes back to addressing me. "Hold on to the belief that he's an amazing man and that loving him may not always be easy, but it'll all be worth it."

I nod. "That makes sense." I swirl the ice at the bottom of my goblet. "The other complicating factor is that my ex-husband showed up at my door at one in the morning the other day and told me he was still in love with me."

"How is that a complicating factor?" Nova asks. "Do you still have feelings for him?"

I shake my head. "*God* no, not at all. I'm just worried he's going to do something crazy to try and win me back."

"Could he win you back?" Nova presses.

"Again, *god* no!" I stare at the table. "If he'd tried years ago, after we first got divorced, maybe. But only because I was still desperate to feel like a family...but I've realized we never really were a family, and that everything he does is about him somehow or another. He told me he's on medication and all that, but yet he shows up unannounced at my front door at one in the morning. Not exactly proof positive that he's really changed."

"What do you think prompted the sudden declaration of love?" Imogen asks.

"Probably seeing me with Ryder," I answer.

Nova frowns. "When did that happen?"

"The weekend before this last one. Ryder picked me up and we went downtown for a date, and then we stayed at a hotel…" I duck my head, blushing. "I sort of lost track of time and was late picking up Nate from his father's—Paul gets visitation every other weekend, and this was his weekend. Ryder took me to Paul's to pick Nate up, and then to basketball practice. That was the first time I've ever brought another guy around Paul, and it must've set him off."

"What about your ex-boyfriend…what's his name? Deke?" Audra asks.

"Derek, and he was never my boyfriend."

Audra frowns. "You dated him almost a year… and you were upset when he dumped you. Sort of makes him your boyfriend."

I sigh. "It's a mental game I played with myself, I guess—it's complicated. The point is, I never brought him around Paul, and the only time he ever saw Nate is when we went out all three of us, and then sometimes we'd go back to my house and hang out for a while, but Derek never stayed the night and never went with me to drop off or pick up Nate from Paul's, and never went anywhere with Nate alone."

"Even after a year?" Imogen clarifies.

I nod. "Derek never really liked Nate, I guess. I didn't see it—I feel like a shitty mother for being so blind and selfish. Derek was cute, and when we were together he was…nice to me."

Nova's eyes narrow. "He was *nice* to you?"

I shrug. "Yeah. He was nice."

"You dated a guy simply because he was *nice*?" Nova's voice rises in intensity.

"Paul was never nice! He was mean, he was selfish, and he was difficult." I'm getting upset now. "He made me feel like he needed me, and I liked feeling needed—at first. But then it turned into a trap, because he *needed* me, but yet I was never enough— nothing I did was *ever* enough. Then we had Nate and I was scared of being a single mom, and Paul needed me, and all I could do was try to survive—take care of Nate, take care of Paul, pay the bills…" I pause, trying to breathe. "I…when I finally bit the bullet and divorced Paul, I was lonely. I'd been lonely for fucking *years*. So yeah, Derek came along and he was nice to me and acted like he liked me, like he wanted me, and I let myself get blinded by that, because for the first time in a long time, I wasn't lonely. He was *nice* to me.

But he wasn't nice to Nate, and all he wanted was to sleep with me—probably because I was so lonely and desperate. And once he got what he wanted, he got bored and moved on. So yes, Nova, I dated a guy just because he was nice to me."

"I'm sorry, I was being judgmental without knowing the facts." Nova is quiet, distant, now. "I get it. More than you know, I get it."

I wave a hand. "No apology needed." I drain my goblet. "I want this thing with Ryder to be real, but now I question my own judgment. What if he's just being nice to me to get me to sleep with him? What if, now that I've given him that, he won't want me anymore? What if I let him take my son out, but it's all just an elaborate ploy? What if he turns out to be just as much of an asshole as Paul and Derek? What if there's something I'm not seeing? What if I let myself fall in love with him and let Nate get attached, and then it just doesn't work for some reason... what if—"

Imogen takes one of my hands, Audra takes the other, and Nova, in a rare burst of humor, puts both of hers on top of all of ours.

"Go team?" Nova says.

I laugh. "So...this is an intervention?"

Aura nods. "Yup. A what-if intervention."

"Very little in life is as destructive and harmful as letting what-ifs rule your decision making." Imogen squeezes my hand. "I'm proof of that. Audra is proof of that. And the relationships we have with Jesse and Franco are further proof that if you can silence the what-ifs and really, truly, clearly see him for what he is, you'll know what's right." She smiles at me. "I'm not saying Ryder is right for you—only you can determine that. I'm just saying that you can't make that decision from a place of what-if."

I look at Audra, who just points at Imogen. "What she said," Audra says. "I lived my life from a place of what-if for twenty years, and it was only when I forced myself to shut that voice up and see what was in front of me that I found the first real, meaningful relationship I've ever had in my life—and the last relationship I'll ever have, too. I'm in it for life with Franco—I don't need a ring or a wedding to know that—and I had to get over constantly asking myself what if to get to this place."

I look at Nova, but she just holds her hands up and shrugs. "Don't look at me," she says. "I'm damaged goods with a baggage train a mile long. I've got zero advice for you—except maybe that I've got a solid bullshit detector, and an even better asshole detector…and both of those tell me Ryder is the real deal. A good guy, and an honest one. For what it's worth, I don't think he's leading you on or playing games. Take that with a grain of salt, though, because

I don't really know him or any of the guys all that well—I'm only here because you three crazy bitches seem to have adopted me and, for whatever reason, I like you and can't stay away."

"It's me," Audra says, cozying up to her. "You're attracted to me and want to have hot lesbian sex with me."

Nova shies away, pushing Audra off with stiffened fingers, as if touching something gross. "You are *not* okay."

"So…that's not it?" Audra says, sounding sad.

"Nope. Not even close." Nova seems to be missing the fact that Audra is obviously just winding her up, or is very straight-faced in playing along. "And please don't do that ever again."

"Damn." Audra snaps her fingers. "I was hoping that was it. You were my chance to try girl-on-girl." She smirks. "I was gonna tape it and show it to Franco."

Nova rolls her head back on her neck. "There's something wrong with you, Audra. You need a psychiatrist, or Jesus, or a nunnery, or something."

Audra breaks into laughter, slugging Nova on the shoulder. "You're so much fun to fuck with—you're so literal."

Nova remains unmoved. "I'm not convinced you weren't partially serious."

"Why? You wanna make out?" Audra leans closer to Nova. "Compare tits?"

"There's no comparison, babe," Nova says, deadpan. "Mine are better."

Audra snickers. "It's hard to tell if you're serious or not. Most of the time you have zero sense of humor, and then every once in a while you say something like that, and I'm not sure if you're kidding."

Nova frowns. "I have a sense of humor." She arches an eyebrow at Audra. "I just don't find being wildly inappropriate literally all the time as funny as you do."

"That's because you're a stick-in-the-mud," Audra says. "You need to get laid. Get a good hard dicking and you'll loosen right up."

"Good...hard...dicking," Nova repeats. "Wow. You know, I can refer you to a good pastor *and* a good psychiatrist."

My phone rings then, and I glance at it—Ryder. "Hello?" I say, answering it, trying to stay calm.

Why is he calling? What's wrong? Is Nate hurt?

"Hey, babe," Ryder says. "We've played laser tag until we're exhausted, but now we're hungry. I was thinking I'd pick up a pizza or two and bring it by your place. Sound good?"

I can't help a smile. "That sounds awesome. Did you guys have fun?"

"I don't know. Nate, did we have any fun?"

"YES!" Nate shouts, so loud I have to pull the phone away from my ear. "I BEAT RYDER BOTH GAMES! I have twenty bucks and you can't keep it this time. Ryder's gonna make me a badass piggy bank to put it in."

"You watch your language, young man!" I scold.

"That's my fault, I said it first," Ryder says. "Sorry. I gotta get a handle on my language, apparently."

"Yeah, you do. If he gets in trouble at school for cursing, I'm blaming you."

"Fair enough." He says something away from the phone to Nate, and then returns to me. "So, I'm gonna call in the pizza. We'll see you at home in about half an hour or so?"

At home.

My heart does a weird melty flip. "Yeah," I whisper. "I'll see you in half an hour...at home."

I'm pretty sure he hears it in my voice. "You okay?"

"I'm great. Really, really great."

"That's what I like to hear." Nate says something, and Ryder addresses me again. "Okay, gotta go. Mister laser tag expert here and I gotta go get supplies to build his piggy bank while we wait for the pizza. Say hi to the girls for me."

I laugh. "How'd you know I was with them?"

"How else were you gonna get through this?" he says, laughing. "Okay, see you soon."

We say our goodbyes, and then I hang up, toss my phone in my purse, and look around to see all the others staring at me with sappy looks on their faces.

"I think that has to be the cutest thing I've ever seen," Audra says. "And I'm generally immune to cuteness."

I blush. "Oh shut up."

"No, for real," Audra says. "It was awesome. I really don't see how you can have any doubts after that. Laser tag, and he's building Nate a piggy bank? *And* he could hear in your voice that you were all gooey over him, which means he really, actually listens to you."

"I wasn't gooey."

"You were pretty gooey," Nova says.

Imogen laughs. "Goo-fest, babe. Own it."

I sigh. "Fine. He just makes me all melty, and I can't help it."

Imogen hugs me. "Don't try to help it. Own it, embrace it, and go with it."

"I'm afraid I don't know how."

"Lead with your heart, think with your pussy, and tell your brain to shut the fuck up," Audra says.

Nova rolls her eyes. "Wow, Audra. Super eloquent advice."

I'm laughing, though, because I was thinking

something similar, just…not quite in those words—
but then, that's what Audra's best at.

We pay the bill, chat for a few more minutes, and
then I head out. And, on the way, I make a stop at the
drug store for a giant package of condoms. Because
Ryder is *so* getting laid as soon as I can figure out how
to make it happen in such a way that Nate won't know.

TWELVE

RYDER DOESN'T GET LAID THAT NIGHT, AND NEITHER do I. By the time dinner was done it was already after seven, and then Nate was begging Ryder to get started on the piggy bank project, so they went out into the garage to start that, which meant I was alone for cleanup, and then it was time for Nate to go to bed. We were just about to have a glass of wine when Ryder got a call from a client with an electrical emergency, so he had to go take care of that.

We text a few times later in the night, we're both pretty exhausted and end up going to sleep in our own beds. So much for getting laid.

The next few days are all fairly quiet and, sadly, Ryder-free, except for texts between us. He's slammed with work—the guys are starting a kitchen remodel and expansion, which means Ryder's services are required pretty much nonstop as they rewire and extend the electrical.

employees have—it's great most of the time...except when you want privacy. Like now. Everyone in the nearby area is listening.

"I can't talk about it right now, Ryder. I'll call you after work, okay?"

"Fine. It's cool—you're at work, and this is personal drama. I get it. Call me later."

"Ryder, you understand, don't you?"

"Yes, I absolutely do understand. I keep my personal shit out of work, too. It's fine. As long as you're okay, I'm okay."

I'm feeling a little trembly, to be honest, but I don't say that. "It's just...a tricky situation. That's all."

"As long we're cool, I'm cool."

"We're totally cool, babe," I say, trying to fake a ditzy Valley Girl voice, and only sort of succeeding.

"Then I'm cool."

I laugh. "This is a silly, juvenile conversation, and I have to go."

Ryder laughs too, and I hear him returning to the work site. "Same. Talk to you later, okay?"

"Okay, bye," I say, and hang up.

I hang up, take the vase of flowers out of my office, and bring them to the receptionist at the front of our office. "Here," I say. "Have some flowers."

The receptionist, Emily, is brand new and very young—fresh out of college, eager to change the world through nonprofit work, and very sweet—she also has a funny and endearing and annoying habit of making statements sound like questions. She takes the flowers, sniffs them, and looks up at me with bright eyes. "Wow, thanks, Ms. Madison. They're beautiful. I love them!" She hesitates. "Why are you giving them to me, though?"

"Well, it's complicated. Let's just say they're from someone who has no business giving me flowers, and leave it at that. They're pretty, so I don't want to throw them away, but I don't want them."

She perks up. "Oh. Well…okay!" She frowns, then. "Um, you know, I was the one who received these."

I blink. "You were?"

"They weren't delivered by a delivery person, and I thought it was kind of weird."

I wait, but she's not forthcoming with any further information. I stare at her. "And?"

"And what?"

"Who delivered them? Why was it weird?"

She tilts her head to one side. "Oh. Well, he was just some guy. He wanted to know if you were available, but you were on that conference call with Mary-Jo, so I told him no, you weren't, and he asked when you would be available, but I was getting a weird vibe from him, so I just said I didn't know." She frowns up at me. "Was I wrong?"

I take my cell phone from my blazer pocket and flip through my old photos until I find one of Paul with Nate from earlier in the summer. "Was this him?"

"The older one, yeah."

I laugh. "Well, it would awful odd if it was my son, seeing as he's supposed to be in school."

"Sorry. My boyfriend says I'm kind of a ditz sometimes."

I frown at this. "That's not okay, Emily. He shouldn't talk down to you like that."

"Well, it's okay because I call him an airhead. He means it with love." She wrinkles her brow. "So, the guy who brought the flowers—he's your ex?"

I nod. "Yup."

"So…why's he bringing you flowers? Are you getting back together with him? Because, like, I know it's none of my business, but going back to an ex is never a good idea."

"I'm not sure why he's bringing me flowers, but I'm definitely not getting back together with him." I have one last question for her. "What was the weird vibe you were getting?"

She shrugs. "I don't know. Just…weird. Not creepy, like I wasn't scared of him, although I probably wouldn't ride in an elevator alone with him. Just weird. He just randomly shows up with flowers and wants to talk to you and you're, like, super business all the time, so it just felt weird."

I think that's about all I'm going to get out of her, so I let it go. "Okay, well, if you see him again, let me know. And definitely don't ever let him back to talk to me."

"You got it, Ms. Madison." She grins at me, all eagerness and sweetness. "Is there anyone I *should* let back to see you?"

I can't help a smile. "Yes. His name is Ryder McCann, and he's a bit under six feet tall, he has huge muscles, red hair, and an awesome red beard."

Her answering grin is mischievous. "I see. And if he ever wants me to help him plan a romantic surprise for you?"

I laugh. "Keep it a surprise, duh!"

"Okay. Should I give you hints?"

I sigh, laughing. "No, Emily. That would defeat the purpose of it being a romantic surprise." I hesitate. "Wait—*is* he planning a romantic surprise?"

Emily goes wide-eyed. "No! I just was wondering. When I got this job, I was hoping something romantic and fun would happen like in the movies. But so far it hasn't."

I resist the urge to roll my eyes. Instead, I pat her on the shoulder. "Stick around, Emily. I have a feeling you'll get your wish."

The rest of the day goes smoothly enough. I finish work and head out to get Nate from school, pop into our favorite coffee shop for a quick snack before he has basketball practice.

I sit on the bleachers and watch him practice, and exchange texts in our girl group.

Imogen: *I need to figure out how to tell Jesse. I'm freaking out!*

Audra: *Ummm, how about: Yo, jesse babe, you knocked me up.*

Nova: *that's fucking stupid, Audra. I swear, you think like a caveman.*

Audra: *excuse me, that's caveWOMAN*

Me: *how about a surprise baby shower? Like, with beer and chicken wings and surprise, we're having a baby*

Imogen: *Actually, Laurel, that's not a bad idea. Act like it's a surprise birthday party, and then when he gets really confused because it's not his birthday, I'm like, oh, oops. And I bring out a cake that has YOU'RE GOING TO BE A FATHER!*

Audra: *Wait, I have an idea!*

Imogen: *If it involves giving him a blowjob, keep it to yourself.*

Audra: *You take the fun out of everything.*

Imogen: *the man gets plenty of BJ's, trust me. I*

need a cute, fun, romantic way of telling him I'm going to have his baby.

Audra: *I was actually going to suggest you let him cum on your belly, and be like, baby-juice on the outside of my stomach, baby-juice on the inside too! Surprise!*

Nova: *I'm literally speechless.*

Audra: *Not as speechless as he'd be.*

Imogen: *Seriously, Audra. You could say Hail Marys til you're 90 and not make up for all the nastiness you come up with.*

Audra: *Sex is my spirit animal.*

Me: ...

Imogen: ...

Nova: ...

Audra: *What? Why are you all sending me ellipses?*

Me: *Because that makes zero sense.*

Audra: *FINE. LET'S PLAN YOUR STUPID FAKE BIRTHDAY SURPRISE BABY SHOWER PARTY.*

Imogen: *Can we get it planned by this weekend?*

Nova: *Did I ever mention I was an event planner in a previous life?*

Audra: *see, again, I'm not sure if you're joking or not.*

Nova: *Not joking. I used to own my own event planning company. Then some shit in my life went sideways, and I had to switch tracks, which is how I ended up in nursing.*

Imogen: *Didn't you also used to be a bartender?*

Nova: *In college, yeah—my first degree was a double major in political science and public relations. I thought I was going to be a politician or something. I was super political back then—a real idealistic, energetic, ra-ra-ra, "I'm gonna change the world" type. And then some shit happened and I discovered by accident that I have a knack for party planning, and ended up starting a company. And then more shit happened and I had to start over. My party planning company didn't quite make enough to make ends meet, so I bartended on the weekends, and when the shit happened, I went back to school for nursing and ended up with my MS. And I am now an assistant to a neurologist, because I'm an overachiever.*

Nova: *Never say I've never shared anything with you, because I think that's the longest text message I've ever sent.*

Me: *Wait, so you have a double major in political science and public relations, AND an MS in nursing?*

Nova: *There's a minor in art history in there too. Like I said, I'm a chronic overachiever who has had zero life, like ever. I was the kid taking college courses in high school.*

Imogen: *not to mention you're six feet tall, ripped, and absolutely gorgeous? ANNOYING.*

Nova: *I offset all that by being a cold, neurotic,*

antisocial bitch.

Audra: *You're not antisocial.*

Nova: *LOL, I notice you're not denying the other two.*

Me: *I wouldn't say you're cold, just a little…aloof, sometimes. But I think it's just because you're hiding a lot of pain and damage and don't trust all that easily.*

Nova: *Or at all. The three of you are the first real friends I've had in years, and making myself leave my apartment to hang out requires an act of will every time.*

Imogen: *We're honored, Nova. We've adopted you because we love you. You're ours now, and you may as well just accept it.*

Audra: *I don't mind you, Nova. I actually kind of identify with you, because I come across as aloof sometimes too. Cold ass bitches of the world, unite!*

Me, with an eye-roll emoji: *Neither of you are cold. It's just a defense mechanism.*

Nova: *quit analyzing us, Laurel.*

Me: *I'm not. I just can't help being observant of human nature.*

Nova: *okay, enough mushy shit. Imogen, would you like me to officially come out of retirement to plan your double-fake surprise party?*

Imogen: *I mean, yeah, I'd love that! But you don't have to. I don't want you to feel obligated.*

Nova: *Having real, actual friends is kind of fun. It would be my pleasure.*

Imogen: *You can't see, but I'm totally squealing like a crazy person right now. I hate planning parties.*

Nova: *I suppose this means I'll have to dust off my sense of fun. It's kind of rusty at the moment.*

Audra: *Hey, I think that was a joke!*

Nova: *Sort of. Okay, not really. I stopped having fun a long time ago.*

Audra: *Well, you let yourself get adopted by the wrong people in that case, because Imogen and I are addicted to fun.*

Nova: *Maybe I let myself get adopted by you exactly because you have fun. Maybe I missed being fun, and having friends, and I'm hoping you guys will help me get out of my cold, neurotic, antisocial bitch shell.*

Audra: *Well if that's the case, then you got it exactly right!*

Me: *Hey, I like fun too!*

Imogen: *I have a feeling this party is going to be the bestest best thing ever!*

Audra: *Will there be strippers? Because there should totally be strippers.*

Nova: *Yes, Audra. Strippers are definitely appropriate for a baby shower.*

Audra: *Strippers are never appropriate, which is why they're always appropriate. And I mean the male kind. If I wanted to see sexy naked bitches, I'd throw us a pajama party.*

Nova: *what the hell does that mean?*

Audra: *you guys all come over, we get drunk and end up naked playing truth or dare while listening to The Greatest Showman soundtrack.*

Imogen: *That sounds fun.*

Me: *Actually, it does.*

Imogen: *I can't drink, but I don't need to be drunk for any of that! Plus, someone would need to babysit you lushes.*

Me: *I have to go, my son is done with basketball practice and I need to feed him. Bye, bitches!*

I put my phone away as Nate trots over, sweaty and grinning. "Hey, buddy! Ready for dinner?"

"Yeah!" he shouts. "I'm starved. Can we have mac 'n cheese with bacon in it?"

I laugh as we head to my car. "Sure. You make the macaroni, I'll make the bacon."

A few minutes later, we're home, and Nate immediately starts making the macaroni. It was the first thing I taught him to cook, and now he's basically a pro.

We're sitting down to eat about twenty minutes later when the doorbell rings.

I sigh. "I'll get it. Go ahead and eat, Nate."

I'm anticipating the worst as I open the front

door. Instead of Paul, however, it's a young man in dirty jeans, a baggy Bears hoodie, wearing a backward Blackhawks hat, and holding a clipboard.

"Laurel Madison?" he asks.

"Yes," I say, my voice trepidatious.

He holds out the clipboard. "I have a delivery for you. Sign at the bottom, please."

"A delivery of what, and from whom?"

He digs in the kangaroo pouch of his hoodie and pulls out an envelope, hands it to me. I open it, and within is a small rectangle of plain white linen paper. On the front is a simple line drawing of a single rose, done in black ink. On the back, in the same black ink, in neat, all-caps block handwriting that I somehow know immediately is Ryder's, is a short message:

If I'm going to send you flowers, it'll look like this.
—Ryder

"Oh dear," I mumble to myself, signing the slip, and then look up to address the delivery guy. "So, you have some flowers for me?"

The young man's eyes widen and he blows out a breath and nods his head. "You could say that."

I frown. "What does that mean?"

He just laughs. "Just…leave the door propped open."

I snort. "Did he go overboard?"

The guy scoops his hat off, scrubs his hand

through his hair, and replaces the hat. "All I can say is, either he messed up *really* bad, or he *really* likes you."

I prop the door open, and the delivery guy enters...wheeling a dolly on which are three giant boxes.

He opens the first box and pulls out a vase filled with a dozen red roses.

Then a second.

A third, and fourth.

The next box contains another four vases, each filled with a dozen roses.

Same with the third box.

I groan and laugh at the same time. "Oh my god. Seriously?"

The delivery guy gives me a stare. "That's just the first load."

"The *what*?"

He grins, indicating the now-empty boxes. "This is just the first three boxes."

I close my eyes, pinching the bridge of my nose. "Of how many?"

The guy glances out the front door at the cube van parked rear-end first in my driveway. "A lot."

"Ohhhh boy."

Ten minutes later, I'm running out of places for the guy to put vases. The poor guy has made four more trips, with three boxes per load times four vases per box, each vase containing a dozen roses each, equals…I'm bad at math. A lot, that's what.

Like, two hundred and forty roses?

When the guy is finished dragging the last three empty boxes out to his truck and comes back in, sweating, sans dolly, I'm laughing hysterically.

"Is that finally it?" I ask, still laughing.

The guy gapes at me. "Yes, ma'am. That's it."

I grab my purse and fish my wallet out of it. "Is this the most flowers you've ever delivered to one person?"

"No tip, please, ma'am. The guy who placed the order paid enough to cover it." He wipes at his forehead. "I did deliver over a thousand roses to a lady, once."

I snort. "A *thousand*? What was the story, do you know?"

He laughs. "I think the guy cheated on his wife, got caught, and was trying to make up for it."

"Did it work?"

He shrugs. "I dunno. The lady was annoyed, though, because it turns out she'd been telling him for years that she hated roses, and he spent over four grand on them."

"Wow. So that was kind of a fail, huh?"

He nods, shrugs. "I guess it seems to me like if you're gonna cheat and get caught, you'd better know what kind of flowers your wife likes." He indicates my houseful of roses. "Your husband mess up or what?"

I blush. "He's not my husband, he's my boy-friend. And no, he didn't."

He grins again. "And do you like roses?"

My smile widens. "I love them."

He removes and replaces his hat once more. "Well, I hope you enjoy them. The vases all have plant food in them, so the roses should last a long time if you keep them filled with fresh water." He waves at me. "Have a nice day, ma'am."

"It'd be impossible not to," I say.

Nate looks up from his homework. "What are you gonna do with all these roses?"

I sigh, looking around at the twenty dozen roses clustered on every available square inch of my home. "I have no idea, bud."

He sniffs. "It's kinda smelly. Like, a good smell, but just…strong. Tickles my nose."

I laugh, ruffling his hair. "No kidding. It *is* pretty pungent."

He stares at me, chewing on the eraser of his pencil. "Ryder must really like you."

I bite the corner of my lower lip. "Yeah, I think he does."

"Do you like him back?"

I nod. "I do."

"Just because he got you a bunch of flowers?"

I shake my head. "No. I already liked him. This just makes me like him a little more."

Nate nods and clears the dinner table before starting on his homework. I stand in my foyer and try to get all the flowers in one picture, but there are too many; I end up having to take a panoramic to get them all in, and then I post the picture in our girls' text thread, which Audra has named "BJ, HJ, Doggy Style, and Cunnilingus."

Me: *so Ryder decided to get me some flowers...*

A message pops up: *Nova has named the conversation "QUIT BEING GROSS, AUDRA"*

Imogen: *Wow. I mean...WOW. He doesn't mess around, does he?*

Audra: *that there is a shitload of roses. I think he may like you, Laurel. Just a hunch.*

Audra has named the conversation "NOVA IS A FUN-SUCKER. SEX IS FOR WINNERS!"

Nova: *I am not a fun-sucker, and I always win at sex...when I choose to do the sex. I am just currently choosing to not do the sex.*

Nova: *IF ANYONE SAYS ANYTHING ABOUT ME AND JAMES I WILL LEAVE THIS THREAD AND BLOCK ALL OF YOU.*

Nova: *Also, Laurel: I think Audra is right...for once. Ryder just MAY like you a little bit.*

Audra: *SUCK HIS COCK*

Me: *Is that ALL you ever think about?*

Audra: *Pretty much, yeah. I'm kind of like a dude, in that I think about sex every thirty seconds.*

Imogen: *You should get that looked at.*

Audra: *I did get it looked at by a PhD, once. Turns out he wasn't a medical doctor, though. Who knew? All he could tell me was that I tasted good.*

Nova: *Imogen, how have you put up with her for so long?*

Imogen: *Because she says what I'm thinking but too chickenshit to say, and it makes me laugh.*

Me: *I'm gonna go call Ryder now.*

Audra: *SEND NUDES*

Me: *If I were to roll my eyes any harder, they'd roll back into my skull and I'd go blind.*

I check in on Nate, who is still doing home-work…along with a lot of doodling ninjas in the margins. He doesn't need my help, and I promised him that he could watch TV once he was done.

I go into my bedroom and lock the door, and then into my bathroom, which I also lock. I've moved vases all over the house at this point, so there are two vases of roses on my bathroom counter. I clench a flower in my teeth and take a fully clothed selfie, and send it to Ryder—only after double, triple, and qua-druple checking to be sure it's going to go to him.

And then I take off my shirt and take another

selfie in just my skirt and bra, with the rose in my teeth, and I send that one.

Next, I take off my bra, keeping one rose clenched in my teeth, and—this next bit of creativity requires a few attempts to get right—wrap one arm around my breasts to squeeze them together; my wrist covers my left nipple, and the rose covers my right nipple. I snap a photo once I get all my bits properly covered, and send it to Ryder.

Thankfully, these roses have had the thorns removed because next, I slip the rose between my breasts and use my arms to prop them together enough that the rose stays in place, and take another selfie like that, with everything from the waist up bared, the rose between my tits.

I send that one, and then wait.

It's only a matter of a minute or so before I see the message notification switch to "read" and then three bubbles bounce and jump.

Ryder: *You got the flowers, I take it?*

Me: *My whole house smells like roses.*

Me: *Where are you? What are you doing?*

Ryder: *At a job, wiring a built-in surround sound system into a man-cave.*

Me: *Are you alone?*

Ryder: *Yes.*

Me: *How alone?*

He sends me a five-second video of himself panning in a circle, and I can see he's surrounded by an explosion of cords and wires and speakers, there's a drill on the floor next to a giant toolbox, and there's a portable work light hooked onto the strut of a ladder. The room is empty, except for him, and the door is closed.

Ryder: *See? Totally, completely alone. I'm the only one at the site, as a matter of fact. Why?*

I go into my room and sit on my bed, and then FaceTime him, making sure the camera is close enough that all he can see is my face.

"Hi!" he says, as soon as the connection is established. It's blurry for a second, and the resolves into clarity.

"Hi, baby," I croon in a singsong voice. "I just wanted to say thanks for the flowers."

"You do mean the roses, right?" he says with a laugh.

I bring a rose into view on the screen. "Yep."

He grins. "I had to be sure. I'd never, ever be so fucking lame as to send a bullshit little bouquet of flowers you don't even like."

"Message received," I say. "Loud and clear."

He looks away, fiddling with something, and then looks back at the screen—the view shifts and I see the ceiling, and then Ryder from a different angle, and the view stabilizes. I realize he propped the phone on something so he could sit down and use both hands while talking to me, and I see his hands every now and then, doing something to a speaker just beneath the bottom edge of the screen.

"So," he says, grinning at me. "Whatcha doin now?"

I shrug, keeping the camera close. "I dunno. Just...hanging around." I arch an eyebrow. "Did you get all four of my selfies?"

His grin is heated. "Fuck yeah, babe. Saved 'em to their own folder titled 'hottest woman alive'."

I pull the phone away a little, just enough that he can tell I'm not wearing a top. "I like the title. You have photos of anyone else in there?"

He pauses in what he's doing. "What? Oh...no. Just...just you."

I pull the phone a little farther away, and now my boobs are entirely within in the frame—I prop them together a bit, for his benefit, since even fake—or, rather, enhanced—boobs sag to the side when you're lying down. "Just me, huh? So, I'm the hottest woman alive?"

"By several orders of magnitude." He blows out a breath. "Laurel...god. You make it seriously fucking impossible to get work done."

I shrug, and his eyes follow the movement of my

breasts. "I just wanted to…show my appreciation."

He rubs his jaw. "I might send you flowers every week if you're going to appreciate me this much."

I laugh. "Oh god, don't send this many again, though. You'll go broke!"

His eyes are fixed on my chest. "Worth every penny."

I bite my lip, hesitating, and then shake my tits at him just for fun. "I have an idea."

He narrows his eyes. "I can't do anything here, Laurel." He groans again. "I absolutely cannot jack off at a job site."

I can't help a laugh. "Oh my god, no. That's a terrible idea." I knead one breast, then the other. "What if you came over tonight?"

He blinks at me. "I…um. I won't be done here until late, Laurel. I really have to get this done." He runs his hand through his hair. "Fuck. Why do you have to tempt me?"

I hesitate, biting my lip, and then forge ahead with my naughty, impulsive idea. "To the left of my front door, in the landscaping bed, there's a little ceramic garden gnome. He's about a foot tall, and he's holding a lamp in one hand—the lamp actually lights up, it's solar powered."

He just arches an eyebrow. "Okay?"

"The gnome's name is Mr. Duckington the

Fourth," I tell him, "and he has a secret."

Ryder stops what he's doing and focuses on the camera. "Oh? Do I get to know what Mr. Duckington the Fourth's secret is?"

I grin. "Mr. Duckington the Fourth is wearing a red hat. If you take his hat off, there's a spare key for my house inside his head."

He lets out a slow breath. "I see. And are you officially inviting me to use your secret key to let myself in?"

I nod, feeling a little shy about the next part. "Do you remember our conversation about you waking me up in a really…ummm…exciting way?"

He groans a sigh. "Fuck yes, Laurel. I remember very, very clearly."

"I'm gonna get Nate to bed, and I'm going to go to bed myself pretty soon after he's in bed." I meet his eyes via the phone screen. "Nate could sleep through the Apocalypse, so don't worry about tiptoeing around."

"You're sure about this?"

I nod, gnawing on my lip again. "Yes, Ryder. I'm absolutely certain I want you to come over tonight."

"Even if it's super late, like after midnight?"

"Yes."

His grin widens, and he rakes his hand through his hair. "Do you sleep naked, Laurel?"

I shrug. "Not usually. But I will tonight."

"I think I'm about to finish this job in record time."

I caress my breasts with my free hand, and I enjoy the agonized desire on Ryder's face. "Don't rush so you make mistakes. I'll be here waiting for you whenever you get done, okay?"

"Fucking hell, Laurel. What did I ever do to deserve you?"

"I keep asking myself the same question about you."

"I'll see you as soon as humanly possible."

"Okay." I give him a look that drips with eager, seductive lust. "And Ryder?"

"Yeah, babe?"

"I hope you're…hungry."

He laughs, but it's a wicked sound, more of a growl than anything. "Laurel, my sweet, sexy darling, I am absolutely ravenous. I plan on *feasting*."

I shiver. "I can't wait."

He blows me a kiss, and I blow him one back, and then we end the call; I drop the phone to the bed beside me, grinning ear to ear. I put a pillow over my face and muffle a scream of excitement, kicking my feet.

I hear a knock on my bedroom door, then. "Mom? I need your help with my homework."

"Okay, I'll be right there!" I call.

I put my shirt back on sans bra, and go out to help Nate with his homework. When he's done, we lounge on the couch together and watch our favorite reality show, about a search for hidden treasure on a remote Canadian island. After two episodes of that, I send Nate to bed. While he's falling asleep, I clean the kitchen—do the dishes, wipe the counters, sweep the floor, then pick up around the living room and make sure everything is neat and tidy.

Solely for my own peace of mind, of course.

Ha, right. I'm totally spit-shining my house for Ryder.

I start on my room—which, to be honest, needed a bit of work anyway. There's a bunch of dirty clothes to put in the hamper, clean clothes that have been languishing in the laundry basket for weeks that I finally put away. I change the linens on my bed, putting clean flannel sheets on. Dust the top of my dresser, hang my collection of frequent rotation bras on a hanger in my closet instead of their usual place on my bathroom doorknob.

There—clean and tidy.

There's something missing, though.

I figure it out, and a smile fixes itself on my face.

I fish my bag of tea lights from under the kitchen sink and position them liberally around my room—on the dresser and side table, and in the bathroom, and then light them all. Then, I rip the heads off of a few roses and sprinkle petals on my bedspread, on the side table, on the bathroom counter and in the sink, and all over the floor in a trail from the bedroom door up to my bed.

My bedroom is now a candlelit sanctuary of romance.

I strip naked and climb into bed…and completely fail to fall asleep.

After an hour of lying there awake, I take my iPad from its drawer and binge on a few episodes of my guilty pleasure: Real Housewives. Finally, I feel myself fading, so I turn the iPad off and put it away.

I drift off, daydreaming of Ryder.

THIRTEEN

W^{H—} What?

Where am I?

Who am I?

Oh…ohhhh god. What's going on?

Why do I tingle all over? Why is my core aching? Why is my belly trembling? Why are my thighs quaking?

Something…something is touching me. Wet, firm, slithery, insistent. Flicking at my clit. Lapping at my seam.

Now there's a presence inside me, not enough to fill me or stretch me, just enough to slide between my lips and curl inside me just so, scraping and massaging against that elusive magical place deep inside me.

Ohhhhh fuck…

My eyes flutter, close, flutter, then I jerk awake as an orgasm slams through me, and I look down to see

Ryder between my thighs, two fingers inside me, slipping and gliding and thrusting and curling, his mouth suctioned around me. He pumps his fingers and his tongue flutters, and the orgasm shifts—at first, it was merely clitoral, just a slashing clenching wave of heat emanating from my center, but then as his fingers move and curl and thrust, the orgasm expands and detonates, becoming vaginal, and I can't help a small, shrill squeal. He doesn't let up as I come—if anything, he intensifies his efforts. My hips rock as I grind against his mouth, and I bite down on my lip to muffle my next scream. I tangle my fingers in his hair and grip hard, writhing rhythmically as the next wave of climax shatters me.

"Ryder!" I whimper.

He lifts up, grinning at me. "Hi, baby."

I hold on to his face as my climax fades, throwing me into shuddering spasms. "You…you're here."

He flicks his tongue against my sensitive center, and I jerk helplessly. "I sure am."

"Best way to wake up," I murmur.

"No kidding."

I shake my head. "No, you don't even understand. I woke up coming."

"Paying you back for when you woke me up with your mouth on my cock."

I grin at him, still gasping for breath. "I hope

you're prepared for a war of attrition, Ryder, because the next time you fall asleep, I'm doing that again."

He slowly laps at me with the flat of his tongue. "Then I'll have to increase my down payment by making you come again."

"You don't have to—ohhhhh god, holy Jesus—Ryder!" I cry out, hips already pumping as he flicks and circles my throbbing core with his tongue.

I wouldn't have known I was even capable of this many orgasms in a row, if not for Ryder's insistence and skill. I find myself rising to the edge of climax within a few seconds, but Ryder draws it out, this time. As I begin to grind and thrust against his face, whimpering, he slows down and uses his fingers inside me, then alternates between his mouth and fingers so I'm teetering on the edge and gasping and writhing.

When I'm there at the edge yet again, I grip his hair in my fist. "Don't you dare stop me this time, Ryder," I groan.

"Why not?"

"Because I want to come one last time so I can get your cock inside me."

"You think this is the last one?" he murmurs, smirking up at me. "What if I want two more from you? Or three?"

I shake my head as my hips writhe and thrust. "No—god, no. I need you."

He just hums a questioning sound—*uh-huh*—and the hum flutters through me, heightening the ache. I'm weak, limp, and shaking from the orgasms I've already had, but the one building inside me as Ryder licks and fingers me slowly to the edge is more powerful than any yet, and I know it's going to leave me shaking and screaming.

"I—oh god, oh fuck—Ryder, I'm gonna come."

"Good, honey, good. Let me have it."

I shake my head, biting my lip. "I...I'll scream," I groan, and then lose myself in ever-loudening whimpers and shrieks. "You have to muffle me, Ryder. I'm gonna come so hard I'll scream, and you have to muffle me."

He yanks the pillow out from under my head at the last second, and I bury my face in it and hold it against my mouth with both hands and let my hips thrust furiously against his face. His hands slide under my ass and he holds me by the hair as I arch off of the bed, screaming into the pillow. He grips my hips and pulls me against his mouth, and I'm sobbing through screams of an orgasm so intense I can't breathe for the power of it. I can't do anything except arch rigid, hips flexed, stomach tensed, lungs deflated, a silent scream trapped in my throat, wave after wave of orgasm shattering and pulsing and exploding, each wave so hard on the heels of the last that it's all one blasting supernova of climactic ecstasy—the kind of pleasure that's so exquisite, so intense, so powerful, so potent that it's almost painful.

When the waves begin to spread out enough that I can breathe, I suck in oxygen with an indrawn scream, hips sagging briefly, only to thrust upward with the renewed assault of his mouth and thrusting fingers.

My scream subsides, and I have to focus on breathing.

He feels me backing away from the edge of ecstasy, and this time, he lets me off the hook of orgasm entirely.

I gasp, limp and helpless, for I don't know how long. I feel Ryder still between my thighs, his beard tickling the tender silk of my inner thighs, his tongue lapping gently and slowly.

I have to stop him—I can't take any more.

And I need him.

God, I need him.

I tangle my fingers in his beard and haul him upward. He crawls almost reluctantly away from me and up my body. I still can't make the rest of my body move—I'm essentially paralyzed from the intensity of the last orgasm…

My hands work, and my mouth works, though. Mostly.

"Ryder," I gasp.

He grins. "Awake, now?"

I huff a laugh. "For the most part."

He's still entirely clothed, a fact that makes me frown unhappily.

"What?" he asks, seeing the frown on my face.

"You're not naked."

He laughs. "No, not yet. Is that a problem?"

I nod sloppily. "Yes. I'm dead—you killed me. But I need you, and I need you *now*."

He lifts up onto his knees, peeling off his T-shirt to bare his beautiful torso and heavy shoulders. "I can take care of that."

Jeans next, and then he's wearing nothing but socks and underwear—he makes quick work of the underwear, and now his gorgeous erection is bobbing bare, bulbous and gleaming.

I laugh, shaking a finger at him. "Ah-ah-ah. No socks during sex."

He slumps to one side, digging at his socks with a finger. "Is that your rule?"

I nod, reaching for him as he finally moves over me. "Yes. It's a rule I just made up right now, because if you're trying to fuck me while wearing nothing but socks, I'll laugh and it'll ruin the moment."

He brings himself into range of my hand, and I grasp him, stroke him greedily. "I don't know—I wouldn't mind laughing as I come."

"Maybe we'll try that, sometime. I'll tell jokes while you fuck me, and see if you can come while laughing."

He kneels between my thighs, reaching for my bedside table—he finds the condoms, opens one, and rolls it on. "That could be fun," he says. "One problem, though."

I frown, taking his shaft in both hands and guiding it against my opening. "What's that?"

"I won't be fucking you."

I frown even harder. "I'm confused."

His smile is…well, loving and tender is the only way to put it. "I won't be fucking you, Laurel." He bends, kisses me with exquisite gentility. "I'll be making love to you."

I turn the kiss hotter, demanding his tongue. "One problem with that," I whisper.

"What's that?"

I push against him, driving him into me in a single sudden thrust. "I don't want you to make love to me right now, Ryder."

"Laurel—" he gasps, head dropping against my breasts.

I push him away, rise up onto my knees. Ryder reaches for me, but I turn away from him on my hands and knees, presenting my ass to him. He moves up behind me, caressing with both hands. I reach under myself and find him, grasp him, bring him to me. Notch him against my opening, then turn and look at him over my shoulder as he palms my ass.

He groans, hands digging into the generous flesh of my hips, and he slams into me, hips slapping loudly against my backside. "Laurel…"

"Please," I groan, writhing backward. "Let me feel you go crazy."

He pulls back, moaning, holds there, just the tip of him left inside me. A few slow thrusts, more of a gentle flutter than anything else…and then, with a resounding spank, he drives in hard—I bury my face into the comforter and let myself wail as he hits me just right, and I touch myself with two fingers, heightening my own pleasure.

Drawing it out, Ryder is still torturing me with those ridiculous fluttering thrusts, only an inch or two sliding shallowly between my clamping channel. I whimper, sob, and now I'm riding the edge, hovering, needing him to fall over. I can't get myself there, not like this, not without Ryder.

"I need you," I sob. "Please, Ryder. Please—"

He caresses my bottom where his spanking has me pink and burning. "Please what, baby?"

"Come—let me feel you come. Fuck me, please, Ryder."

He groans, pushing into me all the way—*slowly*, so slowly I whimper in frustration.

He pulls back, just as slowly…and eases back in. "Like this?" he asks.

"No, god, no…Harder. Please!" I beg, my fingers flying, but I still can't fall over the edge, and I know I won't—not without him, not unless he comes first.

It's maddening, infuriating, delicious. I need him so I can come this one last time—and I've never known this, never needed something so badly as I need to feel him lose control, never needed anyone else's wildness to complete me.

I need Ryder—his completion is mine; his need is mine; his pleasure is mine.

I nod, letting myself move against him, timing it so I thrust backward as he slides in. "I can't—ohhh god, I can't come until you do."

"Didn't seem like you had that problem a minute ago," he grunts.

"It's new," I murmur. "I'm right on the edge, but I can't come—it's…it's like it's stuck."

"And you think me coming will trigger yours?"

I nod raggedly. "Yes," is all I can manage.

"Why?"

I sob. "I—I don't know!"

I'm losing the ability to control my movements, my building, fragmented, stuck orgasm ramping up into madness, into wild fury, making me shake all over, making my movements tremulous and desperate. Every muscle trembles, and I try to stay synched to his thrusts, but all control is gone, and I even need him for this—to take control.

He does.

God, he does.

He growls, and I feel him shudder and now I know it's time—I'm about to get exactly what I've been begging him for.

His grip on my hips tightens and I know I'll have marks—he yanks me backward and pounds in. I cry out, sob with each powerful thrust.

Again, again, and again, each movement more raggedly powerful than the last.

His grunts are nonstop, feral and wild.

He drives into me, grunting and groaning, cursing—and now the sounds become my name, chanted like a prayer: *Laurel—Laurel—LAUREL!*

I'm clamping around him, clenching, squeezing so hard I feel every inch of him.

"RYDER!"

"God—Laurel!"

I'm there, finally, but still teetering on the razor edge. Waiting, waiting, waiting for him. One last time, he slides into me and I ache, squeeze around him, shaking all over, sobbing, trying to push back into his thrust.

Ryder comes with a roar.

I feel it, feel him pulse, and he slams deep, stays there, pushing deeper and deeper. He can't go any deeper—yet I still need more, want more. I come around him, trying to scream but I'm too breathless, my lungs are empty, the oxygen forced out of my lungs.

How long does our merged orgasm last?

I lose track.

All I feel is him, all of him.

Finally, he gasps as if undone, and sags backward. Falls to his side, panting as if he just ran a hundred-meter dash.

I fall onto the bed as he releases me, and I'm still trembling, spasming, shaking, jerking with waves of orgasm. Ryder gathers me in his arms and holds me tightly, our breathing matched—even the ragged gasps for air are united, merged, becoming one.

"Ryder…" I whisper, lips brushing his beard, seeking his face.

"Hmmm?" he asks, vague with delirium.

I find his cheek, kiss just above his beard line, then alongside his nose, and then the other cheek, and his ear, nibble his earlobe and then kiss his shoulder and lick his neck, tasting the salt of his sweat.

Finally, I touch my lips to his.

"Thank you," I whisper.

I feel his lips curl in a smile, and I look up to see him looking at me with a puzzled, happy grin. "Thank you? Why are you thanking me?"

I cup his face. "Just...for you."

He shakes his head. "You're ridiculous."

I frown. "What do you mean?"

"This whole thing has been like some teenage boy's wet dream. You send me pictures of your tits, you FaceTime me topless, you invite me over and let me use your spare key—you ask me to wake you with sex? I come in here and find all these candles lit, rose petals everywhere, and you, naked—the most beautiful woman I've ever fucking seen in my life, and you're waiting for me? I get to put my mouth on you and taste your sweet, perfect pussy? And then I get to watch you come? And seriously, Laurel, the vision of you having an orgasm is pure sex, pure, raw erotic perfection. The way you moan, the way you move? Fuck, I could come without touching myself, just from that. And then, Laurel...and *then* you beg me to fuck you, and when I do, you make me come so hard I think I saw heaven."

I blink up at him, utterly melted. "You saw heaven?"

He grins, a bright, brilliant, ten thousand megawatt smile of utter joy. "Yeah, Laurel, I saw heaven—You, and me, coming together...that's heaven. I watched you come apart for me, and that's heaven. Us, together—that's heaven."

I bite his lower lip, lick it where I bit down. "You're a poet, Ryder."

He shakes his head. "No, you just inspire it in me."

My heart is exploding, shattering with a happiness I didn't even know was possible. "Ryder, I—" I swallow hard, keeping my eyes on his. "I fucking love you, Ryder."

He chokes, somewhere between a laugh and a sob. "That's the most beautiful thing I've ever heard anyone say in my life."

He nuzzles against me, hiding his face in the inky mass of my hair.

I pull away, look at him. There are wet streaks on his face, and I wipe at them. "Don't you dare hide that, Ryder."

"It's fucking embarrassing," he mutters.

"It's not." I kiss him, a dozen quick pecks to his face, and then a slow kiss on his lips. "Talk to me."

"I just..." He sighs, composing himself. "I never thought I'd hear that."

I frown at him. "But—"

"She never said it. She talked about things she loved about me, and I knew, in the rare moments she was lucid and made sense and was anything like even-keeled; I knew she felt it, somewhere in there. But she never said it."

"That's so wrong." I cup his face, brush under his eyes with my thumb, kiss him and kiss him and kiss him. "But I get it. I rarely ever heard it myself. Not never, but rarely." I touch his lips to stop him from saying it. "Don't—not until and unless you mean it wholly on your own. Don't just say it back." I drop my eyes. "I couldn't help myself. I don't know if you even want that with me—"

He silences me with a fierce, wild kiss. "You shut the fuck up with that mess, Laurel Madison," he growls.

"I just—"

He levers over me, his arm under my head, his body on mine, pinning me to the mattress and blocking out the world. "I was in love with you at the barbecue, Laurel. I was in love with you then and I fucking knew it, and that's why I tried to ghost you. I was a scared little pussy, because I didn't think a woman as incredible and perfect and sexy and fucking *normal* and *sane* as you could ever love me back."

I blink tears. "Ryder—"

"So yeah, I want that with you." He brushes his lips against mine in a fragment of a kiss. "I mean it wholly and on my own, not just to say it back, not because what we just did together somehow managed to be fucking and making love at the same time. I mean it because it's what's inside me, because you've managed to capture my heart, and I thought that was impossible—I thought that had been ruined for me forever."

"God, Ryder."

He bends down to kiss me again, and for a moment I'm lost in it.

I whimper, and Ryder pulls back, puzzled. "Already? All I did was kiss you."

I laugh, shaking my head. "No, it's not that. I couldn't come again if the world depended on it."

He frowns. "Then what?"

I glanced pointedly downward. "The condom is leaking on my thigh."

He rolls away with alacrity, vanishes into my bathroom and cleans up, and then comes out with a warm washcloth. Cleans me, kisses me, and tosses the washcloth into the bathroom.

"Want to know the unromantic part of all these candles?" I ask. "Having to blow them all out before bed."

Ryder chuckles. "I got it."

After the candles are all blown out, Ryder sits on the edge of the bed next to me; I reach up and pull at him. "Why are you up there?" I ask. "Come down here and snuggle me."

He hesitates. "I...I probably shouldn't."

Puzzled, I frown up at him. "Why not?"

"Because I'll fall asleep, and I can't guarantee I'll wake up before Nate this time."

"Oh."

"Yeah, oh." He bends down and kisses me. "I don't want to go, but—"

My heart clenches at the thought of him leaving. I let out a sharp sigh, and realize there's no real choice to be made here. I sit up, wrap my arms around his neck and haul him down to the bed. "So don't."

He laughs, struggling against my hold on him. "But, Laurel, you said—"

I wrap my legs around his waist and cling to his neck with both arms, kissing him everywhere I can reach as I keep him trapped in my embrace. "I know what I said," I say between kisses. "But I realized it doesn't apply anymore."

He stops struggling. "It doesn't?"

I shake my head. "Nope." I meet his eyes. "Having admitted that I'm in love with you changes things."

"How so?"

"Well, it's obvious Nate is completely enamored with you, and you seem to like him back—"

"Falling in love with you means loving that kid, too, Laurel." He crawls onto the bed, but stays on his hands and knees above me. "Just needed to point that out. Continue."

I feel my throat close. "Stay, Ryder." I shrug, unable to speak properly. "That's it. Just…stay. Please."

It's his turn to brush dampness away from my cheeks. "If you're sure."

"I've never been more sure of anything in my life."

He lowers himself to the bed, and we make a mess of the rose petals as we slide under the covers and tangle ourselves together. I nuzzle into him, seeking the perfect place…I find it, that nook in the shelter of his arms where I fit like I'm the puzzle piece crafted for him. I sigh, and he murmurs in similarly wordless happiness.

We drowse and flit and drift; a thought bubbles up and out of my mouth. "Hey, Ryder? Are you… clean?"

He hums an affirmative response. "Yeah. Got tested the day after we met."

"Me too."

"Really?"

"Mmm-hmmm. I went to a clinic before work the next day. Just to bc sure."

"Why do you ask?"

"Because I'm on birth control."

"Okay."

I smile against his chest. "Just saying—we're both clean, and I'm on the pill."

He grumbles, an unintelligible mumble, and then I feel him twist, and I open my eyes to meet his. "Are you saying what I think you're saying?"

I nod. "Mmmm-hmmm."

"You and me, and nothing between us?"

I nod again. "Mmmm-hmmmm."

He rests his head back against the pillow. "Have I ever told you how much I love the way you think?"

"May have mentioned it at some point."

"Fair warning, I'll probably last about thirty seconds like that."

I wiggle against him. "Good." I lift up and kiss his chest, then burrow back down against his heavy, powerful chest. "Sex doesn't always have last a long time to be good."

He rumbles a laugh. "You have no idea how good it is to hear you say that."

We drift again, and this time, I'm content to let sleep steal over me and drag me under.

I'm in that place just before falling asleep, that place where you're heavy and warm, where you have no thoughts, just contentment.

"Hey." Ryder's voice, vague and distant.

"Mmm?"

"I love you, Laurel."

I can only sigh, rolling to my side with Ryder behind me. I clasp my hand over his, tangling my fingers
into his, and he clutches my breast possessively, my
heartbeat under his palm; I've never been so happy to
be the little spoon—I feel utterly safe, filled with joy
as I sink into slumber in the protective, loving shelter
of Ryder's arms.

FOURTEEN

G RAY LIGHT STREAMS THROUGH MY WINDOW—THE silver of predawn haze.

Rose petals are strewn everywhere, unlit tea lights on every surface of my bedroom.

For a moment, I'm disoriented—I'm in my bed, in my bedroom. But I'm not alone.

There's a big hard body behind me, a strong hand resting on my hip. Breath on the back of my neck, slow and heavy and rhythmic. A beard tickling my spine between my shoulder blades.

Ryder.

Hey. I love you, Laurel.

God, was that real?

I look over my shoulder at him and know that, yes, it was real.

The clock on my nightstand says 6:01a.m.

Plenty of time to go back to sleep.

I wiggle my ass back into him, and he hums

wordlessly, tightening his grip on my hip. I shift, curling into the comma of his body. Close my eyes and drift.

I'm not sure if I fall asleep or not, just that there's a time of warmth, a fuzzy, hazy fog of drowsiness. An almost drugged sort of happy, joyful, contentedness of not-quite unconsciousness.

Then I feel Ryder's hand clutch my hip. Tighten, release. I hear a murmur from him, feel it on my back. He sighs. Shifts. His hand slides up my side, rests on my belly. After a moment like that, I wonder if he's falling back asleep.

But then he murmurs again. "Laurel?" It's muzzy, sleepy.

"Mmm-hmmm."

"Thank god. Thought I'd dreamed it."

"Mmmm-mmmm."

His hand drifts up to cup my breast, and I smile. I feel him behind me, his breathing telling me he's fully awake now. Something else is awake, too, and my secret smile widens. I don't move, just drowse in the silver shine of dawn, and bask in the rough clutch of his hand, and the hard shelter of his body, and the delicious warmth of our bodies under the covers.

He hardens to full arousal, nestled between the squishy globes of my ass. I draw my knees up and push back against him.

"Mmmm…Laurel."

I lift my upper leg, and he fits a hand between us. Touches my opening. I grasp him, guide him in.

Has anything, ever, felt so perfect as him bare inside me?

Hot and hard and thick, skin on skin and nothing else. I whimper immediately, and he groans. His fingers touch me, and I would tell him I don't need the extra stimulation, but it feels too good so I say nothing. Just move with him. Writhe with him, on my side, him behind me.

It stays slow—he never speeds up past a slow gentle glide. I push back into his thrusts, shuddering as we reach the brink together within seconds. There's no drawing it out, no need, no desire to. We fall over the edge together—I gasp, reaching behind my head to clasp his, twisting to kiss him raggedly, awkwardly as we move.

I roll against him and sob, clutching at his beard. He lets out a soft, shuddery gasp, and that's all the warning I need or want. That gasp, that quiet, gentle, tender in-breath, and then I'm flooded with heat. I feel him tense inside me, pushing deeper, and I'm squeezing in spasms around him, and I feel the spurt as he comes inside me, filling me with his seed. Him coming inside me sets off my own orgasm, and I can't even whimper or sob for the breathlessness of us like this.

We shudder together.

"I—I…" He's barely able to formulate words. "Laurel…god—I love you, I love you, I love you."

I feel him inside me, the wetness trickling out of me.

"Can we wake up like this every morning?" I murmur. I huff a laugh. "Yes, I know—you love the way I think."

"That would be…heaven," he whispers.

"I wasn't being…it wasn't hyperbole," I say. "I know this is jumping into things fast, but…I really do want to wake up with you like this every single morning."

"Say that again when we're not both still shaking from having just come together."

"I don't need to."

He's still inside me, and he finally pulls away. "Laurel, I—"

I look at him, thinking he's going to tell me it's too much too fast. "Ryder, you don't have to—"

He palms my face. "Waking up with you every morning sounds like heaven." He kisses the tip of my nose. "Let me clean you up."

He grabs the washcloth, rinses it with hot water, squeezes it out, and then cleans me with it, each touch gentle and loving.

I pull him down to the bed. "Stay here."

He frowns. "Where are you going?"

"I'm going to make you breakfast."

He grins, and grabs me, hauls me down, kissing me stupid. "Can I make one request?"

I squirm out of his hold. "Anything, love."

"Do it wearing nothing but my shirt?"

I take his T-shirt and shrug into it—it's a plain black V-neck, and it's big enough that it hangs to mid-thigh; the V-neck scoops low, showing off my cleavage. I'm not sure I've ever in my life felt sexier, more beautiful, and more desired.

"Ta-da!" I say, doing a little dance for him. "How's this?"

"Fucking spectacular."

I grin. "Take a shower. I'll make coffee and breakfast, and then after Nate's on the bus, maybe you can help me get clean."

He growls, a feline, rolling-R growl that's at once comedic and lascivious. "I really, really, *really* love the way you think, Laurel Madison."

I sashay out of the bedroom, swaying my butt for him; I make a quick stop in the other bathroom to give myself a little extra cleaning—because *damn*, the man made a serious mess of me, and then head into the kitchen. I hear the shower going a few seconds later, as I grind beans for coffee.

"Mom?" Nate's voice, sleepy and confused.

I kiss him on the forehead as he slumps into a chair at the table. "Hi, honey. Sleep well?"

"Uh-huh," he mumbles. His eyes take in my shirt, and then flick toward my room, where the shower can be heard. "Ryder's here?"

I nod. "Yes, he is."

"He stayed the night?"

I look at Nate. "Yes." I risk a hesitant smile. "Is that okay?"

Nate nods. "Yeah. I like him, and I think he's in love with you."

"I think so too, buddy," I say, unable to hide my joy.

Nate grins. "Are you in love with him back?"

I nod. "Yeah." I ruffle Nate's hair. "Is that okay with you?"

He nods again. "I'm glad."

"You are?"

"Sure. I want you to be happy, and you and Ryder being in love makes you happy."

I kiss him again, and he wiggles away. "I love you, Nate. You know that no matter what happens, that will never, ever change, right?"

He rolls his eyes at me. "Duh. You're my mom."

I laugh. "Exactly!"

I make eggs and toast, and Ryder comes out in

his jeans, no shirt, barefoot, his hair wet and slicked back, beard beaded with water droplets. I only just suppress a moan of appreciation at the raw and rugged sexiness that is Ryder McCann—and my delirious happiness at him being in my home like this.

It feels pretty much perfect, Ryder and Nate and I sitting at my little kitchen table, eating, talking, joking. Nate finishes his breakfast and goes to brush his teeth and get dressed for school. Ryder starts cleaning up from breakfast as I check Nate's backpack, make sure he finished his homework, and then put together a quick cold lunch for him. Nate is pestering Ryder about going to play paintball, and Ryder is ducking his questions, which I realize is because Ryder has plans that he doesn't want to spoil by telling Nate.

And then the doorbell rings.

I'm puzzled for a second, and then dread rockets through me.

No, no, no.

Not now. Not today.

Half of me wants to tell Ryder to hide in my room just so I don't have to deal with the drama, and the other half wants me to ask Ryder to answer the door for me.

Ryder senses something. "Laurel?"

I close my eyes and sigh. "No," I moan. "Please no, not today—not like this."

"Want me to answer it?" Ryder asks.

I shake my head. "No, I'll handle it."

"Want me to go into your room? Give you privacy?"

"I'm not hiding you, or us." I stand up and go to the door, summoning every last ounce of inner strength that I have.

I'm still naked except for Ryder's T-shirt.

The doorbell ding-dongs again. "Laurel?" Paul's voice. He's angry. There's a note in his voice that I recognize, and I don't like it. "Whose truck is that?"

I open the door a sliver, just enough that I can slide my head through. "What do you want, Paul?"

He's disheveled. His clothes show signs of having been worn for several days. He's unshaven, red-eyed. Dark circles rim his eyes. A snarl curls his upper lip.

"Who the fuck is here?" he demands.

"None of your business."

"Mom? Who is it?" I hear Nate ask.

I sigh. I don't want Nate to see his father like this. I turn around and glance at him. "Nate...why don't you go into your room, okay? Please?"

"The bus is going to be here in a minute."

"I'll drive you."

He frowns, sensing something amiss. "Mom—what's happening? Who is that at the door?"

"Nate?" Paul pushes at the door. "It's me—it's Dad."

Nate frowns even harder. "Dad? Why are you here? It's not your turn until next weekend." He takes a few steps closer to the door.

Ryder is behind him, a towel dangling from his hand. "Say the word, babe—I'll handle him," he murmurs, his voice pitched low—he's got his cell phone up, recording this.

"Who is that?" Paul demands, sounding unhinged, pushing at the door.

I put my weight against it. "Go away, Paul. This is enough."

"LET ME IN!" Paul shoves violently at the door.

"Mom?" Nate asks, his voice tremulous. "Why is Dad acting like this? He sounds scary."

I let my eyes plead for me as I fight to keep Paul out. "Paul—please. You're scaring Nate."

"WHO IS IN MY HOUSE? WHO'S BEEN TOUCHING YOU?" Paul shouts, snarling, raving.

I feel hands on my waist—Ryder pulling me away. I resist. "No, Ryder. Don't."

He hesitates, one hand on the door all it takes to keep Paul out. "Why not?" he asks, anger hardening his features.

"It's—it's my mess. I don't want you to—to have to deal with it."

He grins at me, light and unworried despite the anger I see in him. "Babe—this is what I'm here for. Part of being your boyfriend is dealing with your crazy ex." He gently pushes me backward, out of the way, but I cling to his arm. "I've *got* it."

"Ryder, I—"

He touches my lips, the cell phone pocketed now. "I won't hurt him."

I roll my eyes, despite myself. "That's not what I'm worried about."

Ryder lets his fury bleed through. "You should be. I'd really like to—" He glances at Nate, who's watching and listening. "Nate, buddy. Why don't you let your mom and I deal with this, and then we'll talk, okay?"

Nate nods, turns wordlessly and goes into his room, slamming the door.

"OPEN THIS FUCKING DOOR!" Paul screeches.

As soon as Nate's door is closed, I let go of Ryder and back away. "Make him go away, Ryder," I say, my voice hard.

Ryder puts his foot against the base of the door and takes a big step away—Paul is hammering and pushing and kicking, cursing and shouting. I see him mentally count to three, and then Ryder moves his foot, and Paul tumbles inside, off balance at the sudden removal of resistance. He stumbles, and Ryder is there, his big hard hands grabbing Paul by the shoulders and shoving him effortlessly backward, back outside. Paul staggers backward onto the stoop, trips, and falls backward into the grass; Ryder stomps through the doorway to tower over Paul—Ryder seems ten feet tall, somehow, and every muscle is bulging, straining, raw furious power making him positively vibrate.

Bending, Ryder curls one fist into Paul's shirt and hauls him upright, but keeps him off-balance. Paul is abruptly silent.

"Listen to me, you crazy fuck," Ryder snarls. "As it stands, you still get to see your kid. What you don't get to do is show up here, ever again."

"Who—who the hell are you?" Paul stammers, somehow finding the gumption to sound pissed, despite the fury in Ryder's eyes and the obvious threat in his posture and the power in his body.

"Who I am isn't important." Ryder's voice is calm—a deadly, razor-sharp kind of quiet. "What *is* important is that you understand one thing—you are not welcome here—*ever*."

"What are you gonna do?" Paul sneers. "Beat me up if I come back?"

"Much as I'd love to, no." Ryder shakes him. "What will happen is you'll lose what few rights you have left. Maybe you don't really care all that much about the kid in there, but—"

"Don't you talk about my son!" Paul shouts, struggling.

"Quit your squawking, fuck-face," Ryder snarls, and Paul, pale, goes silent. "Here's how this is going to go, okay? You listening? You go away, and you never show up here again. In the meantime, Laurel, whom you will never contact, never look at, whom you will never even *think* about again, will be making a visit to the court, where she'll show the appropriate authorities the video I took of you acting like a fucking lunatic. If you manage to even acquire supervised visitation privileges, I'll be surprised."

Paul goes limp, the fight going out of him. "Let me go."

Ryder keeps him in his grip. "One wrong move and you'll be shitting your own teeth." He lets go and crosses his arms, standing between Paul and my house.

"I'm sorry," Paul whines. "I just—"

I stand behind Ryder. "Go home, Paul."

"I just—I want to talk to you." He's shifted tracks now, trying to wheedle and charm. "I just wanted to talk to you, and I saw the truck and I just—"

"This isn't your house, Paul," I snap. "It never has been and never will be. Who I have in my home is none of your business, and never will be."

"You don't get to fucking—" Paul starts, venomous, and then cuts off and starts over, calmer. "You're my *wife*, Laurel. I don't fucking care what some judge or some piece of paper says. You're *mine*—"

"You better watch yourself, bud," Ryder says, his voice a vicious snarl.

I move aside a little, my own anger getting the better of me. "I'm *not* your wife, Paul! I stopped being *yours* a long time ago. You lost that *years* ago, long before we ever got a divorce. I'm not your wife. I'm not your friend. I'm *nothing* to you—except the mother of your child. We will *never* be together again, Paul. Get that into your head!"

Paul surges forward, eyes blazing, spittle flying. "You fucking played me! You lured me in and seduced me and made me think I could be something I wasn't, and then you dropped me like a rotten egg!"

"What the hell are you talking about?" I'm beyond baffled now; he's not making a lick of sense.

"You got fat, you stupid whore! After you had that brat of a kid of ours, you let yourself go! How was I supposed to feel any desire for you or pretend I loved you when you looked like that? And then once I finally got rid of you, suddenly you look like that!" He gestures at me, at my chest. "You dump me like I'm fucking garbage, and then get all—all sexy? You're hotter now than when we met! It's not fucking fair!"

Ryder steps into Paul's face. "A very thin thread of control is all that's stopping me from breaking you like a twig, Paul." His hand lifts, curls into Paul's shirt, and shoves, once, hard—Paul goes airborne several feet, hits the ground tumbling backward, rolling to land with a thunk on the sidewalk.

I'm shaking, only barely keeping it together. I stop Ryder with a hand to his chest, kneeling in the grass next to Paul. I look at him, and then back at Ryder, who is watching me, protective and powerful and watchful—and peace flows through me.

"Once upon a time, Paul, what you just said would've destroyed me." My voice is utterly calm, my eyes fixed on his. "Once upon a time, when I cared what you had to say. Once upon a time, when you had power over me. Once upon a time, when I was weak." I meet his eyes, and feel only pity, now. "I'm not that woman anymore, Paul. You don't have the power to hurt me. I'm sorry you feel the way you feel, but none of that is my fault. I did everything I could make us work, and I wasn't ever enough for you. So I moved on. It's been over between us for a long time."

Paul's eyes search me, but he says nothing.

"And you know something else? Yes, Paul, I look better now than I ever have. You know why? Because I *feel* better. I'm strong inside myself. I don't need your approval, and I don't care about your dis-approval." Paul reaches for me, but I shrink away. "Don't touch me—*ever*. Don't mistake me being calm for accepting this behavior. I've done my best to facilitate you having a relationship with Nate be-cause you're his father, and regardless of how you've treated me, I know you love him and I want him to know his father. But this? This is unacceptable. You've frightened him, and I'm not okay with that." I harden my voice and stand up, move backward away from him. "I will be asking that your time with Nate be supervised from here on out. Furthermore, if you ever come here again I'll get a restraining or-der against you—it's not an idle threat, but rather a promise."

Paul stands up, scrambling to his feet—I feel Ryder tense beside me, and Paul holds up his hands. "I'm leaving."

I lean into Ryder. "I really do hope you find the help you need, Paul."

He hangs his head. "Don't, Laurel—just fucking...don't."

I shrug. "Okay, then." I sigh, resting my head against Ryder's shoulder. "Goodbye, Paul."

He rakes his hand through his disheveled hair, gets into his car, and, after a long lingering glance at me, drives away.

I wait until he's out of sight, and then I turn into Ryder and wrap my arms around his neck and bury my face in him and breathe him in.

"You okay, Laurel?"

I shudder, but nod. "Yes."

He cups my face. I look at him, let him see all of me as I am in this moment: vulnerable, frightened, upset, but okay. "Are you sure you're okay?"

I nod again. "Yes. I'm okay. A little shaken, but honestly more pissed off than anything." I tighten my arms around his neck and kiss him. "Thank you for being there for me. For protecting me."

He holds me against him, his hands on my back. "I wanted to break his face so fucking bad."

"I know," I murmur. "But that would've only made things worse in the long run."

"That's why his skull is still intact." Ryder glances down at me. "I'm not a violent guy, and I don't typically have a bad temper, but if you threaten me or mine, you'll see the ugly side of me."

I grin up at him. "I don't know—I wouldn't call it ugly. It kinda turned me on." I shiver against him. "It was all caveman and alpha and sexy."

His fingers tighten. "We're on your front lawn, woman. Don't turn me into an exhibitionist."

"Turn *you* into an exhibitionist?" I say, laughing. "I'm the one wearing nothing but a T-shirt out here.

You move your hand wrong, my neighbors are gonna get a nice view of my bare ass."

"Mine," he growls, turning me away, shielding me with his bulk.

I laugh as he throws me over his shoulder and carries me inside, possessively grabbing my ass. "Ryder! Put me down!"

He puts me down once we're inside. "Ooga-ooga. Mine! Ryder no share."

I laugh again, gazing up at him. "For real. You being all possessive and protective is a hell of a turn-on."

Ryder's eyes darken. "Good to know."

I hear Nate's door creak open. "Mom?"

I hurry over to him, kneeling in front of him. "I'm sorry you had to see that, Nate."

"Dad isn't a nice person, is he?" Nate asks.

I sigh. "That's kind of hard to answer, buddy." I think very carefully before answering. "Your father loves you, Nate—I have absolutely no doubt about that. He's just…sick, I guess. He needs help to get better, but he won't do it."

"Why not?"

"I…he…I don't know. He just wants to pretend he's fine when he's not, I think." I hug him. "You spending time with him is going to work a little differently, though, I think. I'm not sure I can trust you alone with him anymore—not after this."

Nate nods thoughtfully. "That's probably a good idea."

I tilt my head and frown. "Why do you say that?"

He shrugs. "Well, just that I don't really think Dad is very responsible. He kinda sucks at being a dad."

I'm torn between wanting to laugh at his blunt observation and wanting to cry that he's had to make the observation at all. "Why's that, buddy?"

"He forgot to make me dinner last weekend. He was in his office working or something, and he just let me watch movies all day. I made myself a P-B-and-J for lunch but then it was dinnertime and Dad was still in his office with the door locked and I was hungry and he just told me to find a snack or something."

I let out a sharp sigh. "Nate, are you serious?" My throat is closed, hot and thick. Guilt rifles through me.

He hears it in my voice. "What? I was fine. I made myself mac 'n cheese."

"You shouldn't have had to, Nate." I try vainly to hold back tears. "Anything else like that you haven't told me?"

"I didn't want you to worry, Mom, that's all. I can take care of myself."

"That's not the point, Nathaniel—or, actually, that's exactly the point! I am your mother—it's my job to worry about you. If I knew your father was locking himself in his office I wouldn't have let you go over there. You're there to spend time with him, and he's locking himself in his office? What's he even doing in there?" I'm working myself up into a rage, and I have to take a few deep breaths and force myself to calm down. "What else, Nate?"

He just shrugs. "He does that a lot. He says he's working, but I don't know what he's doing because he won't let me in there." He scratches his hair. "I have to remind him to buckle his seatbelt, and sometimes in the mornings he doesn't wake up, so I get myself breakfast, and all he has is unhealthy junk food cereal that you say is poison. One time I tried to make scrambled eggs, but they got burned and I had to throw the whole pan away because I was afraid Dad would find out I'd burned his pan and he'd get mad. He brought me to a birthday party at Brian's house one time, and he forgot to come get me. I don't know his phone number so I just stayed the night at Brian's house and he came to get me at like lunchtime the next day."

"*What?*" I screech. "He left you at your friend's house overnight?"

Nate just shrugs and nods. "It was fine, because Brian's parents are really cool, so I got to sleep in a sleeping bag in a hammock in his backyard. Plus, Mr.

McKenna made us banana chocolate chip pancakes for breakfast the next morning."

"Why didn't you call me?" I say, still choking back tears.

"Well, I don't know your number either. Who even memorizes phone numbers anymore? And plus, I didn't want you to worry. It's not like I was out on the street or something, Mom. I was with my friend and his parents."

I can't help a laugh. "You are far too precocious for your own good, Nathaniel Paul Madison." I wrap him in a hug. "Anything else you haven't told me because you didn't want me to worry?"

He shrugs again. "Um…" He gives me a sheepish look. "That kinda stuff happens a lot. Pretty much every time I go over there, he forgets I'm there, or that he is supposed to be taking care of me."

I grab his shoulders and squeeze. "Every single time I picked you up, I would ask how it went, and you said fine. I would ask if your dad took good care of you, and you always said yes." I can't stop the tears. "You should've *told* me, Nate. How can I protect you if I don't know there's a problem?"

He lunges into me, wrapping me up in a tight hug. "I'm sorry, Mom. I just—I didn't want you to worry."

"Were you trying to protect him?" I ask, pulling back.

He shrugs. "Not really. I never have much fun anyway. He lets me watch TV pretty much the whole time, but I get bored of that after a few hours, except there's nothing else to do. I have toys there, but they're all dumb baby toys because Dad has no clue what I like to do."

"Why wouldn't you want me to worry about you, Nate?"

Yet again, the roll of a shoulder. "You work a lot, and until you met Ryder you were always lonely, and I thought if I told you Dad was so irresponsible, you wouldn't let me go over there. And if I didn't ever go over to Dad's, you'd always have me all the time, and I guess I thought that me going to Dad's for visitation meant you'd have some time to yourself when you don't have to deal with me. I know I'm kind of a handful."

I break into sobs—shoulders shaking, incoherent, ugly crying. Ryder is standing beside me, his hand on my shoulder—he knows he can't take this from me, that he can't make it better, that all he can do is be there for me, so that's what he does. It takes a few minutes, but I manage to get myself under control again, and I wipe at my eyes.

"Nate, you listen to me, okay? I'm going to tell

you the truth—the adult version." I brush his hair out of his eyes. "I never wanted to let you go over there— but I had to, because he's your father and he has rights, legal rights to see you, ordered by the court. But he also has rights simply because he's your father—you deserve the chance to know him, to spend time with him, and I thought...well, I guess I thought he was actually using that time to hang out with you. Yes, Nate, I was lonely sometimes, and yes, I work a lot to take care of us, but letting you go over to your Dad's was the worst and hardest part of every month. I was always sad when I dropped you off, and excited when I got to go pick you up, and worried the entire time you were with him." I hold his shoulders. "You're my son, so yeah, I love you because I'm your mom. But I also just like being with you. You're fun, and you're funny, and I love watching our shows together and making dinner together. I have never, ever, not even *one* single time, *ever* felt like having you around was something I had to *deal* with."

"So...I don't have to go over there anymore?" he asks.

"Well, it's not that simple. I can't just not let go you. I have to talk to the court, and you'll probably have to tell some people all the stuff you told me, and I may have to have the McKennas write a letter explaining that he forgot to pick you up. What will

end up happening, most likely, is that you'll have
what's called supervised visitation. I'll bring you to
the library or something like that, and you'll spend
an hour or two with your father there, with someone assigned by the court to supervise the visitation,
and then when the time is up, you'll come back home
with me."

He eyes me, and then Ryder. "Are we gonna go
live with Ryder?"

I smile and look at Ryder. "Um…maybe someday? I don't know. He'll probably be here sometimes,
and yeah, we'll go over there sometimes, but will we
live there? I honestly don't know. I just know Ryder
is going to be around a lot more." I smile at Nate. "Is
that okay with you?"

Nate rolls his eyes at me. "Dude, Mom, you've
asked me this like fifty hundred times already. Yes, it's
okay." He shrugs, a sly smile on his face. "I think it
would be cool if we lived with him. I bet you have all
sorts of cool stuff at your house, huh?"

Ryder laughs. "I think that would be pretty cool,
too, but it's a bit more complicated than that. You and
your mom have your own house where you live." He
ruffles Nate's hair. "But yes, I do have a lot of cool
stuff. I live on a big old farm, and there's tractors to
take apart, a big barn to climb in, and there's even a
rope swing. In the summer, one of my favorite things

to do is swing out and jump off into the creek."

Nate jumps up and down, giddy with excitement. "MOM! We can just move there, right? We don't need this old dump."

I laugh. "Whoa, there. I happen to like this house; so don't go calling it a dump. And we can't just invite ourselves to live with Ryder. Like he said, it's more complicated than that."

Nate rolls his eyes. "Remember what I said about when adults say things are complicated? It just means you don't want to explain it."

I laugh again. "Okay, fine. You're right. The complicated part is that Ryder and I are just starting to really get to know each other. It's a little soon for us to move in together."

Nate waves a hand in an airy dismissal. "Nah. You guys are totally in love. You're gonna get married. We should just move in."

"Nate—" I start.

Ryder interrupts me. "I mean, I'm sort of on his side."

I stand up slowly, my eyes on Ryder's. "What?"

He grins. "I know what I know, baby girl."

I cross my arms and arch an eyebrow at him. "And what is it you know?"

"That it may be crazy, but I'm all-in. As far as I'm concerned, you guys could move in today. One phone call and I'll have the guys with their trucks and trailers, and we'll have your shi—your stuff moved in by dinnertime." He tucks a lock of my hair behind my ear. "But I also get that you may not be ready for that step, and I get that you may not want to leave your house. This is your home, and I can't expect you to just pick up and move in with me. I'm just saying—it may be a little soon, but this whole thing has happened whirlwind fast, and this is par for the course for us, it seems to me."

I search his face, and all I see is genuineness, openness. He's totally serious.

"Ryder—don't—don't…" I'm not going to cry again. Nope, nope, nope.

I turn away, pace into the kitchen and pour myself a fresh cup of coffee, just for something to do while I gather myself. I stir the coffee, even though I didn't put cream or sugar into it.

I feel Ryder behind me.

"Laurel, I didn't mean to upset you, I just—"

I turn, putting my butt to the edge of the counter, holding my coffee mug as a shield between us—mainly for the sake of Nate's innocence. "You're serious?"

"Abso-fucking-lutely," he murmurs, quietly so only I can hear him.

"It's crazy!"

He just grins and shrugs—and the way he does this reminds me of Nate. They're two peas in a pod, in a lot of ways. "Yeah, but when you know, you know. You know?"

I laugh, shaking my head. "Today?"

"Or whenever."

I bite my lip. "Have you thought about this, like really thought about it? Me moving in means Nate moving in. It means you're assuming the role of stepdad, for all intents and purposes." I stare up at him. "It means me and Nate all up in your business, all the time."

He nods. "That has crossed my mind, and I'm not going to lie, being stepdad or whatever to Nate is a little intimidating to think about, but only because I'd be worried about fu—about messing it up."

"I don't mind!" Nate says.

We both laugh, and I cup Ryder's cheek. "News flash, baby—you're gonna mess up. That's called parenting."

"I have zero experience."

I nod, smiling. "I know, but you'll do fine."

Ryder frowns. "Okay, so…is this happening? Are you—are you saying yes?"

I nod. "It's absolutely crazy. It's probably a little irresponsible of us, but like you said, when you know, you know. You know?" I turn to Nate. "What do you think?"

"Can I stay home from school and help pack?"

"I guess that answers that question." I laugh, and have to step away from Ryder so I can think clearly. "This feels rash."

"It's totally rash and impulsive," Ryder says. "But it also is unquestionably the right thing, as far as I'm concerned."

I glance at him. "Do you have enough room for us?"

Ryder laughs. "Yes, Laurel, I have enough room."

I frown at him. "Why is that so funny?"

"Because you haven't seen where I live. It's a giant old six-bedroom farmhouse. It's always been way too much house for one lonely old bachelor, but I bought the place because the barn was already set up as a mechanic's workshop, and it's got a giant pole barn too, so I have somewhere to store projects." He shrugs. "I also just fell in love with the property. It's beautiful, and peaceful, and also not even half an hour from this area where most of my jobs are."

I look at Ryder, and then at Nate, and try to imagine us all living together all the time…

And it's not difficult at all.

"I have a question," Nate says.

"What's that?" I ask.

"Can we get a dog?"

FIFTEEN

RYDER AND NATE ARE WITH JESSE, FRANCO, AND JAMES at a guys-only paintball extravaganza; Nova, Imogen, Audra, and I are with James's daughters Nina and Ella, and the six of us are at a girls-only spa day extravaganza; it's all part of an elaborate plan to surprise Jesse. The men are playing paintball, the women are getting our hair and nails done, and then, later this evening—as far as the men know—we're all going to meet at a local restaurant for what we're calling a "family dinner."

Our original idea was to make Jesse think it was a fake birthday thing, but then we realized how stupid that was, so now we're making him think it's just a get-together after we all have our respective outings. Nova has rented out a private room at a restaurant and the six of us women spent the first part of the day decorating it: there's a tower made of packages of diapers, a bunch of rattles and baby bottles, pink napkins and blue napkins—because obviously Imogen doesn't know the gender yet. And, to top it all off, a massive sheet cake with pink and blue icing, and the words "Congratulations, Daddy!" on it in pink and blue icing.

None of the men know any of this, though. We figured the best way to make sure it stayed a surprise for Jesse was to not let any of the men know, and keep the planning in-house, so to speak.

We're all super excited.

I'm in a spa chair between Audra and Nova, and we're all getting pedicures, the last of our pampering treatments.

Imogen, on the other side of Audra, leans forward to look at me. "So, Laurel…how are things with Ryder?"

I bite my lip, because I've been sitting on my news this whole time, and I'm dying to share it with my friends; I glance at Nina and Ella, James's daughters, who are raptly listening to every word spoken.

"Um, actually…" I grin. "Nate and I are moving in with him tomorrow."

There's about ten seconds of dead silence, and then a chorus of responses from everyone, mostly along the lines of *"What?!"*

Audra narrows her eyes at me. "Are you for real?"

I can only nod. "I know it's a little soon, but…" I

shrug. "It just feels right."

"How did this come about?" Imogen asks. "I know you were trying to figure out if it was safe to let yourself fall for him, but it's quite a jump from that to moving in together."

"Not that much of a jump, honestly," I say. "We both realized the whole idea of 'letting' yourself fall in love is stupid, mainly because we'd both already fallen in love. So the first step was admitting to ourselves, and each other, that we're in love, and that it's safe."

Nova snorts. "There's nothing safe about falling in love."

The other three of us all stare at Nova.

"Someone is bitter," Audra says.

"I'm not bitter," Nova snaps. And then she laughs. "Okay, fine, I'm bitter." She waves at me. "Continue, and please ignore my outburst of un-restrainable bitterness."

I laugh at her, and pat her on the head with a heaping amount of condescending sarcasm. "Ohhh, Nova."

"I'll break your hand," she says, glaring at me.

I just laugh all the harder, and then continue my story. "So anyway, admitting we're in love was step one. And then my crazy ex-husband shows up…" I hold up a hand. "Wait, let me go back. Ryder came over and stayed the night, which was the next big step, because I've never let anyone stay the night, because I didn't want to confuse Nate. So. Ryder stays the night, and we're all in love and everything, and it's great. We wake up and I make us breakfast, and the greatness and wonderfulness and happiness continues."

"And then your crazy ex shows up?" This is Nina, James's older daughter.

I nod. "And then my crazy ex shows up." I sigh. "He showed up at six o'clock in the morning, demanding to know whose truck is in my driveway, and he was absolutely whacked out. Like, totally nuts. Shouting all sorts of craziness and making no sense, and being jealous, mainly because I am, according to him, hotter now than when we were married, and apparently that's just not fair."

"Does he realize the reason you let yourself get…" Audra trails off, hunting for a nice way to put it.

"Fat," I finish for her. "Let's not sugarcoat it, Audra—I was fat."

Audra rolls a hand. "It was his fault, is my point. And you getting in shape so you look all sexy was because you finally found the motivation within yourself to take control of your life, which you'd lost because of him."

I pat her hand. "Yes, Audra, *you* know that, and *I*

know that, and anyone with any kind of sense whatsoever knows that, but no, Paul did not seem to know that."

Ella, at the farthest end of the line of pedicures, pipes up. "Why did Ryder have to spend the night? Was it a sleepover? Papa says sleepovers are dumb because no one ever sleeps and someone always ends up wanting to go home early and they always suck donkey waffles."

We all snicker, and I blush. "Ummm. It was a sleepover, yes."

Nina, older and wiser, leans closer to her sister. "It's a grown-up, thing, Ella. You'll understand when you're older."

Ella sticks her tongue out. "Oh, like you understand any more than I do. You're not a grown-up neither!"

"I'm more grown up than you are! Adults having a sleepover is where babies come from."

Imogen coughs to cover her laughter, while the rest of us try to keep straight faces.

"But Papa told me babies come from the baby gnomes. He said they have a workshop at the South Pole, and that's what Santa does the rest of the year when he's not doing presents."

Nina howls in laughter. "Papa just wasn't ready to teach you about sex."

Ella frowns. "I thought that sounded kinda dumb." She glances at Nina. "What's sex? Is it like kissing?"

"OKAY," Nova says. "That's about enough of this conversation. Nina, Ella, I think this is something you should talk to your dad about, later, *alone*."

"Yeah, *Ella*," Nina says.

Nova arches an eyebrow. "I mean you, too, actually."

Nina rolls her eyes, but then pulls a cell phone out of her pocket. "Dad gave me a cell phone in case we needed him, and he put Netflix on it for us."

"Can we watch *She-Ra*?" Ella says. "I love that show!"

Within a few minutes, the girls are huddled around the cell phone watching a show together.

"How did Ryder handle your ex showing up like that?" Nova asks, returning us to the conversation.

I grin. "Well, let's just say that I discovered he has a protective side, and that I find it very, very attractive."

Audra leans close, lowering her voice. "Men acting protective is equal parts annoying and sexy. Franco gets like that sometimes, and I'm never sure if I want to slap him or fuck him."

I giggle. "Speak for yourself. I know I wanted one of those, and it wasn't to slap him, I'll tell you that much."

"And?" Audra asks. "Did you?"

"My son was in the room, so no." I wiggle my eyebrows. "I did later, though. Twice—once of which was in my bathtub."

Audra covers her mouth to stifle a shriek. "Oh, you dirty girl! In the tub?"

I cackle and nod. "Super messy, though—water got everywhere, and it took us fifteen minutes and all my bath sheets to clean it up."

"Worth it, though, I bet," Audra says.

I blush, nodding. "Hell, yes! *So* worth it." I sigh. "But, back to the point—after Paul finally left, Nate suggested we just move in with Ryder. And I was like, ha ha, no, but nice try. It's a *little* soon and also, we can't just invite ourselves to live with Ryder. And in the middle of this, Ryder's like, well, actually, I'm on Nate's side. Like, come live with me."

Imogen reaches past Audra to grab my hand. "Were you totally freaked out?"

I shake my head. "I should have been, honestly, but I wasn't, somehow. I mean, it's super fast, but this whole thing with us has been fast, which is part of why it was so scary. But once I sort of just accepted that it's real and it's happening and there's nothing I can do to stop it, it got easier to just go with it."

Nova is frowning at me. "I mean, it's not as crazy to me as if you were telling us you were gonna marry him, but it's still crazy to move in together this soon."

I shrug. "I know. But it just makes sense to me, somehow. I don't know. This whole thing with Ryder went from zero to sixty pretty much instantly. To hear Ryder tell it, it was love at first sight for him, which was the whole reason he tried to stop talking to me."

"Well, that does make a certain amount of sense," Audra says. "If you meet someone and fall in insta-love, I can see how you may want to try to run from it. Love is scary as fuck."

"Watch your language, young lady," Nina says, without looking away from the phone.

Audra frowns at her. "Who are you calling a young lady?"

Nina giggles. "Sorry. You watch your language, old lady."

Audra nods primly. "Much better, thank you."

Nina just shakes her head. "You're so weird. I called Papa old man once, and I think his head almost exploded."

Audra laughs, a loud guffaw. "Oh, honey. Something you should learn while you're young— men have very fragile egos. Your papa is probably very sensitive to the fact that he's not a spring chicken anymore."

Nina glances at Audra. "What's a spring chicken?"

Audra tilts her head to one side. "Um, you know,

I have no idea where that phrase comes from. I just know it means he's not exactly young anymore."

Nina nods seriously. "I caught him plucking gray hairs out of his beard the other day." She shrugs. "I told him women like the gray. Grandma was talking about how sexy Anderson Cooper is, and his hair is all silver."

"Ooooohh, *hon-EY*," Audra drawls. "Anderson is all *kinds* of fine. I think James could pull off the silver fox look." She glances at Nova. "What do you think, Nova?"

Nova just gives Audra a death glare. "You're lucky there are kids around, that's what I think."

Audra throws her hands up in the air. "You have the worst case of denial I've ever seen, you know that?"

Nina is watching this exchange very closely. "Papa likes you, you know," she says to Nova.

Nova's eyes narrow, and she shoots another glare at Audra. "You put her up to this, didn't you?"

Audra lifts her hands palms out. "No! I don't know what she's talking about." She tilts her head to one side. "Well, I do, in that I know for a fact James likes you, but I don't know how Nina knows."

"If Papa didn't like Nova, he wouldn't have asked her specifically to keep an eye on us. Normally, the uncles and Grandma and Grandpa are the only ones

Papa lets watch us. But when he brought Ella and me here, he specifically asked Nova to keep an eye on us. It's, like, a sign."

Nova rolls her eyes. "Or, I was the first one here, and the only person available to watch you until everyone else got here."

Nina grins at Nova. "It's okay, you know."

Nova frowns, perplexed by the seeming non sequitur. "What's okay?"

"You and Papa. You can date him. You have my permission."

Nova just blinks, remaining silent for a long time. "Wow. Well…thanks, I guess. That's not happening, though."

"Why not?" Nina asks. "Maybe if you and Papa dated, Papa wouldn't be so cranky anymore. He used to be nicer. Now he's a butt all the time, and it's super annoying." She smirks. "Maybe it would make *you* nicer too."

Nova just huffs in disgust, opens and closes her mouth several times, and then gets up out of the spa chair, her pedicure half-finished, and walks barefoot out of the salon, the pink foam toe separators still wedged between her toes.

Nina is confused. "Why did she leave? Did I say something wrong? I was just teasing her."

Audra smiles at the girl. "I know you were, honey.

It's just that Auntie Nova is kind of sensitive about your dad. We probably shouldn't tease her about it anymore."

"Why is she sensitive?" Nina asks, and then pauses to think. "Is it because she likes him?"

"Honestly, I'm not sure," Audra says. "I just know she is sensitive, and we probably should respect that."

A few minutes later, Nova comes back in and takes her seat, apologizing to the nail technicians—none of whom speak more than a few words of English, and she just smiles and nods at Nina.

She sits in silence for a minute, and then sweeps a glance at us. "Can you all *please* just accept the fact that nothing is going to happen between me and James?"

Nina rests her head against Nova's arm. "I'm sorry, Nova."

"Me too," Audra says. "I like to push buttons, and I don't always know when to stop. So, I'm sorry—I won't bring it up again."

Nova sighs and waves her hand. "You don't need to apologize, you just...you all need to respect the fact that I have my reasons for not dating James, and that I'm not comfortable sharing those reasons right now."

"Are we done getting pampered yet?" Ella asks, apropos of nothing. "I'm hungry."

"Same!" Nina says. "When do we go to the restaurant?"

"Actually our reservation is in thirty minutes," Nova says. "We should probably wrap it up here and head over."

So, once we're all finished with our pedicures, we pile into Nova's SUV and head to the restaurant. We timed it so the boys would get done with their paintball game about an hour before the reservation, so they'd have time to get cleaned up, which means they should be arriving in the next few minutes. While we wait for them, Nova fusses with the decorations, and Imogen has the waitstaff bring the cake in, along with a large knife to cut it with.

And then, five minutes early, Nina, who has been posted at the entrance of the private room as a lookout, announces that they're here.

"Are we shouting surprise?" Nova asks. "I just realized we didn't really discuss what we'd do when they get here."

Imogen suddenly looks nervous. "I—um—yes! Let's shout surprise. It'll be fun. He may have a heart attack, but it'll be fine, right? Right."

Audra laughs, nudging Imogen's arm. "You look like you're about to puke. Is that nerves or morning sickness?"

"Both," Imogen says.

"They're here! They're coming!" Nina whisper-shouts.

"Okay, okay," Imogen whispers, flapping her hands. "He's going to be happy, right?" she asks no one in particular.

Audra hugs her. "He's going to be thrilled! The man loves you so much it's gross."

Imogen takes a few deep breaths, and then waves us all over. "Okay, the men walk in, and we all shout surprise. Ready?"

All six of us cluster together in the middle of the room, with the girls wedged in the middle between Nova and Imogen. We hear their voices, laughing and trading insults, with Nate's smaller, higher voice as a counterpoint; heavy boots clomp on the floor.

The door to the private room opens, and I hear Imogen whisper—"One...two...*three!*"

And then, in perfect unison, we all shout, "SURPRISE!"

All of the men are stunned, and file slowly into the room, taking in the decorations.

Franco is the first to recover. "Um...what? Who—who is the surprise for?"

James is eyeing the decorations. "What's with all the baby stuff?"

Ryder eyes me, quickly putting two and two together and looking at me with a somewhat panicked expression. I can't help laughing, then, and that's the cue for everyone to laugh.

"We decided to play a little game," Nova says, trying to cover the fact that we obviously didn't think this out very well. "It's called, surprise-surprise, where you have to guess what the surprise is and who it's for!"

Jesse is the only one who hasn't reacted—his eyes are on Imogen. "Jen?" he whispers, using a shortened form of Imogen's name I've never heard even Audra use.

Imogen takes a step toward him, and everyone goes quiet, parting to make way for her to walk up to Jesse. "I guess we didn't think this all the way through, did we, ladies?" she says, laughing quietly.

"What's going on?" Jesse asks. Big, gruff, rugged, with shaggy, unkempt black hair and a thick black beard, both shot through with hints of silver, he's the essence of rugged masculinity, but in this moment, Jesse is subdued, quiet, and unsure.

Imogen takes his hand and leads him over to the table where the cake is, stops him to stand in front of it. She gazes up at him. "Surprise?"

He looks at the cake, and reads it out loud, slowly. "Congratulations, Daddy…" A long, silent, tense moment, and then he looks back down at Imogen, who is visibly shaking. "What are you saying, Jen?"

"I'm pregnant."

"Oh, thank fuck," I hear Ryder mutter. I laugh under my breath, and shoot him a look, and he raises his hands. "Sorry, sorry."

Not quite as tall as Jesse or James, nor as heavily muscled, Franco is thin and hard and blond, with sharp, handsome features. He nudges Ryder, muttering quietly: "You said what I was thinking, Ride. Thank fuck!"

"Stop it, you two. Have some reverence for the moment!" Audra hisses.

James is the biggest of the group, standing six-six and built like a grizzly bear ready for winter—heavy with thick, hard, bulging muscle, and short brown hair neatly combed to one side, and a thick brown beard. He hasn't said much after his initial question, and I also notice he's studiously not looking Nova's way.

Jesse is still silent, absorbing Imogen's pronouncement.

She bites her lip, and then reaches up to grab Jesse's big shoulder. "Jesse? Say something."

"You're...pregnant?"

She nods. "Yes. Six weeks."

Jesse is blinking and looking a little pale. "I... you..." He sways on his feet. "We..."

Imogen surges forward, grabbing at him. "Jesse?"

Ryder, Franco, and James all spring into action, just in time to catch Jesse as he faints.

He's only out for a few seconds, and then comes to, shaking his head. "What—what happened?"

James claps him on the back as the three of them heave Jesse back onto his feet. "You fainted."

Jesse holds his head with both hands. "The fuck I did."

Ryder and Franco are both laughing so hard they're holding on to each other. "Holy shit, he actually fainted!" Franco says.

"Watch your profanity, Uncle Franco!" Ella shouts.

"Sorry, Ella-bear," Franco says. "But Uncle Jesse swore first."

"I know, but he has an excuse," Ella says. "He just found out he's gonna be a daddy. I'll let it slide this one time."

Jesse's head swivels to stare at Ella, and then at Imogen. "I'm gonna be a daddy." He says this as if trying to absorb what the words mean. "I'm—I'm gonna be a daddy?"

Imogen is sniffling, trying not to cry. She nods, wiping at her eyes. "Yeah, honey. I'm pregnant. You're gonna be a daddy."

Jesse shoots to his feet and lurches over to Imogen, putting his hand on her belly. "Is it a boy or a girl? When are you due? Should you sit down?"

Imogen laughs, tears falling freely now. "Jesse, Jesse—slow down. Relax, baby." She cups his cheek. "I won't know if it's a girl or boy until about eighteen or twenty weeks. I'm due in April, and no, I don't need to sit down."

"I think *I* need to sit down," Jesse says, and slumps heavily into a chair. He looks up at Imogen. "Maybe this is a stupid question, but...how did this happen?"

Ryder claps him on the shoulder. "Well you see, Jesse, when a man loves a woman, they—"

Jesse whacks him. "Shut up, moron. I know *how*, I was there." He stands up and gathers her in his arm. "I just...I didn't think you...you know...could."

She shrugs, sniffling. "I didn't either. I guess I could, obviously." She searches his face. "Jesse, are— are you...are you upset?"

Jesse shakes his head as if trying to shake away confusion. "Upset? Fuck no!" He glances at Ella apologetically. "Sorry, Ella-bear. Heck no, I mean. I'm just stunned."

"I was so scared to tell you," Imogen whispers. "I wanted to make it special, and I also needed moral support, so we decided on this party."

"Scared? Why on earth would you be scared?" Jesse asks.

She shrugs. "I just...I wasn't sure how you'd feel.

I know I'm not—I mean, neither of us are exactly young, and we never really talked about kids…"

Jesse touches her lips with a finger. "I didn't think it was possible to be even happier than being with you makes me, Jen…" He kisses her softly. "And then you tell me this, and I discover it is possible after all."

She lifts up and kisses him, deeply and passionately. "I love you, Jesse."

He pulls away, rubbing the back of his neck. "You kinda messed up my surprise, you know."

Imogen gives him a puzzled frown. "Your surprise?"

Jesse shoots a look at the guys. "Should I do it anyway?"

Franco snorts. "Duh, moron."

"Do what? Jesse, what are you talking about?"

Jesse takes a step backward, away from Imogen. He reaches into his pocket and withdraws something he keeps clutched in his closed fist. He shuffles awkwardly for a moment, and then drops to one knee—Imogen gasps, hand over her mouth, tears flowing freely now.

"I swear, I had this planned for months," Jesse says. "I've been carrying this ring around in my pocket for weeks, trying to figure out the best time to do this. And I figured today would be perfect, all of us here together in a private room…" He drags his fingers through his beard. "I had a whole speech planned out, and I'm fucking it up."

Imogen laughs through her tears. "No, you're not. You're doing great, baby. Keep going."

He shoves his Oakleys higher on his head, takes a deep breath, and gazes up at her. "I love you in a way I didn't think was even possible, for me or for anyone. I love you so much I don't even know how to handle it most days, and…well, I'm still not quite sure how I managed to convince you to love me back, but I did. So, I want to make this permanent before you change your mind about me."

Imogen laughs again. "I'll never change my mind about loving you, you big idiot."

"Well, I guess that's lucky for both of us, because as it turns out, you're having my baby," Jesse says, laughing, and then opens the ring box in both hands, revealing a glittering princess cut diamond solitaire. "Imogen Catherine Irving…will you marry me?"

Imogen can only nod at first, and then dives at him, going to her knees and wrapping her arms around his neck, sobbing and talking at the same time. "Yes, yes, yes!" She pulls back. "You seriously had this planned for today?"

Jesse nods. "I was gonna stand up at the end of the meal and say this whole big thing I wrote out and memorized."

"So I kind of stole your thunder, huh?"

Jesse laughs, moving to sit in a chair, carrying Imogen with him to cradle her on his lap. "Yeah, but it works better this way."

"I think so too." Imogen frowns. "I just have one question."

Jesse arches an eyebrow. "What's that?"

"Do we get married soon so I'm not a big pregnant whale for the wedding, or do we wait till after and get married with a crying baby at the wedding?"

"If you keep it small," Nova says, "I can have it planned in a month or two."

Imogen looks at her. "For real?"

Nova shrugs and nods, red hair swaying. "Yeah, no problem. I mean, you won't have a big, elaborate thing with five hundred people and swans and all that, but if you're willing to keep it to close friends and family only, yeah, I can pull together something simple, romantic, and beautiful for you pretty quickly." She glances around at Audra, Nova, and me. "Especially if I have help." She laughs. "I'm a little rusty, obviously."

"You know we're in!" Audra says, clearly speaking for the rest of us.

Jesse laughs. "A month or two." He holds Imogen tightly, still laughing. "So, the same day I find out I'm gonna be a father, I propose, and then we're getting married in a month or two!"

"Yeah, well, Laurel and Nate are moving in with me tomorrow," Ryder says, "so obviously none of us do anything the easy or normal way."

Nate, who has, up until now, been watching all this unfold, finally speaks up. "So…when do we get cake?"

And thus the festivities begin. Cake is cut and served, jokes are told, and fun is had by all.

During the party, I look around at this group of people who have, somehow, become like family, and realize I'm deeply, abidingly happy. Mostly, though, it's because of Ryder.

He sits beside me, holding my hand at every possible opportunity, and if he's not holding my hand, he's playing with my hair or rubbing my thigh or curling his arm around me—always touching me in little signs of affection, the kind of affection I'm just now realizing I've craved my whole life.

I elbow him at one point in the party. "Thought it was for you, huh?"

He rumbles a laugh. "It did cross my mind."

"It hasn't even been a week since we…you know, without the…you know," I mutter to him. "I wouldn't even know for a month or two."

"So…it's still possible?"

I laugh, resting my head on his shoulder. "I mean, yes, it's possible, as in no birth control is one hundred percent perfect, but it's very unlikely, especially seeing as that happened a few days before my period, which is when I'm least fertile. I think you're fine."

He sighs. "Don't get me wrong, if that did happen, I'd be all-in and happy, but I wouldn't mind if it didn't happen just yet."

"I agree."

He hesitates, and then looks at me. "So, I, uh…I kind of got Nate a…um…moving-in present."

I sense something in his voice. "And what did you get him?"

He winces, keeping his voice low. "A dog."

I blink at him. "Are you serious?"

He grins sheepishly. "I've wanted one for a long time, but I'm not home enough to justify one. With you guys there, too, it's pretty much the perfect time, because with you both there, I'll be home a lot more."

"What kind?"

He chuckles. "Great Pyrenees. It's just a pup, so it's still with the breeders. I figured it would be a fun surprise to take him to go get it after we get moved in."

"Oh my god, Ryder. A Great Pyrenees? Those things are huge!"

He nods. "I have a big place. Needs a big dog."

He gives me a long, searching look. "I guess I probably should've talked to you about it first, huh?

I laugh, and nod. "Yeah, probably." I nuzzle into him. "But you're in luck, because I've been thinking about getting one for years, but never did for the same reason. He's been begging me for a dog for every birthday and holiday for two years. You have no idea how excited he's going to be."

The evening winds down, and yet we all linger in the private event room, the adults talking, Nate and the girls alternating between running around chasing each other and watching shows on Nina's phone. Finally, the kids start to look droopy-eyed, and even the adults seem to be flagging.

Nova is the one to call it. "Okay, I think it's officially time to call this party a success and go home."

There's a chorus of agreement from everyone, and we all file out and to the parking lot where we all say goodbye and hug and linger a little longer, until finally we manage to drag ourselves away from each other and head home.

Which, for me, means my last night in my little suburban home—tomorrow, Ryder and the gang will swarm this place and empty it of my belongings, and merge my life and Nate's with Ryder's—the week after, I will officially be renting my house out to one of James's clients.

I stand in the darkened parking lot beside Ryder's truck, watching Nate and Ryder talking quietly. I look up and see a bright full moon shining down on us, and thinking about the past few weeks, I cannot believe my good fortune. Life is full of surprises, and with my two best guys by my side, I'm ready for all of them.

EPILOGUE

A month and a half later

I'M WOKEN AT THREE IN THE MORNING TO A FRANTICALLY ringing doorbell. Ryder rolls over, peering at the clock. "Who th'fuck could that be?"

I nudge him out of the bed. "I don't know, but you need to go see."

"Yeah, yeah." The only time Ryder is ever ill-humored is if he's woken up unexpectedly, and even that is funny.

He tugs a pair of gym shorts on and shuffles down the stairs. A few minutes later he shuffles blearily back up the stairs.

"Who was it?" I ask.

"For you." He tumbles back into bed and curls up facing away from me.

I laugh. "Ryder, who *was* it?"

"Nova."

"Nova? What did she want?"

"Dunno. She's bawling her damn eyes out, though."

"Wait…she's still down there?"

"Uh-huh."

"You probably should've led with that, sweetheart," I say, climbing out of bed and shrugging into my robe.

"Sleeping. Night-night."

I laugh, bend and kiss his forehead, and then wiggle away cackling as he grabs at my butt. "You lecherous pervert! You just *had* that less than four hours ago."

He snorts, mostly asleep. "Didn't have your ass. Gonna someday, though."

"Not likely, bub. No backdoor lovin' for you."

He laughs sleepily and then I hear him snoring. I head downstairs and find Nova at our kitchen table, dabbing at her eyes with a paper towel, drinking a glass of whiskey neat.

I sit next to her, rest my hand on her wrist. "Nova? What's wrong?"

She sniffles. "I'm sorry. I just…I need to talk to someone."

"Don't be sorry," I tell her. "This is what friends are for, sweetie. Talk to me."

"I thought I could do this."

"Do what?"

She lets out a shuddery breath. "Plan this wedding."

I frown, confused. "You've *been* planning it. I don't understand."

"Yeah, I've been planning it…and it's killing me."

"You're gonna have to unpack this for me, Nova."

"It's a long story."

"I have time."

"I've had it all locked down for a long time," Nova says, "but this…planning Jesse and Imogen's wedding…it's just—it's bringing it all up inside me for some dumb fucking reason, and I don't know how to handle it."

I hesitate. "I don't want to overstep my bounds, here, but…this is all connected to James, isn't it?"

She nods miserably. "Yeah."

"So…what's the story?"

Nova swirls the last sip of whiskey in her glass. "I'll need another whiskey to get through it."

COMING SOON!

Want more of Nova and Jesse's story, and the world
of Dad Bod Contracting?

SCREWED

The fourth and final Dad Bod Book...

Coming soon!

Jasinda Wilder

Visit me at my website: **www.jasindawilder.com**
Email me: **jasindawilder@gmail.com**

If you enjoyed this book, you can help others enjoy it as well by recommending it to friends and family, or by mentioning it in reading and discussion groups and online forums. You can also review it on the site from which you purchased it. But, whether you recommend it to anyone else or not, thank you *so much* for taking the time to read my book! Your support means the world to me!

My other titles:

The Preacher's Son:
Unbound
Unleashed
Unbroken

Biker Billionaire:
Wild Ride

Big Girls Do It:
Better (#1), Wetter (#2), Wilder (#3), On Top (#4)
Married (#5)
On Christmas (#5.5)
Pregnant (#6)
Boxed Set

Rock Stars Do It:
Harder
Dirty
Forever
Boxed Set

From the world of *Big Girls* and *Rock Stars*:
Big Love Abroad

Delilah's Diary:
A Sexy Journey
La Vita Sexy
A Sexy Surrender

The Falling Series:
Falling Into You
Falling Into Us
Falling Under
Falling Away
Falling for Colton

The Ever Trilogy:
Forever & Always
After Forever
Saving Forever

The world of *Alpha*:
Alpha
Beta
Omega
Harris: Alpha One Security Book 1
Thresh: Alpha One Security Book 2
Duke: Alpha One Security Book 3
Puck: Alpha One Security Book 4

The world of Stripped:
Stripped
Trashed

The world of *Wounded*:
Wounded
Captured

The Houri Legends:
Jack and Djinn
Djinn and Tonic

The Madame X Series:

Madame X

Exposed

Exiled

The One Series

The Long Way Home

Where the Heart Is

There's No Place Like Home

Badd Brothers:

Badd Motherf*cker

Badd Ass

Badd to the Bone

Good Girl Gone Badd

Badd Luck

Badd Mojo

Big Badd Wolf

Badd Boy

Badd Kitty

Badd Business

Dad Bod Contracting

Hammered

Drilled

**The Black Room
(With Jade London):**
Door One

Door Two

Door Three

Door Four

Door Five

Door Six

Door Seven

Door Eight

Deleted Door

Standalone titles:
Yours

Non-Fiction titles:
You Can Do It

You Can Do It: Strength

You Can Do It: Fasting

Jack Wilder Titles:
The Missionary

To be informed of new releases and special offers,
sign up for
Jasinda's email newsletter.